Gerald looked him over for a moment, unmoved but
intensely curious. FRONTISPIECE. *See page* 82.

THE MYSTERY ROAD

By
E. PHILLIPS OPPENHEIM

WITH FRONTISPIECE BY
F. VAUX WILSON

BOSTON
LITTLE, BROWN, AND COMPANY
1923

To
· *the memory of*

WINIFRED TOLTON

the most wonderful secretary and
dearest friend of my life I dedicate
*this story which I dictated to **her***
and which she loved

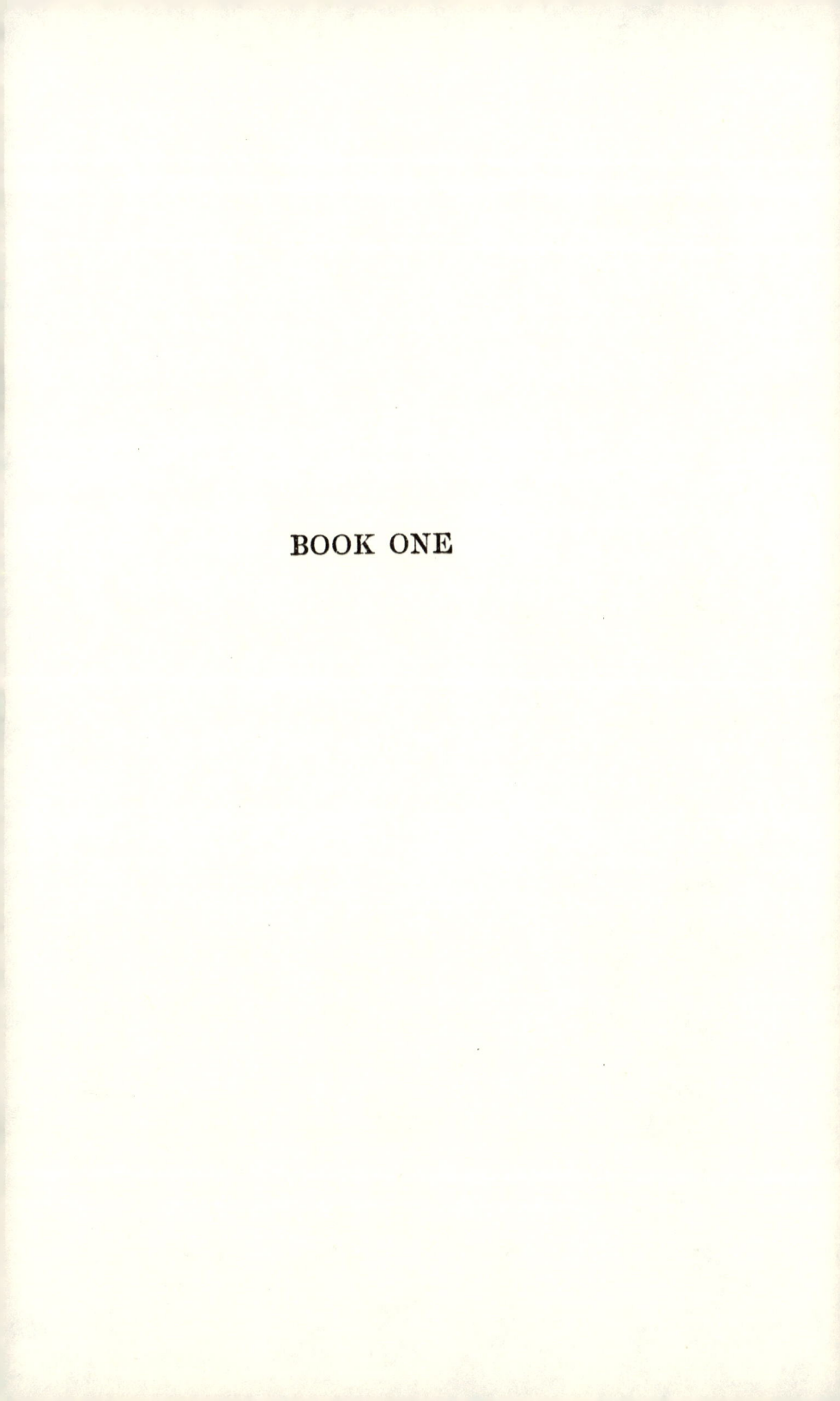

BOOK ONE

THE MYSTERY ROAD

BOOK ONE

CHAPTER I

MYRTILE stood upon the crazy verandah, her eyes shaded by her hand, gazing down the straight, narrow footpath, a sundering line across the freshly ploughed field, which led to the village in the hollow below. The mouldering white stone cottage from which she had issued was set in a cleft of the pine-covered hills; it seemed to struggle against its inborn ugliness and to succeed only because of the beauty of its setting, — in the foreground the brown earth, with its neatly trained vines and its quarter of an acre of fragrant violets; the orchard, pink and white with masses of cherry blossom; beyond, a level stretch of freshly turned brown earth, soon to become a delicate carpet of tender green, and, by the time the vines should sprout, a sea of deep gold. It was the typical homestead of the small French peasant proprietor. Even the goat was not absent, the goat which came at that moment with clanking chain to rub his nose against the girl's knee.

Myrtile's hand dropped to her side. The three figures were plainly visible now. She remained quiescent, watching them with a mute tragedy in her face which, to any one ignorant of the inner significance of this approaching procession, must have seemed a little puzzling. For there was nothing tragic about Jean Sargot — middle-aged, a typical peasant of the district, with coarsened face and weather-beaten skin — or about the companion who hung on his arm, — a plump, dark woman, with black hair and eyes, vociferous and fluent of gesture, with a high-pitched voice and apparently much to say. The third person, who walked in the rear, seemed even less likely to incite apprehension. He was more corpulent than his neighbour Jean Sargot, and he wore clothes of a holiday type, ill suited to this quiet country promenade. His coat was black and long, a garment, it appeared, of earlier years, for it left a very broad gap to display a fancy waistcoat adorned by a heavy gold chain. He wore a silk hat which had done duty at every christening, marriage and funeral in the neighbourhood for the last twenty years, and his whole appearance was one of discomfort. Yet the girl's eyes, as they rested upon him, were filled with terror.

They were near enough now for speech, and her stepfather, waving his hand, called out to her:

"It is the Widow Dumay, little one, and our friend and neighbour, Pierre Leschamps, who come to drink a glass of wine with us. Hurry with the table and some chairs, and bring one — two bottles of last year's vintage. It is not so bad, that wine, neighbour Pierre, I can promise you."

"Any wine will be good after such a walk," the widow declared, panting. "Either the village lies too low, friend Jean, or your house too high. It will be good to rest."

They sank into the chairs which Myrtile had already

placed upon the verandah, Pierre Leschamps laying his hat upon a handkerchief in a safe corner. There were beads of perspiration upon his forehead, for, unlike his friend and host, he was unused to exercise. He kept the little café in the village, and the strip of land which went with it he let to others. His pale cheeks and flabby limbs told their own story. Jean Sargot looked about him with the pride of the proprietor.

" Not so bad, this little dwelling, eh? " he exclaimed. " Four rooms, all well-furnished, a bed such as one seldom sees, and a wardrobe made by my own grandfather, Jacques Sargot, the carpenter. It pleases thee, Marie? "

The widow looked around her with a little sniff.

" It might be worse," she conceded, " but there are the children."

" Three only," Sargot replied, " and in a year or so they will all be in the fields. Think what that may mean. We can sell the timber from the strip behind and plant more vines. Children are not so bad when they are strong."

" The little ones are well enough," Madame Dumay admitted, " but thy eldest — Myrtile — she has not the air of health."

They all looked up at the girl, who was approaching them at this moment with wine and glasses. She was of medium height and slim. Her complexion was creamily pale; even the skin about her neck and arms had little of the peasant's brown. Her neatly braided hair was of the darkest shade of brown, with here and there some glints of a lighter colour. Her eyes, silkily fringed, were of a wonderful shade of deep blue, her mouth tremulous and beautiful. There was something a little exotic about her appearance, although no actual

indication of ill health. The widow looked at her critically; Pierre, the innkeeper, with unpleasant things in
his black, beady eyes.

"Pooh! she is well enough," her stepfather declared.
"Never a doctor has crossed this threshold since her
mother died many years ago."

Myrtile welcomed her father's guests pleasantly but
timidly. Then, after she had filled the glasses, she
would have slipped back into the house but Jean Sargot
grasped her by the arm.

"To-night, my child," he insisted, "you must leave
your books alone. You must drink a glass of wine with
us. It is an occasion, this."

Myrtile looked from one to the other of the two
visitors. She had for a moment the air of a trapped
animal. Madame Dumay made a little grimace, but
Pierre only laughed. She was a flower, this Myrtile,
not like other girls. Even the young men complained
of her aloofness. He knew well how to deal with such
modesty.

"Behold," her stepfather continued, "our two best
friends! Here is good Madame Dumay. A nice little
income she makes at the shop, and a tidy sum in her
stocking."

"Oh, là, là!" the widow interrupted. "What has
that to do with thee, my friend?"

"And also," Jean Sargot went on, without taking
heed of the interruption, "the brave Pierre Leschamps.
Oh, a gay dog, that Leschamps! A man of property,
mark you, child. And listen! Why do you think these
friends of mine are here?"

"I cannot tell," Myrtile faltered.

"Madame Dumay will become my wife. It is what
we need here. And Pierre Leschamps — hear this, little

one — he seeks a wife. He has chosen you. I have given my consent."

Leschamps had risen to his feet. Myrtile shrank back against the wall. The terror had leaped now into life.

"I will not marry Monsieur Leschamps," she declared. "The other — is your affair. But as for me, I will not marry!"

Jean Sargot leaned back in his chair and drank his wine. His two guests followed his example.

"Ho, ho!" he laughed. "Come, that is good! You were always a shy child, Myrtile. Pierre shall woo you into a different humour."

"Ay, indeed!" the innkeeper assented, leering across at the girl with covetous eyes. "We shall understand one another presently, little one. You need have no fear. Marriage is a pleasant thing. You will find it so like all the others."

"It is an institution to be toasted," Jean Sargot declared, filling the glasses and glancing amorously towards the widow. "Trouble not about Myrtile, my friend Pierre. She is thine. We shall drink this glass of wine to Marriage. It will be a festival, that, eh, Marie?"

Myrtile slipped through the open doorway. Her prospective husband looked after her for a moment and half rose. Then he looked back at the wine, flowing into his glass. Myrtile would keep, — wine by the side of Jean Sargot, never! He resumed his seat. In a minute or two he would follow her, — as soon as the second bottle was empty.

Across the stone-flagged floor, out through the little garden and along the cypress avenue to the road, Myrtile fled. She was like a terrified young fawn in the half-light, her hair flying behind her, her large eyes filled with fear. Her feet seemed scarcely to touch the grass-grown track. She fled as one who leaves behind evil things. Only once she looked over her shoulder. No one was stirring, no one seemed to have thought of pursuit. She reached the gate which led out on to the road and clung to it for a moment, as though for protection. On the other side was freedom. Her eyes filled with passionate desire. If only she knew how to gain it!

They were singing now down at the cottage. She heard Jean Sargot's strident voice in some country song of harvest and vintage and what they called love. As she stood there in the quiet of the evening, there seemed suddenly to leap into life a very furnace of revolt. She was weary of her monotonous tasks, — the abuse of her stepfather, generally at night the worse for sour wine and fiery brandy; the care of those motherless children, not of her own stock yet dependent upon her; the grey tedium of a life unbeautiful and hopeless. And now this fresh terror! Her fingers tore at the rough splinters of the gate. Her eyes travelled hungrily along that great stretch of road, passing here and there through the forests, rising in the far distance to the top of the brown hillside, and disappearing in mystery. At the other end of the road one might find happiness!

CHAPTER II

THE two young men adopted characteristic attitudes when confronted with the slight misadventure of a burst tyre and a delay of half an hour. Christopher Bent deliberately filled and lit a pipe, and, seating himself on the top of a low, grey, stone wall, gave himself up to the joy of a wonderful view and the pleasure of unusual surroundings. His companion, Gerald Dombey, stood peevishly in the middle of the road, with his hands in his pockets, cursing the flint-strewn road, the rottenness of all motor tyres, and the evil chance which led to this mishap in the last lap of their journey.

" We'll be on the road again in twenty minutes, your lordship," the chauffeur promised, as he paused for a moment to wipe the perspiration from his forehead. " It's been cruel going all the way from Brignolles, and you've kept her at well past the forty, all the time."

His master nodded with some signs of returning equanimity.

" Don't distress yourself, John," he said. " There's no real hurry so long as we get into Monte Carlo before dark. Come on, Christopher," he added, turning to his companion. " Get off that wall and let us explore."

The two young men strolled off together. On their right was a thickly planted forest of pine trees, fragrantly aromatic after the warm sunshine of the April day. On their left was a stretch of very wonderful country, a country of vineyards and pastures, of wooded knolls and fruitful valleys. And in the background, the sombre outline of the mountains. Gerald paused to point to the little, discoloured house of Jean Sargot.

"Are they real people who live in these quaint cottages?" he speculated. "That place, for instance, looks like a toy farm, with its patch of violets, its tiny vineyard, its belt of ploughed land and this little grove of cypresses. It is just as though some child had taken them all from his play box and laid them out there."

Christopher withdrew the pipe from his mouth for a moment. He was looking at the opening in the little grove of cypresses.

"And there," he murmured, "must be the child to whom they all belong. I think you are right, Gerald. There is something unreal about the place."

Gerald, too, was suddenly conscious of the girl who stood clutching the top of the wooden gate, her face turned a little away from them, absorbed in the contemplation of that distant spot where the road vanished in a faint haze of blue mist.

"We will talk to her," he declared. "You shall practise your French upon this little rustic, Chris. She probably won't be able to understand a word you say."

At the sound of their voices, Myrtile turned her head, and, at the things which they saw in her face, there was no longer any thought of frivolous conversation on the part of the two young men. They stood for a moment indeed, speechless, Christopher spellbound, Gerald, of quicker sensibility, carried for a moment into the world from which she seemed to have fallen. Then his old habits asserted themselves. She was as beautiful as an angel, but her feet were on the ground, and she was obviously in distress.

"Are you alive, mademoiselle?" he asked, raising his cap.

"But certainly, monsieur," she answered gravely. "I am alive but very unhappy."

"You can tell us, perhaps, the way to Cannes?" Christopher enquired.

She pointed to where the thin ribbon of road in the distance seemed to melt into the bosom of the clouds.

"Cannes is over there, monsieur," she said, "and there is no other road save this one."

"You go there often, perhaps?" Christopher ventured.

"I have never been there, monsieur," she answered, with her eyes fixed upon Gerald. "Night after night, when my work is done, I come here and I watch the road just where it fades away, but I have never travelled along it. I have never been further than the first village, down in the hollow."

Gerald came a step nearer to her. He leaned against the gate post. His tone and manner became unconsciously caressing. It was generally so when he spoke with women.

"You are in trouble, mademoiselle," he said. "Sometimes even a stranger may help."

She looked down the road towards where the automobile was jacked up.

"Yes," she admitted, "I am in great trouble. No one but a stranger could help me because I have no friends."

"Be brave, then, and speak on," Gerald enjoined.

There had been no previous time in her life when Myrtile had been required to marshal her thoughts and speak unaccustomed words, yet, at that moment, clearly

and unfalteringly she told her story. She pointed to
the weather-stained cottage behind.

"I live there," she said, "with three half-brothers
and sisters and a stepfather. My mother was the village schoolmistress. She married for the second time a
bad man, and she died. I have taken care of those
children. I have kept the house clean and tidy. I
have done what the curé told me was my duty, and all
the time I have hated it."

"Why?" Christopher asked simply.

She looked across as though surprised at his intervention.

"Because the children are coarse and greedy and ill-
mannered," she explained. "I wear myself out trying
to make them different, but it is useless. It is in their
blood, because my stepfather — is worse. Often he
drinks too much brandy, he is quarrelsome, he is never
kind. There is not one little joy in life, only when I
escape for a little time and come here, and look down
the road which leads to liberty, and wonder what may
lie at the other side of the hills there. You see, I have
read books — many books. My mother and father
were both well-educated. I know and feel that the life
I am leading is terrible."

"There is something beyond all this," Gerald
said. "There is something of instant trouble in your
face."

Again for a moment she was voiceless, a white, dumb
thing stricken nerveless with horror. It was that look
which had surprised the two men. Her breath, as she
spoke, seemed choked with unuttered sobs.

"My stepfather brought home from the village to-
night — the Widow Dumay. He is to marry her — to
bring her to the farm. He brought, too, Pierre Les-

champs, the keeper of the Café. — Horrible! — horrible! "

" Pierre Leschamps," Gerald murmured softly. " Go on."

The girl opened her lips but the words seemed to stick in her throat.

" They propose, perhaps, to betroth you? " he asked, with quick understanding.

Her assent was mirrored in the agony of her eyes.

" He is fat and old and he drinks," she cried. " I would sooner die than have him come near me! "

The two young men turned their heads and looked down at the little farmhouse. The very abode of peace, it seemed, with its thin thread of smoke curling up to the sky, its thatched roof, its reposeful atmosphere. Just then, however, they caught the murmur of discordant voices, a shrill shriek of laughter. The men were singing.

" Look upon us as two friends," Gerald begged. " What would you have us do? "

The girl pointed once more to where the road disappeared amongst the hills.

" If you leave me here," she declared, " I shall walk and run and crawl until I pass out of sight there, and perhaps they may borrow the widow's cart and catch me, and then I shall kill myself. Take me with you as far as you are going — somewhere where I can hide."

The car glided slowly up to where they were standing. Gerald did not hesitate for a moment. He stepped into his place at the driving wheel and motioned to the seat by his side.

"Agreed," he said. " We will start you, little one — tell me, how are you called? "

" Myrtile," she murmured.

"We will start you off on the great adventure of life. It seems to me that there can be nothing worse in store for you than what you leave behind."

The girl pushed open the gate and sprang into the car like a frightened thing. Gerald turned his head. Around the corner of the farm three unsteady figures showed themselves; three voices — two raucous and one shrill — called for Myrtile. There were threats, gesticulations. The girl cowered by Gerald's side.

"Start!" she implored. "Start, please!"

Christopher, however, still hesitated.

"I think," he said, "we should first hear what these people have to say. They have, after all, some claim upon the girl. It might be possible to aid her without bringing her away from home."

Myrtile clung to Gerald. Her eyes were swimming pools of passionate entreaty.

"Start, monsieur," she pleaded. "There is nothing for me but escape. Why does the other gentleman mind?"

"Get in, there's a good fellow," Gerald begged impatiently. "We don't want to have a row with these yokels."

The chauffeur was already in the dickey behind. Myrtile's eyes implored Christopher to take the place by her side. With his feet still on the road, however, he leaned across her to Gerald.

"Gerald," he said, "this is a more serious affair than you seem to think. Who is going to look after the child when we get to Monte Carlo?"

"You can, if you like," was the careless reply. "I'm not thinking of playing the Lothario, if that is what you mean."

"Word of honour?"

" Word of honour. Don't be an ass, old chap. It's up to us to give the girl a chance."

Christopher stripped off his coat and wrapped it around Myrtile. Then he took the place by her side. Gerald slipped in the clutch and they glided off.

The twilight overtook them swiftly. The lights of Monte Carlo, as they commenced the long descent, were like pin pricks of fire thrust through a deep blue carpet. Out in the bay, the yacht of an American millionaire was illuminated from bow to stern. From the back of the twin range of hills on their left, the golden horn of the moon was beginning to show itself. Myrtile, whose eyes had been fixed upon the flying milestones, leaned forward now with a little exclamation of wonder.

" It is fairyland! " she cried.

Gerald looked down at her indulgently.

" You live so near and you have never been even as far as this? " he asked.

" It is as I have told you," she answered. " I have never travelled ten kilometres from the farm in my life."

Christopher was almost incredulous. Gerald, however, nodded sympathetically. Both young men had taken it for granted from the first that their charge understood no English.

" In France they are like that," Gerald remarked. " It is the sous that count. But this child — isn't she amazing, Christopher? Except for her clothes, there isn't a thing about her that suggests the peasant. She is like a child Madonna — an angel — who has stolen into the clothes of a girl gone for her first communion."

" I should still like to know what you are going to do with her when we arrive? " Christopher asked bluntly. "Are you going to take her to the Villa? "

"Later on, perhaps," was the careless reply. "Certainly not this evening."

"Why not?" Christopher persisted. "Your sister is very kind-hearted. It seems to me, as long as we have the girl on our hands, that she is the proper person to look after her."

Gerald smiled slightly.

"My dear Chris," he said, "you and Mary are pals, I know, but I am not sure that you altogether understand her. She doesn't like surprises. We must pave the way a little before we ask for her help."

"And in the meantime?"

Gerald yawned.

"What a persistent fellow you are!" he observed.

"You can't imagine that they will take her in at the hotel, without any luggage and in our company?"

Myrtile had been looking from one to the other of her two companions with a sense of growing trouble in her eyes.

"Messieurs," she interrupted, "it was wrong of me not to tell you before. I speak a little English. I understand very well."

"You are a most amazing child!" Gerald exclaimed, looking down at her in genuine astonishment. "You have never been ten kilometres from your homestead, and you speak a foreign language! That comes of having a schoolmistress for a mother, I suppose. However, have no fear. We shall dispose of you pleasantly."

"To-morrow," she said timidly, "I can find work."

"To-morrow be hanged!" Gerald replied. "Look about you, little one. We are entering the town. If your story is true — and we know that it is," he added hastily, " you see for the first time shops, villas, hotels. The building in front of us is the Casino. Now you see the lights that fringe the bay."

" It is amazing," Myrtile murmured.

They drew up at the side door of the hotel where the two young men were to stay. Gerald descended.

" Take care of the child for a few minutes, Chris," he begged. " I am going to interview one of the housekeepers."

He disappeared into the hotel. Myrtile watched his tall, slim figure until he was lost to sight. Then the fear seemed to return. She shivered.

" I am a trouble to him," she faltered. " He will hate me for it. I only meant that you should drive me somewhere where I could lose myself. Perhaps I had better go, monsieur. Can I not slip away before he returns? "

" He would be very angry if you did," Christopher assured her. " He has gone to arrange for some one to look after you for the night. To-morrow I think you will do well if you try to find some work. If you wish it, I will help you."

Her eyes still devoured the door through which Gerald had passed.

" Tell me his name? " she begged.

" His name," Christopher replied, " is Gerald Annesley Dombey."

She repeated it after him, a little hesitatingly.

" I shall always think of him as Gerald," she said. " It is a very pretty name. Tell me, why did the chauffeur say ' your lordship '? "

" Because he is the eldest son of an earl and he is entitled to be called Lord Dombey."

" He is noble, then? I am not surprised. He seemed

like that to me. — And you, monsieur? May I know your name? "

" My name is Christopher Bent," he replied, " plain Christopher Bent."

" ' Christopher ' is a very nice name," she said, with a trifle of unconscious condescension, " but of course it is not like ' Gerald.' "

She looked longingly back towards the crowded doorway, and the young man who stood by her side was aware of a curious and altogether inexplicable sensation. He suddenly found himself envying Gerald's careless but fascinating manners, his good looks, his light, debonair manner of speech. Even this little waif picked up at the roadside was already under his spell. Then Christopher remembered other things about his friend, and his face grew stern.

Gerald returned presently with a neatly dressed young woman. He held out his hands to Myrtile and assisted her to alight.

" It is all arranged, child," he announced. "Annette is a chambermaid here, and the niece of one of the housekeepers, whom I know well. She will take you to some rooms close at hand, where you will be made comfortable. To-morrow morning early, Christopher and I will come and see you."

" Mademoiselle will be entirely well suited," the young woman declared. " It is but a few yards away."

Myrtile, still wrapped in Christopher's coat, looked a little pathetic as she stood upon the pavement by Annette's side.

" I shall not see you again to-night, then, Monsieur Lord Dombey? " she asked shyly.

" Not to-night," he laughed. "And ' Monsieur Gerald ' is quite enough from you, petite. To-morrow we

will have a long talk.   Have no fear — you shall not
return to the farm unless it is your wish."

Myrtile stooped and with a sudden, passionate gesture raised his hand to her lips.   Then she dragged
Annette off, without looking behind.   Gerald laughed a
little consciously.

" Our village maiden is somewhat demonstrative," he
remarked lightly.   " Come on, Chris.   A cocktail whilst
they unpack our clothes.   I've telephoned to the Villa.
We must do a duty dinner there first, but afterwards I
will show you the land where the pleasure-seekers of the
world have built their Temple."

CHAPTER III

LADY MARY DOMBEY was a young woman of very pleasing appearance, but there were occasions upon which she could look stern. This was one of them.

"I am never surprised at anything that Gerald does," she told Christopher, who was seated next her at the dinner table, "but I must say that I should never have expected you to have been mixed up in one of his escapades. What are you going to do with the girl?"

"We rather hoped for some advice from you," was the somewhat rueful reply.

"You are welcome to it. Send her home."

"You wouldn't talk like that if you'd seen the state of terror she was in when we found her, Mary," Gerald remarked from the other side of the table.

"Is she very beautiful?" his sister enquired.

"Wonderfully," Christopher pronounced.

Gerald shrugged his shoulders.

"She is of an age when all girls are beautiful," he observed. "Perfectly filthy time she seems to have been having, though."

"We hoped," Christopher ventured, a little doubtfully, "that you might be able to make use of her as a kind of under sewing maid, or something of that sort."

"Thank you," Lady Mary replied, without enthusiasm, "I am perfectly satisfied with the services of my own maid. Besides, the servants' quarters here are ridiculously cramped. They are all complaining, as it is."

Lord Hinterleys, who had taken only a languid interest in the conversation, intervened for the first time.

"Where is the young person now?" he enquired.

"In some rooms one of the housekeepers at the hotel found for me, sir," Gerald replied.

"Perhaps the housekeeper can find her some employment," his father suggested.

"We'll dispose of her all right," Gerald declared confidently. "She may wake up in the morning and feel homesick, and, if so, we'll send her back."

"You know very well that she won't do anything of the sort," Christopher protested.

Lady Mary rose to her feet.

"I can't quite decide," she said, "which of you two has lost his heart to this paragon of village loveliness. However, I feel sure that my advice is the best. Send her back to her people."

Gerald strolled to the door with his sister and returned to his place, fingering his cigarette case irritably.

"I have always thought," he remarked, with mild sarcasm, "that a barrister should be a person of infinite tact and perceptions. It appears that I was wrong. I never dreamed that any one could be such a blithering ass as you, Chris."

"Thank you, Gerald," his friend replied, helping himself from the decanter which Lord Hinterleys had passed around. "In what respect have I merited this severe criticism?"

"Why, by talking about the girl as though she were something unusual! Mary's a good sort, and all that, but no girl likes the man who is sitting next her at dinner time to rave about his latest discovery of violet eyes. You'd probably have had those violet eyes to

look at every time you came down to stay at Hinterleys, if you hadn't made such an ass of yourself."

Lord Hinterleys sipped his wine thoughtfully. Gerald, who was longing to smoke, watched its leisurely dis-
appearance with impatience.

" I am not suggesting for a single moment," the former observed, " that your attitude towards this young
woman is not and will not always be entirely irreproachable, but at the same time you must remember that we
are in a country where such adventures are likely to be
misunderstood. I feel inclined, therefore, to endorse
your sister's advice. It is very possible that the young
woman, at the time you discovered her, was indulging
in a passing fit of petulance. I should do all that I
could to encourage her to return to her people."

" We'll talk to her in the morning, sir," Gerald promised. " Wonderfully this port has travelled."

" We brought it out six years ago," his father remarked. " Martin laid it down himself, and it has not
been disturbed since. — There, I have finished my two
glasses. I shall retire to the drawing-room and persuade Mary to sing to me, and you two young fellows
can smoke to your hearts' content. Give me your arm,
Gerald."

" Don't think we shall stop long, if you'll excuse us,
sir," Gerald confided, as he rose to his feet. " It's
Christopher's first night in Monte Carlo and I want to
show him the ropes. Come along, old chap, and make
your adieux," he added, turning to his friend.

Lord Hinterleys nodded as he leaned on his ivory-
topped stick.

" You young men choose weird games at which to lose
your money, nowadays," he observed. " Filthy places,
all Casinos — no ventilation, foul atmosphere, reeking

of scent and tobacco, and, to say the least of it, a very dubious company. Still, if I were your age I suppose I shouldn't notice these things. — Did you do any good with those two hunters you bought from Loxley, Gerald? One of them I thought was good enough for some of these country steeplechases."

Father and son became temporarily absorbed in a subject of common interest. Lady Mary made room for Christopher by her side. She was scarcely possessed of her brother's good looks, but her complexion was good, her features unexceptionable, her eyes clear and as a rule sympathetic, her tone and manner attractive. Her figure, especially in a riding habit, was undeniable, her skill at golf and tennis far above the ordinary amateur. It was not for lack of offers that, at twenty-four years of age, she was still unmarried.

"Must you rush off so soon on your first evening?" she asked reproachfully.

"Not so far as I am concerned," he assured her. "I would rather stay here and listen to you sing. It's Gerald who is dying to lose his money."

She made a little grimace.

"Every one goes to the Casino or the Sporting Club at night," she said, "and for the first few times it is amusing enough. I hope you won't spend all your time there. When shall we play golf?"

"To-morrow afternoon?" he asked.

She nodded.

"I'm taking father out to lunch at the Club," she said. "We'll play directly afterwards, if that suits you. Tell me, have you had any interesting cases lately? I saw that you won the libel suit you were telling me about."

They talked for some time with interest. Lady

Mary's wit was keen and her insight unusual. During a pause in their conversation, Lord Hinterleys looked across the room through his horn-rimmed eyeglass.

" Your friend seems to get on very well with Mary," he remarked.

" They've always been pals," Gerald acquiesced.

" Doing pretty well at the Bar, isn't he? "

" Thundering well. They say he's certain to be one of our youngest K. C's."

" I knew his father," Lord Hinterleys reflected. " He was at Eton with me. Very good stock, though not remarkably prosperous."

" Christopher isn't well off," Gerald admitted. " You don't make a lot of money at the Bar your first few years."

Lord Hinterleys said nothing for several moments.

" Mary has her aunt's hundred thousand pounds," he said at length. " She is a difficult young person to marry. Knows her own mind, though. I should never interfere."

" Chris is a good fellow, but I don't fancy he has any thought of marrying just yet," Gerald remarked. " You won't mind if I take him off now, sir? We shall meet for lunch at the Golf Club to-morrow."

Christopher obeyed his friend's summons without enthusiasm. Gerald, however, was both insistent and impatient, and the two young men took their leave a few minutes later.

Christopher, quickly impressed with the charm of the place, would have willingly spent the remainder of the evening seated outside the Café de Paris, watching the passers-by, listening to the music, and marvelling at the amphitheatre of lights which fringed the bay and dotted the whole background of hills with little specks of yellow fire. Gerald, however, was too anxious to do the whole honours of the place. He dragged his friend into the bureau of the Casino, where they obtained their tickets for the Cercle Privé, and afterwards on to the Sporting Club, the Mecca of Gerald's desires for the evening, at any rate. Christopher breathed a little more freely here than in the Casino; the atmosphere was less pernicious, the crowd by which he was surrounded far more attractive. After Gerald had taken a seat at the baccarat table, he wandered around for some time, fascinated by this strange, cosmopolitan gathering, their diversity in class, manners and dress. Presently he found a seat in the little bar, ordered a whisky and soda and leaned back to watch the never-ceasing stream of pleasure-seeking loiterers. Suddenly, without any warning, his thoughts played him a queer trick. The walls of the thronged room fell away; its murmur of silvery voices, its tangle of exotic perfumes, were non-existent. He was back on the cool, sunlit hillside, with the odour of the violets and the pines in his nostrils, and the girl looking over the gate. She turned her head and he saw her face, — her beautiful eyes, with their passionate, terrified appeal; her quivering lips, her child's figure; the tender appeal of her, the soul and sweetness of her innocent youth clinging like some fresh, sweet perfume to her trembling body.

Gerald stood suddenly before him, his face aflame, his eyes brilliant. His voice quivered with excitement.

"Christopher, you moonstruck old dodderer," he cried, "wake up! I have seen the most wonderful creature on earth. I won't leave this place until I find out who she is."

"What, another adventure?" Christopher exclaimed. "Sit down and have a whisky and soda."

" Don't talk to me about whiskies and sodas," Gerald
replied, sinking into the vacant chair, however, and calling a waiter. " I tell you she's the most amazing person I ever saw — a revelation! "

" You're not thinking about Myrtile? "

" That child? No! " was the impatient rejoinder.
" I tell you it's some one here to-night. She's either
French or Russian or Italian — I can't make up my
mind which. She is with an older woman, who seems to
be a sort of attendant. Every one's talking about her,
but no one seems to know who she is."

" This place is full of that sort of people, isn't it? "
Christopher asked, not greatly impressed.

" That sort of people! " Gerald repeated contemptuously. " Wait till you see her! I'm not easily led
away. I've seen the most beautiful women in most of
the capitals of the world. I was at Vienna and Rome
before the war, you know, but I never —— Don't
move, Chris. Don't look as though I've been talking
about them. Here they come! "

Christopher watched the approach of the two women
with an interest casual at first but real enough as they
drew nearer. The younger of the two walked slightly
in advance. She was rather over the medium height,
and her carriage, although she was not in the least as-
sertive, was full of the simple dignity of one who has
been accustomed to command respect. She was slim,
yet the outlines of her figure were so soft as to become
almost voluptuous. She wore a dress of perfectly plain
black lace, against which the skin of her neck and shoulders seemed of almost alabaster whiteness. Her only
ornament was a long, double string of pearls of unusual
size. Her hair, glossy and absolutely jet black, was
brushed from her forehead and around her ears so that

it seemed almost like a sheath. Her complexion was absolutely pallid, her lips a natural scarlet. Her eyes were of a deep shade of brown, inclined to be half closed, as though she were short-sighted. Her eyelashes were long and silky; her eyebrows looked as though they had been pencilled, and yet left a conviction of entire naturalness. Such details as remained of her toilette were unique yet simple. The woman who followed her possessed also an air of distinction, but she was middle-aged, with grey hair and somewhat unwieldy figure. She carried herself with an air of deference towards her companion.

" Well? " Gerald whispered excitedly.

" She is very beautiful and very unusual," Christopher admitted. " Have you no idea who she is? "

" If I had found any one who knew who they were, I should have been introduced before now," was the blunt reply. " Freddie Carruthers has gone down to ask the Superintendent."

The two women subsided on to a couch. The elder one gave an order to a waiter, the younger one glanced indifferently around. Her eyes rested for a moment upon Gerald. There was nothing personal in their regard — her manner was, indeed, if anything, austere — but Christopher was conscious of a sudden indrawn breath, almost a sob, which escaped from his companion's lips.

" I wish Carruthers would come," the latter muttered impatiently. " I didn't exaggerate, did I, Chris? "

" No," the latter admitted, " I can't say that you did. She is very wonderful and very interesting. It is quite your day for adventures."

Gerald laughed scornfully.

" You're not comparing our little protégée from the hills with — with her, are you? " he demanded.

" Each has her charm," Christopher replied.

Gerald leaned back in his chair and laughed long and heartily.

" Our little wild rose," he said, " is like a thousand others — a pretty face, a fascinating age, confiding manners. In twenty-four hours she would have taught you all that she could know of love and life. She is as much a yokel intellectually as this girl is a mystery. Are there any queens or royal princesses wandering about the world nowadays, Chris? I swear that she looks as though she had stepped down from a throne. Thank heavens, here comes Carruthers! "

A young man who had been staring in at the doorway recognised Gerald and came across to them.

" No go, old thing," he confided, leaning down. " They are registered here as Madame and Mademoiselle de Ponière — aunt and niece. The old buffer downstairs, however, admitted that he believed that to be an assumed name."

" Couldn't you bribe him, or something? " Gerald asked eagerly.

" Old Johnny fairly cornered me," Carruthers explained. " The two ladies, he told me, had declared their desire to remain incognito. It was not, therefore, the business of a gentleman to be inquisitive. Whereupon I came away with my tail between my legs. All the same, I don't believe he has the least idea who they are."

" They can't possibly escape for more than a few days, in a place like this, without being recognised," Gerald declared.

Carruthers stroked an incipient moustache.

" One gets nasty knocks sometimes," he observed. " There was a milliner and her head mannequin who fairly knocked them all silly at Biarritz last season."

" Don't be a blatant ass, Freddy! " Gerald exclaimed contemptuously. " Mannequins can learn to strut but not to walk. That habit of walking into a crowded room as though you were the only person in it isn't picked up in Bond Street or the Rue de la Paix. I ——"

Gerald was suddenly on his feet. The younger of the two women, in turning towards her companion, had swept a small lace handkerchief, which she had laid upon the table in front of them, to the floor. She made no effort herself to regain possession of it, but glanced towards the waiter. Gerald, however, already held it in his fingers.

" I believe this is your hankerchief, mademoiselle," he ventured:

She accepted it with a very slight but sufficiently gracious smile.

" I thank you very much, sir," she said, speaking in English, with a slight foreign accent.

Some casual remark was already framing itself upon Gerald's lips, but it remained unuttered. The girl had turned and resumed her conversation with her companion. She had the air of not realising that there was another person in the room. The young man, with a little bow, returned to his place. He hid his feelings perfectly, but his two companions could guess at his discomfiture.

" It's no good, old chap," Carruthers assured him confidentially. " They simply aren't taking any. That Italian Prince with the swivel eye, whom all the women are raving about, tried his best to get into conversation.

Managed to get one of his pals to address him by name,
so that they knew who he was, but there was nothing
doing.   Dicky Gordon tried to get a word in edgeways
at the roulette table, but it didn't come off.   One of the
croupiers, whom he knew, went out of his way to whisper
to him that the ladies did not desire acquaintances."

Gerald sighed.

" I shall know her sooner or later," he muttered,
" but it's such a waste of precious time."

The woman and the girl rose presently to their feet
and turned towards the door.   Gerald, for the first time
in his life, felt himself guilty of an impertinence.   He
watched them descend the stairs, watched a bowing
servant run and fetch a waiting automobile.   He even,
from his position at the top of the steps, leaned forward
to hear if any word of address was spoken.   He was un-
rewarded.   A footman opened the door of the car, closed
it and mounted to the side of the chauffeur.   The car
drove rapidly away in the direction of Nice.   Gerald
waited for the porter to remount the steps and slipped
a ten franc note in his hand.

" Do you know who those two ladies were? " he asked.

" They call themselves Madame and Mademoiselle de
Ponière," the man replied, after a moment's hesitation.

" Call themselves? " Gerald repeated.   " What do
you mean by that? "

The man shrugged his shoulders.

" There are many who come here who do not desire
their presence to be known, monsieur," he said cau-
tiously.

" Criminals, perhaps, — or royalty? " Gerald ventured.

The man looked imperturbably through the revolving
doors.

" Many of all sorts, monsieur," he assented. " Monsieur will excuse."

He hastened off on some excuse connected with a waiting automobile. Gerald had no alternative but to rejoin Carruthers and Christopher, whom he found watching the play at one of the roulette tables.

" Any luck? " the former asked eagerly.

" Not an iota," Gerald confessed. " I tipped the man who saw them off, but he either knew nothing or would tell me nothing. — I shall have a plunge at baccarat," he added. " I feel like gambling this evening."

" You won't forget that we promised to go and see Myrtile early? " Christopher reminded him.

Gerald stared at his friend.

" Myrtile? Who the devil —— Why, the child from the violet farm, of course! I'd forgotten all about her."

CHAPTER IV

MYRTILE came flying to the door. Christopher saw her eyes travel over his shoulder, he saw the sudden cloud upon her face. A queer little stab of pain startled him by its very poignancy.

"Monsieur Gerald, he is not with you?" she asked disconsolately.

Christopher shook his head.

"He was up late last night," he explained. "I went to his room but he was fast asleep. I dare say he will come on presently."

The girl looked at the clock — a brazen, loudly ticking affair of bright gilt.

"He promised to be here early," she said. "Has he spoken of me? Has he said anything about sending me back?"

"Nothing," Christopher assured her. "Do you still feel that you don't want to go back?"

She stood quite still in the middle of the little apartment and looked at him. Something about her was altered. It seemed almost as though she had passed from girlhood to womanhood in the night.

"I will not go back," she declared fiercely. "It is not that I mind poverty or hard work. It is Pierre Leschamps. I could not bear him near me. He shall never come near me, otherwise I shall die. Even you, Monsieur Christopher, you do not wish me to die."

Her eyes were swimming with tears. She leaned a little towards him and Christopher patted her encourag-

ingly.   Her lips were very close to his, fresh and sweet
and quivering.   Christopher, conscious of a rare and almost overmastering temptation, turned away brusquely.

"Come outside," he invited.   "I will take you on the
Terrace, and we will sit in the sunshine."

She clapped her hands, herself again almost immediately.

"Oh, I am so anxious to go down to the edge of the
sea!" she cried.   "It is so wonderful.   You will not
mind, monsieur, that I have no hat and that my clothes
are very poor?   If you should meet your friends, they
will wonder what place I have with you."

"I have no friends here," Christopher assured her,
"and if I had, it would not matter.   Presently I will
try to find Gerald again, and we will make up our minds
what to do with you."

"Monsieur Gerald will arrange everything," Myrtile
said confidently, as they walked out into the sunshine.
"He will find me some work — I am sure of that — only
I hope that it will not take me far away.   I should like
to be near him."

They wandered down from the fashionable part of the
promenade to the pebbly beach and along the sands.
Myrtile was never tired of the wonder of it all.   Often,
however, she cast an anxious look backwards.

"You do not think Monsieur Gerald will be searching
for us?" she asked timidly.

Christopher was conscious of a curious sense of an-
noyance which he could not altogether explain.   He led
the way up the steps and on to the Terrace.

"We will take a seat here," he suggested.   "We can
see the hotel and the turning to your lodgings, and you
can watch for him."

She acquiesced willingly, and for the next half-hour

she divided her attention between the entrance to the hotel and the passers-by. At the end of that time she became a little self-conscious.

" It is not right, Monsieur Christopher," she said, " that I sit here with you in these clothes and without a hat. People look at us so strangely."

" You look very nice," Christopher assured her, " and besides, it is no one else's business but our own."

" Then why do they look at me so strangely? " she persisted. " It must be because I have no toilette, no hat, my shoes are ugly. Indeed, monsieur, it is no place for me. Here are friends of yours coming, I am sure — the beautifully dressed young lady who looks at me so curiously."

" It is Gerald's father and sister," he whispered.

She was suddenly very white and frightened. Christopher rose to his feet. Lady Mary nodded a little coldly, Lord Hinterleys acknowledged his greeting with some surprise.

" Where is Gerald this morning? " his sister asked.

"A little lazy, I am afraid," Christopher replied. " When he got your message that there was to be no golf to-day, he went to sleep again."

"And this is your little protégée, I suppose? " Mary remarked, looking at Myrtile.

" This is Myrtile," Christopher assented. " We are waiting for Gerald now to decide what to do with her."

" You wish to leave home, I understand? " Mary asked, turning to the girl, who had risen to her feet.

" I will never return there," Myrtile replied, — " no, not even if Monsieur Gerald himself commanded me to. I would sooner throw myself into the sea."

" Isn't that a little extreme? " her questioner rejoined coldly.

"The misery I should have to face if I returned would also be extreme," Myrtile declared. "I am hoping to find some work here."

"That should not be difficult," Mary observed. "Give Gerald our love, Christopher. I was sorry to have to put off the golf, but dad didn't feel equal to Mont Agel this morning."

"Nothing serious, I hope, sir?" Christopher enquired.

"Nothing at all," Lord Hinterleys replied. "I was a little tired, and I always feel the air up there rather strong. Tell Gerald I hope we shall see him some time during the day."

He raised his hat and they passed on, Mary with a nod to Christopher which lacked much of its usual cordiality. Myrtile looked after them and there was trouble in her face.

"They do not like me," she said. "They do not think that I ought to be here with you. They are right, of course. I am just a little peasant girl in peasant girl's clothes. Let us go."

Christopher's remonstrances were in vain. She turned and walked away, and he was obliged to follow. Just as they were leaving the promenade, however, they came face to face with Gerald, issuing from the hotel. He gave a little start as he recognised Myrtile. Except for a careless thought when he had first awakened, he had forgotten all about her. It was characteristic of him, however, to behave during the next few minutes as though he had been thinking of no one else.

"So Christopher has been stealing a march on me!" he exclaimed. "Has he shown you all the sights, Myrtile?"

"I waited a long time for you," she replied. "We

have been sitting on the Terrace. Monsieur Christopher thought that you would come there."

"And Myrtile has been a little troublesome," Christopher said. " She is going back to her rooms to hide because of her clothes."

" Clothes? " Gerald repeated. " Why, of course she must have clothes. We ought to have thought of that when we brought her away."

" But, monsieur," she began timidly, " even the clothes which I have at home — my communion gown ——"

Gerald waved his arm.

" Come along," he invited. " We will transform you. What a joke! "

" Oh, monsieur! " Myrtile cried, with glistening eyes.

" I suggest," Christopher intervened, " that if we are going to buy her a frock we go to one of those shops higher up in the town."

Gerald waved aside the suggestion.

" We will go to Lénore's," he said. " Madame Lénore is a great pal of mine. Myrtile, you shall have clothes fit for a duchess."

" Then they would not be fit for me," Myrtile objected doubtfully.

" Nor, I should think," Christopher added, " would they help her to obtain a situation."

Gerald, however, would listen to no remonstrances. He ushered them into a quiet but sumptuous-looking little establishment, only a few doors from the Hôtel de Paris. A Frenchwoman, dark and attractive, came forward to welcome them. As soon as she recognised Gerald, the conventional smile became one of real welcome.

"Ah, monsieur — milord! " she exclaimed. " It is

good to see you again! Her ladyship was here only three days ago. I ventured to ask if you were to be expected. Milord does me a great honour by this visit. Will you please to sit down?"

"Madame," Gerald declared, "I am here on business. We have with us a princess — the Princess Myrtile."

"A princess?" Madame repeated, with a wondering glance at the girl.

"A princess in everything but clothes," Gerald explained. "That is your part. We hand her over to you. Dress her, Madame. We will return in an hour."

Madame's eyes sparkled. To the real Frenchwoman, every feeling gives way when it becomes a question of profit. She looked at Myrtile appraisingly.

"Mademoiselle will be worth dressing," she assured them joyfully. "Return, as you say, in an hour, milord, and I can promise that mademoiselle shall be all that you would desire."

Christopher for the first time intervened.

"Look here, Gerald," he said, "I don't think that you are giving Madame quite the right idea."

"In what respect?"

"Mademoiselle is the daughter of working folk," Christopher explained. "She requires clothes of good quality, if you will, but clothes in which she can seek a situation. That is so, is it not, Myrtile?"

The girl's eyes were fixed anxiously upon Gerald.

"I should like to have what Monsieur Gerald would wish me to have," she replied.

"Mademoiselle has a figure so fashionable," Madame Lénore murmured, "so slim yet so elegant, and an expression altogether spirituelle. I have some frocks only this morning arrived from Paris, in which she would seem a dream."

" We do not desire mademoiselle to become a dream,"
Christopher said stoutly. " We have the charge of her
for a short time only, and the sort of toilette which you
have in your mind, I think, Madame Lénore, would be
highly unsuitable. Am I not right, Gerald? "

" Oh, I suppose so," the young man agreed. " I'd
rather like to see her in one of Madame Lénore's crea-
tions, though."

" Milord and monsieur," Madame said, " leave it to
me. Return in an hour. There shall be two costumes
ready. You shall take your choice. If mademoiselle
will have the goodness to step this way ——"

The two young men wandered out. They made their
way back to the Terrace, where Lord Hinterleys walked
for a time, leaning on Gerald's arm. Mary drew Christopher on one side.

" So that is your little protégée," she remarked.

" That is she," Christopher admitted.

" I do not wish to seem a prude," Mary continued,
" or anything else disagreeable, but do you really think
that you are doing the right thing, Christopher, in sitting about on the Terrace with a peasant girl dressed
— er — according to her position? The whole escapade, I think, is ridiculous. I am not so surprised at
Gerald but I am surprised at you."

Christopher was conscious of some irritation. He
liked and admired Lady Mary, but it seemed to him
that her attitude was a little unsympathetic.

" I can quite understand the whole incident seeming
ill-advised," he admitted, " but, looking back at it, I
honestly cannot see what else we could have done."

" You could have left the girl where she was," Mary
insisted.

Christopher shook his head.

" You didn't see her," he replied. " No one could have left her. When I think of what we saw in her face, even now I am inclined to shiver."

" Is she different, then, from other girls faced with an uncomfortable home situation? "

" I think that what I am going to say may sound absurd," Christopher admitted, " but she is different. She may be only a peasant by birth, but she has a soul."

" Really! " his companion murmured.

" No actress could have simulated the horror we saw shining out of her face," he persisted. " I don't think that I should ever have thought of bringing her away — it was Gerald who did that — but I think that he was right, and I should never consent to sending her back unless she were willing to go."

"And exactly what do you two young men propose to do with her, then? " Mary enquired. " The girl is very attractive. You are aware, I suppose, that the situation lends itself to misconstruction? "

He looked at her reproachfully.

" I suppose there are very few of our actions which might not be misinterpreted in one way or another," he replied.

She accepted the challenge of his eyes, looking him squarely in the face.

" It is not you I am so much afraid of," she said. " It is Gerald."

" But you don't believe ——" he began.

" I believe that Gerald's intentions are always good," she interrupted; " he is capable, even, of idealism. On the other hand, he is fatally weak, especially where women are concerned. I fancy," she went on, " you will find that you have assumed a dual responsibility, and I fancy, too, that some day you will be sorry for it."

They slackened their pace. Just ahead, Gerald and his father had met two women, old friends, with whom they were exchanging greetings. Lord Hinterleys was talking with the elder; Gerald to her daughter. The slight air of boredom, which the latter so often wore, had completely disappeared. He was leaning towards the girl tenderly, almost affectionately. His eyes were holding hers, he was talking earnestly and apparently with conviction. Lady Mary touched her companion's arm.

"That is the Gerald whom you have to fear," she said. "You might trust him in any other walk of life, but, although he is my own brother, I don't believe that he has a grain of conscience where women are concerned. He doesn't care about that girl, she is not the sort of person he ever would care for, yet she will go back to lunch to-day convinced that she has made a conquest, thinking of what he has said to her, and finding every one else's manner and words ordinary. Gerald has the spirit of the philanderer in his blood. If the girl attracts him sufficiently, you, at any rate — and probably he — will be sorry you did not leave her to her village lover."

"You have described Gerald correctly when you called him a philanderer," Christopher admitted. "I put myself in court, and on his behalf I plead guilty to the charge. On the other hand, I have greater faith in his kindness of heart and his sense of honour than you seem to have. This child is helpless and innocent. For that reason I believe that she will be as safe with Gerald as with me."

Lady Mary sighed. The look of trouble still lingered in her eyes.

"I hope that you may be right," she said. "I am

not a superstitious person, but I have some sort of foreboding about that child. I feel that she is going to bring trouble, somehow or other. — In any case, let us change the subject. The Rushmores have arrived and want some tennis. Shall we play — say — Wednesday afternoon?"

"Delighted!" Christopher assented, already pleasantly conscious of a changing atmosphere.

CHAPTER V

It is a fact that when the two young men reëntered the establishment of Madame Lénore, they both failed utterly to recognise the girl who was standing in a distant corner, talking to the proprietress. It was not until she detached herself and came hesitatingly up to them that they realised, with varying sensations, who she was. Gerald laughed with pleasure and held out both his hands. Christopher's admiration was tempered with a certain amount of distinct disapprobation.

" Well, what does milord think? " Madame demanded.

" My congratulations! " Gerald replied enthusiastically. " My dear Myrtile, I wonder if you realise how charming you are? "

The girl looked shyly up at Gerald, her face soft and eloquent with pleasure.

" Mademoiselle, like that, can go anywhere," Madame continued. " She can lunch, if you will, with a prince at the Hôtel de Paris, spend the afternoon at the Sporting Club, or attend the reception which the Spanish Ambassador is giving this afternoon. She is absolutely correct and in the latest môde."

The two young men still contemplated their charge. She was clad in a fine white serge costume, trimmed with silver braid. Her lace blouse was delicately filmy and transparent, the cut of her skirt as scanty as the last word from Paris had decreed; her white silk stockings and suède shoes, procured from a neighbouring establishment, irreproachable; her large hat, a gossamer-like confection of tulle and lace. Of the charm of her appearance there could be no possible question, but, in exact proportion with Gerald's satisfaction, Christopher's disapproval seemed to grow.

" I do not criticise your clothes, Madame, or your taste," he said, " but we have given you the wrong idea. Mademoiselle is in search of a situation. She is a working girl for whose future as a working girl my friend and I are anxious to provide. Those clothes are entirely unsuitable."

Christopher's words fell like a bombshell in the little establishment. Myrtile's eyes slowly filled with tears. Gerald was frankly angry. Madame shrugged her shoulders.

" I did not understand that the position of mademoiselle debarred her from being dressed becomingly," she said, a little drily. " In any case, it is a great waste not to give mademoiselle the advantage of charming clothes. Her figure — why, it is adorable; of her complexion and carriage you can judge for yourselves. Mademoiselle, dressed as she is now, and with one or two evening gowns which I have in my mind, would make the sensation of the season in Monte Carlo."

" And what good would that be to her? " Christopher demanded. " Mademoiselle has need to earn her living, and to earn it honourably."

" Look here, Chris," Gerald interrupted, " you're taking this thing too seriously. We know very well that Myrtile must be found something to do later on, but in the meantime she may as well have a little fun. Can't you see for yourself how wonderful she is? She will puzzle the whole of Monte Carlo for a week."

" And after then? " Christopher asked.

Gerald turned impatiently away. Madame held up a wonderful confection of white lace and silk.

"This is what I figure to myself for mademoiselle's first evening frock," she said, — "this and a hat of black lace, with a string of pearls which I could perhaps borrow. I promise you that she would make a sensation you do not dream of."

"It is not our wish that she make a sensation of this sort," Christopher persisted harshly. "It appears to me that you both wish to provide the child ——"

He stopped short. Gerald's eyes were filled with sudden fire; the girl was trembling.

"You're talking like an ass, Christopher," Gerald declared. "This is my affair."

"It is nothing of the sort," Christopher rejoined stubbornly. "It is our affair. I claim an equal right in disposing of Myrtile, and I will not have her decked out in these clothes. What we need for her is a plain blue serge suit and a small hat. She will always look charming, she will always be attractive, but nothing in her future walk of life justifies our arraying her in clothes like these."

Madame shrugged her shoulders more disparagingly than ever.

"It is as milord and monsieur desire, of course," she said. "I can provide such garments as monsieur describes."

Gerald looked at Myrtile once more. The admiration in his eyes this time, at any rate, was absolutely genuine.

"I can't see the harm in having the child properly turned out for, say, one week," he protested, turning to Christopher.

"And at the end of that week, what?"

There was a deadly directness about Christopher's gaze. Gerald, although there was no definitely formed thought of evil in his mind, avoided it.

" If you are proposing to marry Myrtile," Christopher continued, " then the clothes you have selected are suitable. Unless you have made up your mind to do that, I beg that Madame will show us something different."

There was a somewhat hectic silence for several moments. Frenchwoman though she was, and full of tact, Madame Lénore could scarcely conceal her contempt for the crudeness of this puritanical Englishman. Myrtile herself felt as though a dream of Paradise were fading away. Gerald, because he was good fellow enough at heart, felt further insistence impossible. He was quite content to drift into danger; he was not casuist enough to evade a plain warning.

" Well, I suppose we shall have to let this disagreeable fellow have his way," he declared. " Take her along, Madame, and see what you can do. You hear my friend's idea — plain blue serge buttoned up to the throat, cashmere stockings and square-toed shoes."

" There will be a compromise," Madame declared firmly. — " And for the rest, little one, do not trouble too much," she whispered, as she led Myrtile away. " I shall keep these clothes just as they are, until the other gentleman has made up his mind to meddle no longer. Come to me when you are ready. I can make you look so that milord will take notice of no other woman."

Myrtile's eyes were swimming with tears.

" It was just for him that I wanted to keep these clothes," she said. " I wanted him to take me out and to feel that I looked like other girls. As for Monsieur Christopher, I detest him!"

"Mademoiselle has reason," the woman murmured.
"He has not the chic of milord. It is a pity that he
should interfere. Perhaps later on milord will bring
you here without him."

Myrtile's eyes shone. Reluctantly she stretched out
her arms and felt the dress slip away from her.

In the showroom outside, neither of the two young
men was particularly disposed for conversation.
Christopher felt a distinct return of his first apprehension concerning Gerald's attitude towards Myrtile,
whilst Gerald himself was conscious of a vague sense
of resentment at his friend's interference, the more
poignant, perhaps, because of its wisdom. Anything
in the nature of an explanation between the two was
rendered impossible by the smallness of the room and
the presence of the shop assistants. So Gerald contented himself with lighting a cigarette, while Christopher studied a book of fashions. Suddenly an event
happened which created a new atmosphere in the little
place. Gerald relinquished his cigarette, Christopher
laid down his volume of fashions, the shop assistants
and mannequins, figuratively speaking, stood to attention. The manageress came hastening forward. An
automobile had stopped outside, a footman had thrown
open the door, Madame and Mademoiselle de Ponière
entered. The latter was simply enough, though richly
dressed, and she entered the shop with the air of one
conferring a peculiar honour upon the establishment.
She carried a little Pekinese dog under her arm; the
footman remained standing outside as though on guard.
The greeting of the manageress was almost reveren-
tial.

"Mademoiselle desires to see our new models?"

The newcomer glanced half unconsciously towards

the two young men, who had risen to their feet. Then
she passed on, followed by the older woman, to the
most distant corner of the room. It appeared that she
wished to look at hats, and the whole establishment
seemed at once infected with an eager desire to serve
her. Hats were produced on every side, and passed
from hand to hand with an air of deep anxiety. Mademoiselle, however, it transpired was not easy to please.
She sat watching the various confections which were
produced for her inspection, with an air of tolerant indifference. Gerald moved to the side of the bookkeeper,
who alone remained at her place behind the little
desk.

"Tell me," he whispered, "who is that young lady?"

"She appears in our books, milord, under the name
of Mademoiselle de Ponière," was the discreet reply.

"But what is her real name?" Gerald persisted.
"Who are her friends? Is it possible to make her acquaintance?"

The woman looked at him with a slight smile. She
had a tired and rather faded face, and her hair was
lined with grey.

"One hears only rumours as to whom she may be,"
she answered. "For the rest, milord should apply to
Madame herself."

Gerald waited for Madame's reappearance with a
new impatience. Presently Myrtile came out to them
once more. The transformation was still amazing, but
the blue serge costume was absolutely plain except for
its thick edging of braid, and the little toque, with its
dark blue quill, absolutely free from ornamentation.
Yet it seemed almost incredible that this graceful girl
who came towards them a little shyly but with perfect
self-possession should indeed be the peasant child who

had been under their care for rather less than twenty-four hours.

"Mademoiselle is transformed," Madame Lénore declared. "She has natural elegance. In the simplest clothes I could give her, she would still create an impression. I have done my best, milord and monsieur. I trust that you are satisfied?"

"Entirely," Gerald assented. "But, Madame Lénore, I want a word with you."

"If milord would excuse me for one moment," Madame begged, with a glance towards the further end of the shop. "One of my most valued clients has arrived."

Gerald drew her on one side. Myrtile glanced a little anxiously into Christopher's face.

"Monsieur Gerald does not seem satisfied," she complained. "He has no longer any pleasure in looking at me. He does not like me in these clothes."

"Nonsense!" Christopher replied. "Believe me, they are far more suitable than the others."

Myrtile was still not altogether satisfied.

"They are very wonderful," she acknowledged, looking at herself in the glass, "and I am very, very grateful, but when I came before, his whole face seemed alight with pleasure, and this time he scarcely took any notice of me at all."

"There is something else on his mind," Christopher assured her. "I am certain that he is satisfied."

Gerald found Madame Lénore quite obdurate.

"It is impossible, milord," she declared firmly. "With many of my clients, yes. There would be no cause for hesitation. But to present you to mademoiselle would be impossible. She would not respond. She would never pardon the liberty."

" Then will you tell me who her friends are? " he
persisted. " Let me know, at least, where I should be
likely to meet her? "

Madame's manner had lost much of its amiability.
She seemed genuinely worried.

" Milord," she said, " none of these things are possible."

" But who is she, then? "

Madame Lénore turned away.

" No one knows," she answered under her breath.
" It is not for us to know. Milord will excuse me."

Gerald rejoined his companions with a cloud upon his
handsome face. Myrtile watched him timidly.

" You do not approve of these clothes? " she ventured.

" I approve of them so much," Gerald announced,
pulling himself together with an effort, " that I am
going to take you to Ciro's to lunch. Come along,
Christopher. Madame Lénore is a disobliging old cat."

CHAPTER VI

THE two women sat on the terrace of their wistaria-covered villa, — Madame de Ponière hunched up in her chair, smoking a cigarette through a long tube; Pauline, her reputed niece, her coffee and cigarette alike neglected, gazing fixedly seawards. Their immediate environment suggested at once a taste for luxury and the means to gratify it. The linen and silver on the little table at which they had just lunched was of the finest possible quality, — the former lace-bordered and adorned with a coronet. A bowl of pink roses occupied the centre of the table. The coffee had been served in little cups of the finest Sèvres china. In the background, a single servant was standing, dressed in plain black livery, a man grey-haired and with lined face, but tall and of powerful build. He possessed to the full the immobility of feature of the trained English servant, but there was something entirely foreign in his sphinx-like attitude and expression. He had the air of one who neither saw nor heard save at his mistress's orders.

"I am weary of everything here except the sun," Pauline declared deliberately.

The woman opposite knocked the ash from her cigarette. Hers was an aged and withered face, but her black eyes were still full of life and fire. Her long, thin hand, on which flashed several strangely set rings, was suddenly extended towards the waiting servant. Without a word he bowed and disappeared.

"One must wait," Madame de Ponière declared.

"For what?" the girl asked lazily.

The older woman's eyes glittered for a moment.

" For what will surely come," she declared. " The portents are all there. The writing is no longer upon the wall — it blazes to the sky."

" And meanwhile," Pauline murmured, " the sun shines, my heart beats in tune to it, and I feel all the time the weariness of the days."

" It is the insurgence of youth," the older woman conceded indulgently. " I suppose the greatest must feel it some day."

" There was a girl in the dressmaker's shop," Pauline went on. " The good Madame Lénore amused me by speaking of her. She is a peasant, it seems, picked up on the road by two young Englishmen and brought here for the first time in her life only yesterday. These young men have amused themselves by decking her out in the clothes of another class. The girl is beautiful, and she sees fairyland everywhere. She is in love with one of the young men, of course. One could see that in her face."

" A very ordinary affair," the older woman observed. " What of it? "

" Nothing except that I rather envy the girl."

Madame de Ponière's black eyes glistened dangerously.

" It would be easy to change places with her," she said coldly. " You are probably as beautiful, and the trifle of breeding you possess might be considered an asset."

Pauline smiled, and her face was at once more attractive than ever. There were little creases about her soft brown eyes, her mouth lost its discontented curve and became at once tremulous and gentle.

" It is an encouraging thought," she murmured,

" especially as the young man whom the girl appears to fancy has already endeavoured to make my acquaintance."

" It is the worst of this place," Madame de Ponière declared, a little viciously. " The men are all *boulevardiers. Canaille!* "

" The young man in question happens to be an aristocrat," Pauline observed, her eyes fixed upon the adjoining villa.

" The more reason for care," the woman muttered.

Pauline sighed.

" I might perhaps save him from the peasant girl. They tell me that these young Englishmen often regard an intrigue of this sort differently from our own people. He might even be led to marry her. He looks like a man of weak character."

The older woman thrust another cigarette into her tube and lit it. She inhaled with the long, regular breaths of the confirmed smoker. Her delicately shaped but talon-like fingers were stained with nicotine.

" Zubin arrives this week," she announced.

Pauline yawned.

" More mysteries," she murmured, " more false hopes, more exaggerated stories. Nothing good will come of Zubin's visit but the money he brings, unless by any chance he has news of Stepan. — Meanwhile, dear Madame, I bore myself. I rather wish that I had been born an American."

The woman showed no sign of anger, yet somehow or other she seemed to diffuse an atmosphere of contempt.

" It is perhaps a pity," she admitted, " that you are descended from one of the greatest rulers the world has ever known. It is perhaps a pity."

"Give me something to rule over," the girl declared, "and I will be repentant — the souls and liberties of a few million people, or the hearts of a few men. I am twenty-three years old and the sun is warm. And then there is the music, our one resource when there is no money to gamble with. What is the use of music, Madame, to one who lives behind the bars? It simply makes one pull at them a little harder. I am as badly off as Stepan himself, who loves me from behind the fortress walls. Sometimes I wish that I were there with him."

Madame de Ponière reached for an ivory-topped stick and rose to her feet. Almost as though by magic, from somewhere within the dim, cool recesses of the room beyond, the grey-haired manservant was by her side. She leaned upon his arm.

"We drive at four o'clock, Pauline," she said. "Afterwards, we will watch the play at the Sporting Club."

Pauline shrugged her shoulders. It was the same yesterday afternoon, and every day behind. It would probably be the same to-morrow, — the same for her, but not for that peasant girl. For her there was no stereotyped routine. She looked intently across the narrow gorge towards that other villa. A two-seated car had turned in from the road and was crawling up the winding avenue. She stretched out her hand for the field glasses which lay on the table by her side. The young man at the wheel was the young man at whom the peasant girl had looked.

Pauline rose to her feet. Almost as mysteriously as the manservant had appeared a few moments before, a black-robed maid hastened towards her. Pauline shook her head.

" This afternoon I do not wish to rest," she decided. " I shall walk in the gardens."

" Mademoiselle desires that I shall attend her? " the maid asked.

Her mistress hesitated.

" I desire to be alone," she announced.

Pauline descended the stone steps, crossed the drive, and plunged into a narrow footpath which wound its way through a plantation of stunted but sweet-smelling pine trees, downwards towards the sea. The path was not an easy one, and Pauline's shoes were scarcely designed for such an adventure. Nevertheless, she persevered. She had almost to push her way through a grove of oleanders, and to wrap her skirts carefully around her as she passed between some spiky cactus trees. As last, however, she gained her end. She stood upon the little strip of sand, besprinkled with rocks, which bordered the sea. Only a few yards away the shimmering blue water rocked towards the land in little wavelets. She turned and looked back. The villa from which she had come seemed like a doll's house shining out of its sheltering clump of cypresses. More directly above her now was the far more extensive residence of Lord Hinterleys. She looked towards it searchingly. There were several people upon the broad verandah, amongst them the slim figure of a young man at its farther edge, gazing intently in her direction. She smiled a little as she picked her steps across the yellow sand to the edge of the sea and clambered on to a rock. There was a breeze here which she had scarcely anticipated. For the first time she realised that she was bareheaded, ungloved, — she to whom usualness in all things was almost an instilled religion. A queer fit of heedlessness, however, was upon her. She stood upon

the top of the slippery rock, finding a strange pleasure
in the salt-laden air and the wind which brought a
thousand ripples of light to the trembling blue sea,
which blew her skirts about, and even brought disar-
rangement to her smoothly bound hair. This temper-
ing of the sunshine brought a new joy to its warmth.
She stood there basking in a purely sensuous pleasure,
forgetful for a moment of the depression of the morning. The sound of tumbling stones in the little gorge
behind scarcely disturbed her. It was not until she
heard footsteps upon the strip of beach that she turned
her head. Coming towards her, already only a few
yards away, was a young man of personable appearance and unwontedly determined expression. For once
in his life, Gerald had made up his mind.

CHAPTER VII

GERALD, although he was in reality brimful of confidence in all his relations with the other sex, had sometimes a not altogether unattractive appearance of shyness. He stood bareheaded for a moment, looking up at Pauline.

"I am so sorry if I startled you," he said. "I was looking for my sister. I know this is a favourite place of hers, and when I saw you standing there I rather jumped to the conclusion that you must be she."

"Really?" Pauline replied. "Are we so much alike, then?"

"Not in the least," he declared frankly.

"That seems to make your explanation a little insufficient, does it not?" Pauline remarked.

Gerald settled down to business.

"I know that I ought to have turned back," he said, "but, after all, wasn't it much more natural of me to come on? I have been trying, ever since I first saw you, to get some one to introduce me — we are, after all, as I have just discovered, to my great delight, neighbours — and this is the Riviera, not Berkeley Square. May I tell you that my name is Gerald Dombey, that my father and sister have the villa up there, and that, from the moment I saw you, I have been anxious to make your acquaintance?"

She looked at him in silence for a moment, half critically, half thoughtfully. There was nothing absolutely discouraging in her attitude, and yet Gerald somehow conceived the idea that this might not, after all, be so easy an affair as he had hoped.

"Are you used to enlarging your acquaintance in this manner?" she asked.

"I very seldom feel the desire to do so," he assured her. "Don't be annoyed, please. I am really quite a respectable person. I will call upon your aunt, if she will give me permission."

For the first time Pauline smiled. It was rather a cold smile, but the fact that it was a smile at all was encouraging.

"I fancy that you had better dismiss that suggestion from your mind altogether," she said. "My aunt does not receive here, and she certainly would not welcome you as a caller."

"Why not?" Gerald enquired, a little perturbed.

"Because you are a young man," Pauline replied. "There are two things which my aunt dreads more than anything else in life, — a bad throat for herself, and young men for me."

"I don't see how she can hope to keep young men away from you altogether," Gerald declared. "You don't mind my saying, do you, that you are the sort of girl whom young men would want to know?"

Her smile returned. She even laughed slightly, showing some very wonderful teeth.

"Really, you are a most singular person," she observed. "Do all young Englishmen talk to casual acquaintances in this unrestrained fashion?"

Gerald was puzzled. Pauline was not altogether falling into line with the conclusions he had arrived at concerning her.

"I don't know that I am very different from the others," he said. "Tell me, what is your nationality?"

"Why should I tell you anything about myself?" she asked, a little coldly.

"It appeared to me that it might — er — help our acquaintance."

"Have I acknowledged the acquaintance?"

"Well, you are talking to me, anyhow," he pointed out, with a slight twinkle in his eyes.

"I scarcely see how I could help it," she replied. "If you are really curious about my nationality, I will tell you that I have some French blood in my veins. France, however, is not my native country."

"And you live — where?"

"Nowhere," she answered, a little sadly. "At present we are wanderers — what you call in England adventurers."

Gerald raised his eyebrows.

"That is scarcely the word," he murmured.

"My aunt has a curious objection to meeting people upon our travels," Pauline continued. "I myself find her aloofness sometimes a little tedious. That is why I am misbehaving to the extent of letting you talk to me."

"Your aunt seems a very difficult person," Gerald sighed. "I don't see why I can't make her acquaintance and ask you both out to dine."

"Do not think of such things!" the girl enjoined hastily. "Before I say another word to you, promise me that you do not present yourself at the Villa or give any indication of knowing me, if we should meet at the Club or anywhere."

"But why on earth not?" Gerald demanded. "If your aunt is such a stickler for propriety, surely I can find some one to present me?"

"If you do not promise me what I ask," she threat-

ened, holding her skirts in one hand and looking as
though prepared to jump down from the rock, " I
shall leave you at once."

" I promise, of course," he assented. " Meanwhile,
may I be allowed to ask, as between us two, — do I
know you or do I not? "

" We are complete strangers," she declared.

" Accept my profound apologies for addressing you,"
Gerald begged, with a low bow.

Pauline reflected for a moment.

" As a matter of propriety," she said, " you certainly ought to leave me at once. As a matter of fact,
I was about to propose something else."

" Let me hear it, at any rate," he insisted.

" I watched you drive up to your father's villa in
your car. Will you take me a little way in it? "

" Rather! " he assented eagerly. " Where shall I
pick you up? "

" Outside the Villa gates," she replied. " My aunt
is absolutely certain to sleep for two hours. It is the
only liberty I have during the day. Please go at once
and fetch the car."

She dismissed him with an imperative wave of the
hand. As soon as he was out of sight, she jumped
down from the rock, crossed the little strip of sand,
and commenced her leisurely ascent to the Villa. Once
or twice she laughed softly to herself.

It was an excursion which Gerald pondered on many
times afterwards. Pauline had settled down in the low
bucket seat by his side and leaned back with an air of
absolute content. She had, in fact, the appearance of
one enjoying a rare pleasure. As soon as Gerald slackened speed, however, with the idea of entering into conversation, she became curt and almost rude, and his

proposition that they might take the higher road and
have tea at Nice she promptly negatived. When, after
an absence of about an hour and a half, they drew up
at the gates of the Villa, she left him with the merest
nod of farewell.

"You will come for another ride soon — perhaps to-
morrow?" he asked anxiously.

She shook her head.

"I can make no plans," she replied. "I should think
it very improbable. I thank you so much for your
kindness. Your car is quite wonderful."

She walked away with the air of one who has con-
ferred a great favour. Gerald drove slowly back to
the Villa d'Acacia and joined his sister on the terrace.

"Do you know anything about the two women at
the next villa, Mary?" he asked.

She looked up from her novel doubtfully.

"One never knows one's neighbours here," she answered. "I saw them driving, the other day — a
strange-looking old lady and a very good-looking girl.
Isn't there something queer about them, or is it my
fancy?"

"There is something unusual," Gerald replied.
"They seem curiously indisposed to forming acquaintances, which is odd in a place like this. I happened to
be talking to the younger woman for a few minutes.
She gave me the impression, somehow, that they were
people of greater consequence than their manner of
living here would indicate."

"I expect I am uncharitable," Mary observed. "An
elderly lady with no friends, who takes a rather beautiful young woman about with her to public places, does
certainly invite comment, doesn't she? Tell me about
your little protégée?"

" We lunched with her, Chris and I," Gerald replied.

" Goodness gracious! Where? "

" At Ciro's. We bought her some clothes at Lénore's, this morning."

Lady Mary lit a cigarette and threw down her book.

" I am not the guardian of your morals, Gerald," she observed drily; " a girl, nowadays, has all she can do to look after her own — but I honestly think you ought to send that child back to her people."

" Too brutal," he replied. " They wanted to marry her to some horrible old man."

" Whatever the position was, your interference was most uncalled for," his sister declared. " As for Christopher, I am really surprised at him. Where is he this afternoon, by-the-by? "

" I left him with Myrtile," Gerald replied. " You'd better talk to him. He's been lecturing me all the time — kicked up a row, even, because I wanted to buy the child pretty clothes."

The butler came out on to the terrace.

" Mr. Rushmore has telephoned from the tennis club, my lord, to know if you and her ladyship will make up a set. They are waiting now for a reply."

Mary rose to her feet.

" I am all for it, if you can, Gerald," she declared.

" Tell Mr. Rushmore that we'll be down as soon as we can change," Gerald directed the butler. " You needn't order a car. I'll run you round in the coupé, Mary."

" Shan't be ten minutes," his sister promised.

On their way up the hill, they passed Christopher and Myrtile. Gerald rather enjoyed his sister's look of amazement.

"Doesn't she look a topper!" he remarked, as he turned to wave his hand.

"She has an amazing flair for wearing clothes," Mary admitted drily. "I think you two young men ought to be thoroughly ashamed of yourselves for what you are doing, and I shall just look forward to an opportunity of telling Christopher so."

Gerald glanced at his sister's profile and chuckled.

"Good old Chris!" he murmured. "I'll let him know what's coming to him!"

CHAPTER VIII

MYRTILE was suddenly tired. She seated herself upon the trunk of a tree, and Christopher followed her example. Below them stretched the motley panorama of Monte Carlo, the wide bay and the glittering sea. The hillside and all the country within sight was dotted with villas. There was one especially, overhanging the sea, towards which she gazed wistfully.

" Do you know," she said, " that I have not seen Monsieur Gerald for three days? "

" He has been busy," Christopher answered shortly.

" Busy? " she queried.

" He plays golf and tennis every day. Then his father and sister take up a good deal of his time."

" You always find time to come and see me every morning," she said. " Besides — it was not his sister with whom I saw him motoring yesterday."

" You must remember," Christopher reminded her, " that Gerald had many friends before you came here."

" I know," she answered. " I cannot hope to count for very much. But why cannot he be at least kind like you? If only he knew how long the days seem when I do not even catch a glimpse of him! "

Christopher braced himself for an effort.

" Myrtile," he began, " you know that I am fond of you."

" You have been very kind," she answered listlessly.

" Because I want to be kind, I am going to say things that may sound harsh," he went on. " You are a very foolish girl to waste your time thinking and dreaming of Gerald. You should only let your thoughts dwell upon one man continually when there is some chance in the end that that man may become your husband."

Her listlessness passed. She settled down to the subject seriously.

"But, Monsieur Christopher ———"

"Christopher," he interrupted.

"Christopher, then — you ask me to do what I plainly see no one else does. Wherever you have taken me here — wherever we go — there are men and women together who are fond of one another. One only needs to look at them to see it. It is so in the restaurants, in the gardens where we sit, in the cafés. I have seen love in the eyes of many girls since I have been here. They do not all expect to marry the men they are with."

Christopher leaned over and laid his hand upon hers.

"Myrtile dear, will you listen to me?" he begged. "Look at me for a moment. I am twenty-six years old. I have lived in cities as well as the country. In London I am what you call an *avocat*. I have to use my brains every day, I have to understand my fellow creatures. Will you get that into your head?"

"It is not difficult," she assured him, with a little smile. "I think you are very clever, and you know many, many things."

"And as for you, Myrtile," Christopher went on, "when one thinks of your upbringing, it is amazing to realise how much you have read, how much you know. But listen to me. Nothing that one reads can teach one what life is like. You spent many hours wondering what was at the end of the road. You think now, because you have passed over the hill, that you are there.

My dear, you are not even at the beginning of the way."

She plucked some grasses and twined them round her fingers.

" Go on," she whispered.

" This is not life that you watch day by day. Mostly it is a very garish imitation of it. And in the same way, that light which you see is not always love. It is sometimes a very unworthy imitation of it."

" They seem very happy," she murmured.

" They are not happy — they are only gay," Christopher insisted. " Sometimes they are only pretending to be gay. Sometimes their pretence comes from very unworthy motives. There are dancing girls who smile upon a king, but there is no love in the matter."

" You mean that these people who seem so happy are not in earnest? " she asked.

" I mean that if they are in earnest," he explained, " it is only for the moment. It is a sham earnestness which spoils the real thing when it comes. What you see here is not life. It is not even a very wonderful reflection of it. Mostly it is a little company of pleasure seekers, come to cast aside for a time the serious side of life and gamble with their pleasures as they do with their money."

" But some must be in earnest," Myrtile protested.

" One of them who is not in earnest is Gerald, and I tell you so, although Gerald is my friend," Christopher said. " He is here to amuse himself, and he would prefer to amuse himself without giving any one else pain. If that is impossible, however, he is sufficiently reckless not to count the cost where the other person is concerned."

She drew a little away.

"That does not sound like the speech of a friend," she reminded him reproachfully.

"But I can assure you that I am his friend, although a candid one," Christopher declared. "All that I have said to you, I have said to him, and a great deal more. You will let me finish?"

She made no reply. She had gathered herself up into an attitude which in any one else would have been ungraceful, her chin resting upon her hands, her back curved. Her eyes were fixed upon the exact spot where the sea seemed to melt into the clouds. The grace of her slim body lent beauty even to the hunch of her shoulders.

"You are like a child who has been let out of a dark room," Christopher went on. "Everything seems beautiful, but you don't see clearly — your eyes aren't strong enough yet. What you imagine to be love is a worse thing. Gerald does not love you. He can never marry you. He belongs to that world at which you are looking with blurred eyes. — Myrtile, how old were you when your mother died?"

"Ten years old."

"I thought so!" Christopher exclaimed, in despair. "I am certain your mother was a good woman, Myrtile."

"I know she was," Myrtile answered.

"I wish to God she were alive!" he groaned. "Myrtile, don't you want to be good?"

"I want to be happy," Myrtile replied. "I shall always be good."

"How do you know that?"

"Because I am all good inside," she said. "I couldn't do any of the things that wicked people do."

Christopher sat for a moment in puzzled thought.

" Look here," he went on, " if you love Gerald, and Gerald doesn't love you, and you are content with the pretence of his love, and you go on loving him, and you know that you cannot be his wife, then you are not good any longer."

She shook her head.

" There is only once in my life," she said, " that I have ever come near sin, and that is when I thought of staying at the farm and marrying Pierre Leschamps. I love Gerald. All that I need to be happy and good is that he should love me."

" But Gerald does not love you and never will," Christopher declared bluntly. " He is far too selfish. At the present moment he takes some one else for a motor ride every afternoon, and doesn't get up in time to come and see you in the mornings because he is entertaining the young ladies of the Russian Ballet at supper every night."

She looked at him sadly.

" And you are his friend," she reminded him again.

" Dear, stupid little girl," he said, " don't you see that because I am his friend, and because I am your friend, and because I share the responsibility of having brought you away, I insist upon your realising the truth. Gerald, at the present moment, at any rate, is incapable of a stable affection, and if he were capable of it, his people would not allow him to marry you."

" I do not wish him to marry me," she declared, with a little choke in her voice.

" Perhaps not," he replied. " In that case, you should listen to me more patiently. I want you to leave this place and go to some friends of mine in England."

" What, alone? "

" Alone."

She shook her head.

" Christopher," she said, suddenly slipping her arm through his, " I think you want to be kind to me. I believe that you are very good — perhaps you are better than Gerald. But so long as Gerald wants me near, I shall stay. Even if he goes about with other people, he thinks of me. He has told me so, and he has promised to take me to one of those supper parties this week. I am looking forward to it more than to anything else in the world."

Christopher's face hardened.

" You will not go to one of those supper parties, Myrtile," he insisted. " I would rather take you back to the farm."

She turned her head and looked at him. There was something in her eyes from which he shrank, — something very much like hate.

" If you try to stop me," she threatened, " I shall hate you for ever."

She saw the pain in his face and she was suddenly remorseful. She clung to his arm again. Her cheek almost touched his.

" Christopher — dear Christopher," she pleaded, " I did not mean to hurt you. I know how good you are, but just think how wonderful it would be for me to go with Gerald, to meet other girls, to laugh and talk, to sit by his side, his guest, to dance, perhaps — oh, it would be Paradise! Everybody else goes to parties, Christopher."

" I will take you to the Opera," he promised.

Her eyes glowed.

" It would be wonderful," she murmured, " but you must not prevent my going to the party."

"Myrtile," he pointed out, "the young women whom you would meet there are not fit for you to know."

"But what harm can they do me?" she persisted. "I know that they are not nice. I went to the hotel for a few minutes with Annette last night — she had to go and give her keys to her aunt — and in the distance I saw Gerald, and I hated the people he was with. But what does it matter? Gerald will take care of me."

Christopher rose to his feet. There was a certain hopelessness about his task that he was slowly beginning to realise.

"Come," he said, "it is time we went back. I am playing tennis with Gerald's sister this afternoon."

She took his arm as they scrambled down into the road.

"You are not cross with me, Christopher?" she ventured, a little timidly.

He shook his head.

"No, I am not cross."

"You look so gloomy — even a little miserable," she went on, clinging to his arm and looking up into his face. "I am a very great trouble to you, I fear. Are you not sorry that you ever brought me away?"

"I am not sorry yet, Myrtile," he answered. "I only hope that I never may be."

Her mood suddenly changed. She laughed gaily.

"Oh, là, là!" she cried. "If you look so glum, I shall sing and dance to you, here in the road, as we do at festival time. Gerald says that I must have dancing lessons. He is going to send me to a woman here."

She pirouetted lightly on one foot, a miracle of buoyancy and grace. Then she went suddenly rigid, took her place by his side and clutched at his arm. An auto-

mobile whizzed past them, on its way up the hill: Gerald
was leaning back in the low driving seat, the sun gleaming on his dark, closely brushed hair, his head bent towards his companion; Pauline sat a little aloof,
haughty, unbending, her beautiful face cold, unrelieved
by any light of sympathy or interest. Her eyes swept
carelessly over Christopher and his companion, as they
passed. Gerald did not even see them.

" Who is she? " Myrtile whispered.

" No one knows much about her," Christopher re-
plied. " She and her aunt have the next villa to
Gerald's father. She calls herself Mademoiselle de
Ponière."

Myrtile laughed quietly. She was already herself
again.

" Mademoiselle is a very stupid girl," she declared.
" Gerald was looking at her and she looked only at the
road. She does not care. Gerald will find that out."

Gerald came to the tennis courts, an hour or so later,
and played several sets almost in silence. He had lost
for the moment all that light-hearted gaiety which made
him, even amongst the foreigners who frequented the
place, easily the most popular of the tennis-playing
fraternity. He played brilliantly at times, but with
obvious carelessness. He had the air of a man whose
thoughts are busily engagéd elsewhere. He took Christopher on one side, during one of the periods of rest,
and flung his arm around his shoulder.

" Chris, old man," he confided, " that girl is driving
me mad."

" Myrtile? " Christopher asked, with wilful obtuse-
ness.

" Don't be an ass," was the impatient reply. " You

know very well that I mean Pauline de Ponière. — Tell me, are you dining at the Villa to-night? "

" Not to-night. Your people are dining with the Prince."

" I am engaged to Carruthers but I shall throw him over," Gerald said eagerly. " I want to talk to you."

" And I have a few words I want to say to you," Christopher rejoined.

" We're in this set," Gerald pointed out, rising to his feet. " Let's be alone somewhere, then — Ciro's Grill at eight-thirty."

CHAPTER IX

GERALD and Christopher were a little disappointed with their rendezvous, so far as regards its possibilities for intimate conversation. Although it was twenty minutes to nine when they entered the place, there was still a fair number of loungers around the bar, drinking cocktails, and many of the little tables around the room were already taken. They chose as remote a one as possible, however, and seated themselves side by side, with their backs against the wall. Gerald ordered the dinner and the wine. Then he started the conversation with a somewhat abrupt question.

" Chris," he asked, " exactly what do you think of Mademoiselle de Ponière? "

" I don't know her," Christopher reminded him.

" As a matter of fact, neither do I," Gerald declared, a little bitterly. " She permitted me to introduce myself down on the sands below the Villa, and she has been for a ride with me in the car every afternoon since; yet she does this secretly, and if I meet her with her aunt I am not allowed to speak to her or to expect recognition. I am not permitted to call at the Villa, I don't know where they come from, I don't know even her nationality. Furthermore, they do not appear to know a soul in Monte Carlo, nor have we ever stumbled across a single mutual acquaintance."

" The situation seems peculiar," Christopher admitted. " I can't see the faintest reason why she shouldn't introduce you to her aunt."

" Neither can I," Gerald agreed. " I flatter myself that for my few but well-spent years I have seen something of the world and its snares, but I honestly cannot place these two women."

" What is mademoiselle's attitude towards you when you are alone? " Christopher asked.

" Ridiculously reserved," Gerald answered. " I once touched her fingers and I thought she would have struck me. Humiliating though it may be, I am half inclined to believe that it is the motoring alone which attracts her in the slightest degree, and that I represent very little more to her than the man who is driving the car."

" Do you wish to represent more? " Christopher asked bluntly.

" I don't know," Gerald answered, after a moment's hesitation. " She attracts me horribly. She has done so from the first."

Their conversation was momentarily interrupted by the arrival in the place of a newcomer, a stranger to both the young men. He was tall and broad-shouldered, sallow-skinned, with a mass of black hair, good features, but with hard, almost brutal mouth. Although the night was warm, he wore a huge overcoat, from which he seemed to part with some reluctance. He was in morning clothes of fashionable cut, and he wore a singular number of rings upon his massive fingers. Immediately he had been relieved of his coat, he made his way to the bar, drank two cocktails in rapid succession and lit a cigarette. Then he wandered to the table adjoining the one at which the two young men were seated, and, having given his order for dinner, busied himself making calculations upon some scraps of paper which he tore up as soon as they were filled with figures.

Gerald spoke to the waiter who served them, with whom he was well acquainted.

"A stranger here, Charles?"

The man glanced over his shoulder and lowered his tone.

"A Russian gentleman, milord," he announced, "staying at the Hôtel de Paris — Monsieur Zubin, he calls himself. They say that he has been playing very heavily."

"Russians who play high are no great novelty here," Gerald remarked, under his breath. "There are not so many of them with money, nowadays, though. — Chris," he went on, as the man left them, "you asked yesterday what was the matter with me. I'll tell you. It's this uncertainty about Mademoiselle de Ponière. It's an absolute torment to me. It's getting on my nerves."

"Define the exact nature of your uncertainty?" Christopher suggested.

"Define it? What the devil do you mean?" Gerald answered gloomily.

"Is it the character and reputation of these ladies concerning which you cannot make up your mind, or is it mademoiselle's lack of reciprocation to your overtures which you find distressing?"

"For God's sake, chuck that legal tosh!" Gerald begged. "It's both!"

"Has she ever mentioned the subject of money, directly or indirectly?" Christopher asked.

"Not once," Gerald replied. "She always has the air of having plenty, and her clothes are quite wonderful. Furthermore," he went on, helping himself to wine, "she doesn't encourage me in the slightest. I wish to God she would! She really seems to look upon me just as a chauffeur."

Christopher laughed quietly. There were people who called Gerald the most spoilt young man in London, and his present predicament had its humourous side. Gerald himself made a little grimace.

" It's all very well, Christopher," he said, " but I am a great deal too near being in earnest over this. Pull yourself together and suggest some way of getting hold of the truth."

" If the girl herself won't help you," Christopher replied, " how can any one else? "

" I suppose you're right," Gerald assented gloomily.

" Ask her pointblank where she was brought up and how it is she knows no one here," Christopher went on.

" I'll try it," Gerald agreed. " The worst of it is, she has such a terrible way of looking at you when you ask anything she doesn't approve of; she makes you feel as though you'd been guilty of an impertinence. Only yesterday, I suggested Mary's calling on her. I'm not at all sure that Mary would have played up, but I risked that. ' My aunt is not receiving here,' was her only reply. Hang it all, you know, Chris, I'm not a snob, but that does seem a trifle offhand, considering all things."

" I should call it a little ominous," Christopher pronounced. " If she and her aunt really are wrong 'uns, she'd be jolly careful not to put you in a false position by letting your sister call upon her. She knows quite well that's the sort of thing a fellow doesn't forgive."

The place had become very crowded indeed. A small orchestra was playing in the far corner. Several unattached young ladies, who preserved an air of haughty indifference towards the company generally, but seemed to be on remarkably good terms with the head waiter, had brought colour into the little assembly. The large man who was reputed to be a Russian had called for pen and ink, and between the courses was writing a letter. The *maître d'hôtel*, who knew Gerald, stooped and whispered in his ear.

" Monsieur Zubin, the large gentleman you asked me about, milord," he announced, " has just won two million francs over at the Casino. Some of these people have followed him over. He must have the money in his pocket."

To Christopher the scene was a novel one, and he leaned forward in his seat. Two young ladies had seated themselves at the next table to the Russian, and the nearest was glancing tentatively at him now and then, without, however, evoking the slightest response. A rather seedy-looking individual, seated upon a stool before the bar, had made one or two moves in the same direction and was apparently only waiting for the Russian to finish his letter before he addressed him. On every side were signs of a sort of parasitical hero worship. People from all quarters were whispering together and glancing towards him. The object of all these attentions continued to write his letter unmoved. Presently he called for a *chasseur*, thrust his letter into an envelope and addressed it. The boy made a prompt appearance and stood, cap in hand, waiting for his orders. The man who had just won two million francs handed him the letter, gave him some brief directions and a handful of coins. The *chasseur* saluted and hurried off. Gerald gripped his companion by the arm.

" Did you hear that, Chris? " he whispered.

" I heard nothing," Christopher replied.

"I saw the address, too," Gerald continued eagerly. "The letter is to Madame de Ponière, Villa Violette!"

The dispatch of the letter was the signal for certain almost imperceptible advances on the part of those who had been watching the great man. The young lady at the next table leaned over and congratulated him on his good fortune, an overture which was received a little gruffly and without enthusiasm. Mademoiselle smiled, however, and did not take the rebuff to heart. A bottle stood in ice by her neighbour's side, and she judged that a more propitious moment would arrive. The seedy-looking stranger slid from his stool, leaned over the table and whispered a few words in the Russian's ear. He was a sandy-haired man, with puffy cheeks and a nervous manner. His clothes had once been well enough but were now shabby. He had the gambler's restless air.

"Sir," he began, "forgive my addressing you."

"What do you want?" was the blunt rejoinder.

"I stood behind your chair in the Rooms. I flatter myself that I brought you fortune, as I have brought it to many others. I have been an immense loser at the tables, but, in proportion to my own losses, my friends have always won."

"What of this?" the other asked brusquely.

"The fortunes which control winning or losing are strange ones," the sandy-haired man continued. "There are many who contend that they are influenced by the good or evil will of a bystander. I admired your courage, monsieur. I willed you to win. I have lost as much at the tables as you have won. Will you grant me the loan of a meal?"

"Go to hell!" was the brutal reply. "I have nothing to do with cadgers."

The man staggered as though he had received a shock. He was used to rebuffs, but not such rebuffs as this.

"Monsieur!" he stammered. — "Perhaps five hundred or even two hundred francs ——"

"Not a sou, and be off. Do you want me to complain to the manager?"

The sandy-haired man went back to his stool, a little dazed. He held out his hand as though for a drink, which the bartender forgot to serve. A young man dressed in the height of fashion rose from his place at the other side of the room, and came over to talk to the two girls for a few moments. Then he turned to the Russian, addressing him courteously and with an air of respect.

"I congratulate you, monsieur," he said, "upon your splendid gambling. I watched you for an hour this afternoon. It is not often that one sees the bank broken four times."

The Russian looked at the newcomer with his bushy eyebrows drawn together. His champagne had been served and he had drunk a couple of glasses of the wine. His expression, however, seemed colder and more menacing than ever.

"My gambling is my own affair, sir," he said. "I do not discuss it with strangers."

The young man smiled. He was not in the least offended.

"There is a freemasonry here," he explained, "which sometimes dispenses with introductions. All of us visitors who measure our wits and our pockets against those of Monsieur Blanc are in a sense allies. When one triumphs, it is permitted to the others to congratulate him."

" My experience is," the Russian declared, unmoved,
" that, after the congratulations are over, a little request usually follows. I do not acknowledge the alliance you speak of. I play for myself, my own pleasure
and my own profit."

" It is your right," the young man acknowledged, his
tone still good-tempered, although there was a malicious
twist at the corners of his lips. " Since my congratulations offend you, I withdraw them. May you lose back
again your two millions, and may some of it flow into
our pockets."

The Russian laughed mirthlessly.

" Whatever of my two millions flows into your pockets," he replied, " will come via Monsieur Blanc — I can
promise you that! I am a stranger here, and I desire
no acquaintance. Your table, I think, is on the other
side of the room."

The young man edged away. The smile remained
upon his lips but his expression was curiously malevo-
lent. Gerald smiled as he saw him cross the floor.

" Horribly bad character, that," he remarked to
Christopher. " I missed him here last season and asked
where he was. They told me that he was in prison for
stabbing his mistress. — I suppose I shall get it in the
neck, Chris, but I've got to talk to the old brute. I
can't afford to miss an opportunity of speaking to some
one who knows Pauline."

" I shouldn't, if I were you," Christopher advised.
" You see he isn't in the humour to talk to anybody,
and if there really is any mystery about the De Ponières, he won't care about being asked questions about
them."

Gerald was, for him, however, determined.

" Those others were all wrong 'uns, and he probably

knew it. The fellow's manner is brutal, but I believe he's a personage. I shall try my luck in a moment or so."

Mademoiselle returned to the attack. She leaned once more towards her neighbour.

"Monsieur's wine appears to be excellent," she ventured.

The Russian, who had begun to eat seriously, summoned a waiter without raising his head.

"Serve two bottles of wine," he directed, "to mademoiselle and her friend, and bring me another."

"Monsieur is a prince," the girl murmured.

The big man flashed a sudden look at her. Then he went on with his dinner.

"You are welcome to the wine," he said. "It does not please me, for the moment, to converse. Besides, I am hungry."

Mademoiselle murmured another word of thanks and turned back to her companion. She knew her world and she was content.

"Monsieur must not be interfered with," she declared. "He has been playing since the Rooms opened, and he is weary. The fortune of some people is marvelous," she went on, watching the coming of the wine. "If I were to win a mille, I should be crazy with delight."

Gerald waited for several minutes, until his neighbour had entered upon another course. Then he leaned a little towards him.

"A trifle communistic, the ideas of the world about here," he remarked.

The Russian looked at him and shrugged his shoulders.

"I come from a country where I have learnt to hate

that word," he said. "Be so good as not to repeat it
in my hearing."

"You are a Russian?" Gerald ventured.

"It is entirely my business of what nationality I am,"
was the cold reply.

"Naturally," Gerald agreed. "At the same time, we
are all human. The man who wins a couple of millions
here is a public character. You will probably find old
ladies rubbing their five-franc pieces against your coat
sleeves, as you enter the Rooms."

"So long as they do not attempt to talk to me, I
shall be content," was the curt retort.

"You are not exactly looking for acquaintances, I
perceive," Gerald remarked.

"I have none here, nor do I desire any."

Gerald smiled. He had reached the point at which
he had been aiming.

"That," he observed, "is not strictly true. You
have just dispatched a note to some ladies of my acquaintance."

Monsieur Zubin had so far met Gerald's tentative
overtures with the cold rudeness of one who recognises
an equal. At his last words, however, a look almost of
fury flashed into his face. He struck the table with his
fist.

"I ought to have remembered the sort of people by
whom I was likely to be surrounded here," he declared.
"One comes to beg for alms, another to tout for a loan
or to pave the way for a robbery, and you, who look as
though you ought to know better, cast sneaking glances
over my shoulder to read the superscription of a private
letter. What a riffraff!"

Gerald bit his lip. He kept his temper perfectly.

"I saw the address, I assure you, entirely by acci-

dent," he said. " I happen to be acquainted with one
of the ladies or the name would not have attracted my
notice. Madame and mademoiselle occupy the next
villa to my father's."

"Acquainted? That is a lie!" the Russian exclaimed.
" The ladies of whom you have spoken have no acquaintances in Monte Carlo."

Gerald shrugged his shoulders.

"At least," he said, " I will agree with you so far as
to admit that this is no place in which to discuss them."

Monsieur Zubin rose deliberately to his feet. One
realised then his extraordinary height. He must have
been at least six feet, four inches, and broad in proportion. Gerald, although he himself was considerably
over average height, seemed like a child by his side.

" If you mention their names again," he threatened,
" I shall throw you out of the place."

Gerald looked him over for a moment, unmoved but
intensely curious. The mystery of Madame and Mademoiselle de Ponière had only been increased by this
chance meeting.

" Pray sit down," he begged. " You are making
every one uneasy. I have no wish to quarrel with you.
I simply took you for an ordinary human being."

The Russian resumed his seat. Mademoiselle raised
her glass and laughed into his eyes. Gerald called for
his bill.

CHAPTER X

DURING their short walk to the Sporting Club, where the two young men had arranged to spend the rest of the evening, Christopher endeavoured to bring the conversation round to the subject of Myrtile.

"It is time," he insisted, "that we did something a little more definite about Myrtile."

"What can we do?" Gerald replied carelessly. "She'll find a job presently."

"She won't unless we help her," Christopher replied, "and meanwhile this life is horribly bad for her. She is all the time unsettled and uneasy, and I don't wonder at it. You don't take her seriously enough, Gerald."

"In what way?"

"She told me this afternoon that you had promised to take her to one of your supper parties."

Gerald was not altogether at his ease.

"It was rather a rash promise," he admitted, "but after all, why not? She'd create quite a sensation."

"That child's immediate future is a charge upon our honour," Christopher said sternly. "You and I know the class of young women you invite to your parties. They're smart enough — the best of their sort, without a doubt. At the same time, they're not fit companions for Myrtile. She's full of hysterical impressions, as it is. She mustn't come near them. She mustn't breathe the same atmosphere."

"Are you in love with Myrtile?" Gerald asked curiously.

Christopher loathed the question but he remained outwardly unperturbed.

"Myrtile is a child," he said. "It will be time enough to think of such things when she has become a woman. The one deadly and pernicious certainty is that she is in love with you. Be careful, Gerald. You don't want to walk on the floor of hell."

They had reached the steps of the Sporting Club. Gerald ran lightly up.

"My dear Chris," he said, turning around as he prepared to divest himself of his overcoat, "don't be a melodramatic ass. We're in the wrong atmosphere for that sort of thing. Jupiter! Here is the family!"

"Well, you might appear a little more pleased to see us," Mary declared. "Dad and I looked in here on our way back from the dinner party. Dad met an old friend there — Sir William Greatwood — and he insisted upon our coming. It seemed so ridiculously early to go home. They've hurried in to make sure of places at the first roulette table."

"Let's find a corner in the bar and have some coffee," Christopher suggested. "Gerald is too electric to-night for a man of my staid temperament."

"I'm not so sure of your staid temperament as I was," Mary rejoined. "However, I'd like some coffee. We'll take those two easy-chairs."

Gerald soon drifted away and the two were left alone. Mary leaned back in her corner and studied her companion thoughtfully.

"Christopher," she began, "I am not at all sure that you two young men are behaving nicely in Monte Carlo. Father was saying this afternoon that we scarcely saw you at all except at tennis."

" Will you play golf and lunch with me to-morrow morning, Lady Mary? " he begged.

" With pleasure," she replied. "And now that you have made your peace, do tell me about Gerald. He seems to have an extraordinary craze for taking the mysterious young woman next door out motoring every afternoon. Who is she? "

" I haven't the faintest idea," Christopher confessed. " Neither has he. That, I think, is part of the attraction."

" Does any one know her? " Mary asked, a little doubtfully. " She looks all right, but, after all, ours is such a very small world that it seems odd no one knows anything about her."

Christopher shook his head.

" I believe that Madame Lénore — the woman from whom we bought the things for Myrtile — knows something about them, at any rate."

Lady Mary played with the pearls which hung from her neck.

" To leave the subject of our mysterious neighbours, then, have you succeeded in finding any employment for your little protégée yet? " she enquired, looking up at her companion.

" Not yet," Christopher replied. " I have written to a cousin of mine in London, who goes in for that sort of thing, to see if she can find her a post as nursery governess. The housekeeper at the hotel would take her as a chambermaid, but for once I agree with Gerald — I think she is far too good for anything of that sort."

" I can't imagine what you two young men think you know about it," Mary remarked. " The girl has lived all her life as a peasant, and I am still old-fashioned

enough to believe that it is exceedingly unwise to pitch-
fork any one into a position to which he is unaccustomed."

"The girl is altogether unusual," Christopher
pointed out. "Her father and mother were both
school-teachers. Sometimes I feel inclined to regret
that we ever discovered her, but so long as we did, and
brought her here, we must try and start her properly."

"In Monte Carlo?" his companion observed, a little
drily.

"I shall send her to England, if my cousin agrees to
take her," Christopher declared.

"And, in the meantime, the poor little fool is hope-
lessly in love with Gerald. Well, you both know what
you are doing, I suppose. I should be sorry to have
your responsibility. — I think I ought to go and see
how dad is getting on with his mille."

"Wait one moment," Christopher begged, laying his
hand upon her arm. "I want you to watch this."

She looked up curiously. Gerald had just entered
the crowded little room, and, at the same moment,
Mademoiselle de Ponière and her aunt appeared on the
other threshold. Madame was dressed in black clothes
of old-fashioned but distinctive cut. A wonderful black
lace shawl drooped from her shoulders. Her ears and
fingers blazed with gems. She leaned, as she walked,
upon an ivory-topped stick, and her eyes had their usual
trick of wandering around the room as though she saw
no one. Pauline's wonderful figure seemed sheathed in
a black net gown, which fitted her with almost magical
perfection. From the curve of her large hat, which
framed her pale face and heavily-fringed eyes, to the
tips of her black and white patent shoes, she seemed to
represent a perfection unobtrusive but inevitable. Ger-

ald, who had been on his way to join his sister and
Christopher, paused at their approach, as though bent
on challenging some recognition, however slight, from
the girl. In this, however, he was disappointed. Without any appearance of avoiding him, without even turning her eyes away from his direction, she passed by as
though in complete unconsciousness of his presence, and
followed her companion through the other door. Gerald stood for a moment in silent fury after they had left.
The cigarette which he had been holding between his
fingers slipped on to the carpet, crushed to pieces. He
set his heel upon it and crossed the room. Lady Mary
recognised the sense of disturbance in him and welcomed
him with the tactful smile of one who has noticed nothing unusual.

"Tell me whether to play *trente et quarante* or roulette to-night, Gerald?" she said. "Or shall I go and
play baccarat? If only the people there weren't so
alarming!"

Gerald looked across at Christopher. He seemed as
though he had scarcely heard his sister's words.

"Did you see that?" he asked, in a low tone.

Christopher nodded.

"Personally," he admitted, "I should find it intolerable, but then, as you know, I hate all mysteries. I
should feel inclined to go up to the young woman and
ask her if she were tired after her motoring."

"I believe I have an average amount of pluck," Gerald declared, "but I tell you honestly I couldn't face it.
I believe I should get the most colossal snub which has
ever been inflicted upon a human being."

"The girl is extraordinarily attractive," Mary observed. "Shall I really be brave and call, Gerald?
One doesn't do that sort of thing abroad, but she must

be lonely. If they aren't what they should be, it won't
hurt me."

"No good, old dear," Gerald groaned. "I've suggested something of the sort already, but she only threw
cold water on the idea."

Lady Mary laughed softly.

"After all," she decided, " there is something humourous in the situation. I always look upon Gerald as being the most woman-spoilt man I know. Quite a new
experience for you, dear, isn't it? I can't think how
you ever progressed so far as you have done."

" Sheer British pluck," Gerald declared. " I can assure you I never shivered so much during my three years
in France, as I did when I walked up to the rock where
the girl was standing. I don't remember, even now, how
I made the plunge."

" You probably asked her if her name wasn't Smith
and if you hadn't met at the Jones' ball," Mary remarked. "After all, there have been other people in the
world who haven't wished to make acquaintances. They
are both in half-mourning, too."

" I should cheer up, old fellow," Christopher advised.
" They won't hold out for ever. You will probably find
that to-morrow afternoon the young lady will shyly invite you in to meet her aunt."

" You don't know what you're talking about," Gerald
growled. " There! Did you see that? "

Through the open doorway, Madame de Ponière and
her younger companion were plainly visible, making their
way towards one of the roulette tables. They had come
face to face for a moment with a little Frenchman, who
stopped and bowed with every mark of respect. Both
of the women acknowledged his salutation graciously.
Gerald sprang to his feet.

" That's Henri Dubois, Monsieur Blanc's representative there ! " he exclaimed. " He knows them ! Thank heavens, I've come across some one at last who does ! "

He crossed the room in half a dozen strides, and accosted Monsieur Dubois in the private way leading to the Hôtel de Paris. The usual civilities were exchanged.

" Monsieur Dubois, you can do me a favour," Gerald confided, as he drew him towards the bar and ordered two liqueur brandies.

" If it is possible, it is done," Dubois declared. " If it is impossible, it shall be done."

" I want you to tell me," Gerald continued, " who the two ladies in black were, to whom you just bowed — Madame and Mademoiselle de Ponière, they call themselves ? "

The courteous smile faded from the lips of the little man. He was watching intently the pouring of the brandy into his glass.

" Milord," he regretted, " I cannot tell you anything about those two ladies."

Gerald was a little staggered. Monsieur Dubois was a well-known gossip, to whom he had been indebted for the history of many of the visitors to the place.

" You, too ! " he exclaimed. " What on earth is the mystery about them ? "

The Frenchman looked at him in bland surprise.

" Mystery, milord ? " he repeated. " Is there one ? "

Gerald avoided a fruitless discussion. He laid his hand on his companion's shoulder in friendly fashion.

" Look here, old fellow," he said, " I will ask you one question, and one question only. What are their real names ? "

Monsieur Dubois smiled. His difficulties were at an end.

" Milord," he declared, " you wrong those very respectable ladies in imagining that they would present
themselves here under names to which they had no right.
Both ladies, who are, as you have doubtless surmised,
related, are entitled to the name of De Ponière. The
first Christian name of the older lady is Anastasie, of
the younger — Pauline. I am happy to be able to satisfy milord. A thousand excuses. They call me from
the baccarat room."

Gerald returned dejectedly to the room where his
sister and Christopher were waiting expectantly.

" It appears that there is no mystery at all," he announced. " Dubois assures me that they are related
and that their names are indeed De Ponière."

CHAPTER XI

MYRTILE rose in the morning, as was her custom, at a little after seven o'clock, carefully made her bed, dressed, and walked for an hour upon the Terrace. These early diurnal wanderings were tempered with a certain sadness, although she was always finding something new — new beauties or new sores — in this amazing spot to which she had been transported. She saw the mists which wreathed the hilltops before the sun had power to burn them away, — mists grey some mornings and opalescent on others, but always of wonderful shape, always fantastic, dissolving sometimes at unexpected moments to reveal unexpected beauties, hanging down the hillsides at times in long, ghostly arms, to sever the pine woods, the strips of pasture and the small vineyards. The little town itself had the air of being in déshabille, of somewhat resenting this early riser's curious gaze. Where the coloured lights had burned last night, and the music of violins made sad and sweet the throbbing atmosphere, was a desert waste, — tables piled on one another, chairs turned over, the débris of cigars and cigarette ends and burned-out matches still littering the ground. There were water carts in the streets and sweepers upon the pavement. The beshuttered and becurtained shops looked with blank eyes upon this scene of renovation. It was too early, as yet, even for the mannequin or the seamstress; the streets were filled only with the ghosts of last night's giddy throngs. The Casino itself, closed and silent, seemed brooding over that hive of passion, of disappointment and strident joy of a few hours ago. The villas on the hill were barely opening their eyes. A ragpicker stole along the Terrace, making his furtive collection. To Myrtile, whose life as yet was composed mainly of externals, everything was still beautiful. The sun warmed her with the promise of love. She was never tired of watching the little waves breaking upon the sandy strip, and the million scintillating lights upon the bay. She looked up with a glad smile at the silent hotel where Gerald was sleeping. Perhaps he was dreaming of her at that very moment. Love had crept into her life and found her very ignorant. As yet it was a beautiful and simple thing. That it was capable of change and division never even occurred to her. She loved Gerald, and, although he sometimes disappointed her, it must be that Gerald loved her. She had few doubts about it all. All her confidence, all her will, went freely with that warm, sweet impulse which filled her heart and thoughts, and which seemed to her the sweetest and most wonderful thing in life. She was intelligent, almost brilliantly intelligent, and, even in those few days, the sordid and ugly side of other people's lives and aspirations had sometimes been revealed to her, only to be brushed aside as something very remote, something from which love made her forever free. Gerald's attitude often puzzled, sometimes even distressed her, but she put his vagaries down to her own lack of understanding. She was convinced that all would be well when she saw more of him, and she harboured a dull sense of resentment against Christopher, who she believed was always working for some unknown reason to keep them apart.

At half-past eight she returned to her rooms and deliberately attacked a great mass of sewing, which was sent to her daily from the hotel, and the payment for which, by arrangement, provided her with board and lodging. From that time onwards, she sat in the window with but one hope, — the hope of seeing Gerald. Once or twice he had come and taken her out to luncheon, but Christopher was unfailing in his visits. He presented himself every morning at about the same time, and even if Gerald appeared, he always accompanied him. Gerald once, obeying a curious impulse, had sent her a great box of roses, over which she had wept with delight, and which she kept alive by every known artifice. Christopher brought her, day by day, the little things she needed, — gloves, stockings, handkerchiefs, and often a few simple bonbons and flowers. Despite her resentment against him, it was always a pleasure to hear his firm tread and to watch his tall, broad-shouldered figure and good-humoured, intelligent face as he crossed the road, invariably with some small parcel in his hand. He seemed to have much more time to spare than Gerald, a fact which, womanlike, she half resented, ignorant of the fact that Gerald sat up half the night enjoying himself in his own fashion, and that Christopher often gave up his morning round of golf to be her companion. She found an evil counsellor, too, in Annette, the maid at the hotel, who occupied the other bedroom in the little cottage and generally looked in for a few minutes on her way to work. Annette, who was thoroughly French, was completely puzzled by the situation. She could account for it in her own mind only from the fact that the two young men were English and therefore presumably mad. Of her own preference she made no secret.

"But how mademoiselle is industrious!" she exclaimed, looking in at the door soon after Myrtile had

returned from her early morning walk and settled down
to her sewing. " I hope my stingy old aunt pays you
well for all that sewing."

" She gives me my board and lodging here," Myrtile
replied, with a smile. " That more than contents
me."

" Board and lodging! Oh, là, là!" Annette declared,
sinking into her accustomed chair. " That would not
content me. Even one's salary at the hotel is not sufficient. It is the tips from which one can buy one's
clothes."

" Soon I shall have to think of clothes," Myrtile confided. " At present Monsieur Gerald has given me all
that I need."

" It is a very chic costume and doubtless expensive,"
Annette admitted, " but for evening clothes mademoiselle
has nothing."

" I do not go out in the evenings," Myrtile replied,
a little wistfully. " Monsieur Christopher took me once
to the Opera, but we sat in a box."

" Monsieur Christopher!" the maid repeated, with a
little shrug of the shoulders. " He is well enough but
he is heavy. He speaks French like an English school-
boy. But Milord Dombey — ah, he is superb! He
speaks French like a Parisian, he dances divinely, he is
gay all the time. Oh, if he were on my floor, that I
could see him sometimes, I should be happy!"

Myrtile said nothing. She had learnt that the best
way to make Annette talk was just to listen.

" It amazes me," Annette continued, " that mademoiselle does not ask Milord Dombey for some evening
frocks and attend one of his supper parties. Charles,
the head waiter, brings me news often of them. They
are of the most amusing. There are artistes there, and

all manner of wonderful people. Has mademoiselle no curiosity to see life? "

Myrtile threaded a needle carefully before she replied.

" Milord Dombey," she said, " would, I believe, take me, but Monsieur Christopher does not think it well that I go to those parties. He declares that they are for people whom I should not meet."

Annette threw herself back in her chair, revealing to the full her silk-stockinged legs. She clasped her hands behind the back of her head. She was vastly amused.

" Oh, là, là! " she exclaimed. " That is so like Monsieur Bent! What does he make of life, that young man? Does he think it well for a girl as beautiful as mademoiselle to sit here alone at night and creep into bed, while monsieur who adores her spends his time with other women? Pooh! Mademoiselle should have courage."

Myrtile laid down her work. Her heart was beating fast.

" Tell me, Annette," she begged, " who are these guests of Milord Dombey? Why do they keep me away from them? "

" It is not Milord Dombey's fault," Annette declared. " He is a *beau garçon*, that. It is the stupid Monsieur Bent who should have stayed at home in his dull London. They are all well enough, these guests of Milord Dombey's. Some sing at the Opera; others, perhaps, have seen life in Paris, but for that what are they the worse — what harm can they do? It is perhaps Monsieur Bent's idea that he keeps you away from Milord Dombey, who is so attractive, and takes you back to his stodgy England and marries you there himself. Oh, if I were mademoiselle, I should submit no longer!"

"What should you do, Annette?" Myrtile asked, half fearfully.

"I should put on all my prettiest clothes," Annette replied, entering into the matter with animation, "and I should come to the hotel. I should find my way to Milord Dombey — that would be for me to arrange — and I should just tell him that I had come, that I was tired of being left at home. Then I would whisper one or two of the nicest little things I could think of into his ear, and I would put my arms around his neck, and — well — I know Milord Dombey — he would not send me away — not if I were mademoiselle."

The work had fallen from Myrtile's hands. She was sitting up in her chair, her eyes very bright, her lips a little parted. How fortunate it was that Annette had come! Without a doubt, she would do this. Only one must beware of Monsieur Christopher. He was full of droll ideas. It was, perhaps, as Annette had suggested. He must be made to understand. Presently Annette departed, and when, a little later on, Christopher arrived to pay his morning call, Myrtile was seated as usual at her work, her manner unaltered except that she was a little gayer than usual, perhaps a little more kindly. Christopher, on the other hand, was inclined to be serious.

"Myrtile," he announced, "I have heard from my cousin in England. She thinks that she will be able to find you a place in about a month's time."

"That is very kind of her," Myrtile answered, without enthusiasm. "What does Gerald say about it?"

"I have not mentioned it to Gerald yet," Christopher

replied. "He was dining out last night and had a supper party afterwards at the Carlton, and as a matter of fact he was fast asleep when I came out. I have no doubt, however, that he will be glad."

The girl made a little grimace.

"He may not be so glad to get rid of me as you," she remarked.

"We shall neither of us be here in a month's time," Christopher reminded her. "Certainly I shall not, and Gerald, I believe, is due to go on to Biarritz before then."

Myrtile sewed industriously for a moment.

"Perhaps," she suggested, "he may want me to go on to Biarritz with him."

"You must not talk like that, Myrtile," Christopher said sternly. "You must not say such things. If Gerald goes, it will be with some other young men to play polo. There would be no possible place for you in such a company."

Myrtile proceeded calmly with her sewing. She was beginning to be sorry for Christopher. He understood so little.

"We must tell Gerald about it," she conceded. "You understand that I should not do anything without his approval?"

"Quite," Christopher acquiesced. "We are both equally your guardians, Myrtile. Gerald is just as fond of you, I am sure, as I am."

She smiled without looking up. Some day he would know the truth, this kindly but rather foolish Englishman. He would know that she and Gerald loved one another. He should always be their friend, though. He was very good, in his way, only he would not understand.

"What about a short walk before lunch?" he suggested.

Myrtile dropped her work at once.

"We will go along the Terrace," she proposed, "and while I sit upon a seat, you shall go in and wake up that lazy Gerald. You shall tell him that I am waiting, and I am sure that he will hurry out."

Christopher assented, a little sadly. Once or twice before they had carried out the same programme, and he was wondering whether it would not have been better to have told Myrtile the truth, — that on two occasions Gerald had absolutely refused to join them, and that on the third he had been brought out almost by force. There was a little pang in his heart as he watched Myrtile's gay preparations. Life was so wonderful to her that it seemed a shame to destroy a single illusion.

"We'll try and rout him out, at all events," he promised.

CHAPTER XII

MYRTILE was seated alone at the far end of the Terrace, outside the Hôtel de Paris, when the tragedy happened. Her first impression was that some very unusual people had found their way on to the promenade, — a fête-day excursion, perhaps, from one of the neighbouring villages. And then the colour seemed slowly drained from her cheeks. She would have got up and fled but her limbs absolutely refused their office. Her slight movement, however, had attracted the attention of the two men. With exclamations of incredulity, they hurried towards her. The incredulity turned swiftly to joy. Myrtile, in such clothes, represented, without a doubt, boundless wealth. It was a morning of good fortune, this!

"Myrtile, thou little rascal!" her stepfather cried, gripping her pearl-coloured gloves in his horny fist. "Pierre, thou seest. It is she indeed. Amazing! It is veritably amazing!"

Pierre Leschamps was not so fluent. His narrow, covetous eyes looked over Myrtile's slim body lasciviously. What he had lost! He was filled with self-pity.

"It is an escapade, this," he said. "Thou art ready to return, Myrtile?"

"Never!" the girl declared passionately.

"Oho!" her stepfather exclaimed. "We shall see about that. There is the law, little one. The law does not allow an honest man to be robbed of his daughter — ay, stepdaughter, if you will," he went on, checking a passionate protest on Myrtile's lips. "Now, then, out with it, my child. Where did those clothes come from? Who brought you here? Who is supporting you?"

"I am supporting myself," Myrtile answered. "I sew all the mornings and most of the afternoons."

The two men laughed unpleasantly. Her father laid his hand upon her shoulder.

"Listen," he said, "you were carried away from home by two Englishmen in a motor car — rich Englishmen, by all accounts, with much luggage. Where are they?"

"What do you want with them?" Myrtile demanded.

"That is not for thy silly head, little one."

"There is a matter of compensation," Pierre growled. "Tell us where to find these Englishmen?"

Myrtile looked wildly around. She scarcely knew whether she prayed for or dreaded Christopher's return. Then suddenly she saw him close at hand, accompanied, to her infinite relief, by Gerald. She gave a little cry of joy. Now, indeed, all would be well. Gerald would arrange everything.

"So these are they?" her stepfather muttered, as the two young men approached.

"They look like gentlemen of wealth," Leschamps echoed.

"The stepfather of Myrtile, as I live," Gerald muttered, under his breath. "Heaven grant that we may escape a brawl out here! Must we ——"

"Of course we must," Christopher answered curtly. "Can't you see that the child is frightened to death? We'll have them in the police station, if they make any trouble. The police here haven't much sympathy with their class."

Myrtile called to them softly.

" This is my stepfather," she said, " and his friend, Pierre Leschamps."

" Mon Dieu! " Gerald exclaimed, in frank horror. " Are you the man whom Myrtile was to marry? "

" I am he, indeed, monsieur," the innkeeper acknowledged. " I have gone to great expense in the matter. My house was painted and whitewashed and my bedroom papered. The neighbours were all bidden. I had even laid in wine for the feast."

" Then you ought to have been ashamed of yourself," Gerald declared. " Why, how old are you, my friend? "

Leschamps patted his stomach.

" I am but fifty years old," he replied, " a man in the prime of life. Myrtile was promised to me. There is no one else like her. I am without a wife. It is a very serious position for a man with an inn to look after."

" And what about me? " her stepfather intervened, his voice rising with the recollection of his wrongs. " For many years I have kept that child. I have fed her and clothed her all that time. Now that she is eighteen, now that she is of some use in the world, how does she show her gratitude? What can I do without her, I ask? I was to marry the good Widow Dumay. Now she says ' no! ' She declares that, without Myrtile, the care of the children is too much for her. She refuses to allow me to arrange for the wedding, unless either Myrtile returns or she has at least five hundred francs with which to arrange for help."

" Five hundred francs! " Leschamps groaned. " What is that for a wife like Myrtile! It is a blow to me, this. My health has suffered. I am gloomy. My business decreases. The neighbours will no longer drink a bottle of wine with a man who cannot sing a song or smile once during the evening. They go elsewhere. My connection tumbles to pieces. And there are my rooms all painted and my bedroom papered, and I have no wife."

"It appears to me," Gerald proposed, "that we had better discuss this matter in my rooms over a bottle of wine — a bottle of champagne, eh? What do you say, gentlemen?"

"Let it be this moment," Myrtile's stepfather insisted. "Let us know where we are without further delay. This matter makes me sad. I cannot sleep or eat. I have dug deep into my savings to come here. Oh, it has cost me much money, this journey!"

"And I," Leschamps declared, "I who have never been in a train before, who have never spent ten sous on my own pleasure, it is ruin, this journey. And I have been sick of the stomach."

"Follow me, gentlemen," Gerald invited.

He led them into the hotel, much to the amazement of the liveried servants, took them up in the lift, in which both nearly collapsed upon the floor, and ushered them into his sitting room. For a few moments, effrontery and avarice were alike powerless. They were dumb with amazement. They looked around them, muttering inarticulate words. Leschamps dabbed at the perspiration on his forehead with a bright, cherry-coloured handkerchief. Her stepfather looked helplessly across the room to where Myrtile was seated side by side with Christopher. Gerald ordered champagne, which was brought in by a servant dressed in knee breeches and silk stockings. Leschamps secretly pinched himself. Gerald, the central figure of the little party, towards whom every one turned and on whom Myrtile's eyes were unswervingly fixed, began to rather enjoy the situation.

"Now, gentlemen," he said, after he had moved them up to the table and placed the bottle of wine between them, "let us deal with this question in a few words. Your stepdaughter, Myrtile, is not coming back to you, Monsieur Sargot; neither will she become your wife, Monsieur Leschamps. She will be well taken care of and that is all that concerns you. We would like, if possible, to arrange this matter pleasantly, although we admit no claim. At what price do you, Monsieur Sargot, place your daughter's services? And you, Monsieur Leschamps, at what figure do you put your expenses in preparing for your wedding which will never take place?"

"It is a hard question," Myrtile's stepfather declared, seizing the bottle and pouring himself out another glass of wine.

"It will be a great loss for me," the innkeeper groaned.

"Myrtile did all the cooking," Jean Sargot continued. "There was no one made such a ragout, and the children with her were like angels."

"That is not true," Myrtile intervened calmly. "The children were always bad-tempered and difficult to manage."

"She has lost her head, the little one," her stepfather lamented.

"There is not another girl in the valley one would marry by the side of her," the innkeeper muttered.

Gerald waited until they had finished. He was leaning against the back of a sofa, smoking a cigarette which he had just lit.

" Well, gentlemen," he said, " it is for you to name a sum. All that I ask is that Myrtile be left in peace."

" The Widow Dumay," Myrtile's stepfather said, watching Gerald closely, " declared that I ought to have in the stocking another two thousand francs, if I am deprived of Myrtile."

Gerald opened his pocketbook.

" Will the same sum content you, Leschamps? " he asked.

Pierre Leschamps tried to sigh. His eyes, however, betrayed his greedy satisfaction.

" I will accept it," he said. " May Myrtile be happy! "

Myrtile's stepfather struck the table with his fist.

" Look here, all of you," he expostulated, " this is all very well, but why should Pierre Leschamps have as much as I — I who have lost my daughter —— "

" She was to have been my wife," Leschamps growled.

" It was I who was to give her to you," the other retorted. " You have lost nothing because she never belonged to you. Five hundred francs would pay you many times over for all the expense you have been to in your miserable little house. The rest of your two thousand should come to me."

The faces of the two men were aflame. Pierre Leschamps was tugging viciously at his little black moustache. There was a purple flush on Sargot's cheeks. They seemed about to fall on each other. Gerald struck the table with the flat of his hand.

" Look here," he enjoined, " unless you both want to be ordered out of the room without a sou, hold your peace."

No threat could have been more effective. They stood looking at him like dumb animals. He silently filled the glass of each with more wine.

"Now remember that you are friends and comrades," he begged. "There is, after all, something in what Jean Sargot has said. To lose a stepdaughter is more than to lose a promised wife. I will add a thousand francs to your amount, Jean Sargot."

"And I shall have my two thousand?" Leschamps cried.

"You shall have your two thousand," Gerald promised.

Their eyes hung upon his pocketbook like the eyes of sick animals. Gerald counted out the money but retained it in his hand.

"You, monsieur," he said, addressing Myrtile's stepfather, "will sign a paper which my friend here will write out, promising to resign all claim to Myrtile and never to attempt to see her again."

"I will sign it," the man agreed.

Christopher sat at the desk and wrote out a few brief sentences. Jean Sargot signed it without even confessing his inability to read. They stood up to receive the money. Myrtile, and even Christopher, watched them, fascinated. Their brown, nailless fingers clutched and trembled as they counted the notes. Each in turn buttoned them into the inside pocket of his coat. It was more than they had dreamed of, this. Myrtile, a village child, to be worth a fortune!

"It is finished, then, this affair," Sargot declared, as he drained his glass.

"It is finished," Gerald agreed. "I will ring for a page to show you out."

"You need have no anxiety about Myrtile," Christo-

pher said. " She will be found a suitable home and she
will lead a suitable life."

Jean Sargot suddenly remembered that he was her
stepfather. He brushed his coat sleeve across his
eyes.

" Little one," he cried, " embrace me. This is, then,
farewell."

Myrtile rose to her feet but she remained at the other
side of the table.

" I wish you farewell and I wish you good fortune,"
she said. " I would rather not embrace you. You have
been hard and cruel to me, as you have been to others.
Try and be kinder to your own children. And as for
you, Pierre Leschamps," she went on, " do not dream
for a moment that I would ever have married you. I
would sooner have thrown myself into the quarry."

" The little one was always strange," Leschamps
muttered, almost apologetically.

They stumbled out of the room after the page who
presently arrived. Gerald broke into a shout of laughter as they disappeared. Myrtile's eyes, however, were
filled with tears. Christopher, too, was grave, but it
was to Gerald the girl turned.

" I have cost you a great deal, I am afraid," she
said. " Now I belong to you."

She leaned towards him. Christopher intervened almost harshly.

" To us," he declared, throwing down a little bundle
of notes upon the table. " You and I are Myrtile's
joint guardians, Gerald. That was our understanding.
I shall hold you to your promise."

Myrtile's head was buried on Gerald's shoulder.
Gerald himself was for a moment half embarrassed, half
carried away by Myrtile's calm assumption. He looked

into Christopher's grey eyes, however, and he pulled himself together.

"That's all right, old chap," he promised. "We'll steer clear of trouble — somehow."

CHAPTER XIII

GERALD found Pauline waiting for him at the accustomed spot, after luncheon that afternoon. As he slowed down his car to pick her up, he was conscious of a return of that feeling of irritation which had been growing stronger with him, day by day, — an irritation based upon her obvious desire to escape recognition when with him and to keep their acquaintance as far as possible a secret. She was waiting in the shadow of a great magnolia shrub, dressed in inconspicuous grey, with a veil thicker even than the exigencies of motoring necessitated. In the background was the same black-gowned maid who always attended her as far as the avenue and took her silent leave at his approach.

Pauline stepped lightly into the place by his side, without waiting for him to vacate his seat.

"Turn round, please," she directed. "We will go the other way. I do not choose to pass through the town."

Gerald obeyed, although her request only added fuel to the smouldering fire of his resentment. He turned away towards the mountain road and maintained a silence which was not without its significance. His companion, after a few minutes, glanced towards him indifferently. He was leaning back in his place, his eyes, as usual, fixed upon the road, his left hand firmly grasping the steering wheel. The humourous twitch, however, had gone from his mouth. There was a distinct frown upon his forehead.

"You are perhaps weary to-day?" she suggested. "You would like to shorten our drive?"

Gerald turned and looked at her.

"I am not weary," he replied. "I am puzzled. I hate mysteries."

"The old complaint," she yawned.

"With a new reading," he retorted. "I have shown myself ready, as you must know," he went on, "to study your rather peculiar whims in every way, but when it comes to meeting you face to face at the Club and receiving nothing but the stoniest of stares, I must admit that the situation grows beyond me. You could surely find a hundred reasonable excuses for the most formal sort of recognition. I am not — well, I am not a disreputable acquaintance, am I?"

She laughed quietly.

"Not in the least. You belong to what they call in England the middle-class aristocracy, do you not, — two or three centuries old, with a damp house in a park and an armful of undistinguished titles? I suppose that sort of thing counted for something before your tradespeople and lawyers and bankers were all admitted into the magic circle."

"Are you a socialist?" Gerald enquired, a little taken aback.

"Not at all," she replied curtly. "I am an aristocrat."

"Are you afraid to present me to Madame de Ponière?" he asked, after a moment's pause.

"Terrified," she admitted frankly.

"Because my quarterings are insufficient? I might remark that my father is the ninth Earl and that I am his only son."

"It is not that at all," she assured him indifferently.

"There is really no reason why we should not meet in a place like this on equal terms, but my aunt is a woman with only one idea in her head, and for the successful development of that idea it is advisable that we make no acquaintances whatever here. There, my Lord Dombey, have I not been kind to you? I would see more of you if I could, because in a place like this the escort of a man is an advantage. As it is, I can assure you that I risk a good deal in taking these afternoon rides."

"You have explained nothing," he insisted, a little doggedly. "I still do not see why I may not be recognised in public, why it would not be in order for my sister to call and invite you to tennis, why you and your aunt should not allow me to entertain you at dinner. I am just as far from understanding you as I ever was."

She sighed.

"Well, do not be cross with me, please," she begged. "If you knew how wearisome my life was and how grateful I really am to you for these few hours of escape, you would feel more kindly towards me. See, I give you my hand. Let us be friends."

It was the first time during all their acquaintance that she had accorded him the slightest mark of favour. The touch of her fingers thrilled and surprised him. He held her hand unresistingly for several moments. Then she drew it quietly but firmly away.

"Well, that is settled," she said. "Now talk to me about other things. Is there no news at the Rooms? Has no one been breaking the bank?"

"There was something I was going to tell you," Gerald replied, with a sudden flash of recollection. "I sat next to a man at dinner last night in Ciro's Grill, who they say broke the bank several times during the afternoon. I believe they said that he was a Russian. I suppose you know all about him, however."

" I? " she exclaimed. " Why should I? "

" Because, between the courses of his dinner, he wrote a letter and sent it off by messenger. He was at the next table and it was impossible for me to avoid seeing the envelope. It was addressed to Madame de Ponière."

She looked at him, amazed.

" To my aunt? " she repeated. " But we received no letter from any one last night."

" I saw it sent off about twenty minutes to ten," Gerald assured her.

" We left for the Club at half-past nine," Pauline reflected, " but I am quite sure that there was no note waiting for us when we got back. What was this man like? "

" They said that he was a Russian and that his name was Zubin," Gerald replied. " They also said that he had won two million francs in the afternoon."

" Zubin! " she exclaimed, with a little start. " Describe him at once, if you please."

" That is easy," Gerald acquiesced. " He must have been at least six foot three or four, and he had tremendous shoulders. He was one of the most powerful looking men I have ever seen in my life. He had a sallow complexion, a lined face, black eyes and a mass of black and grey hair."

She put her hand upon his.

" Stop the car, please," she begged. " Turn round as quickly as you can. I must go home."

Gerald ran on to an adjacent widening of the road, reversed the car, and headed back for Monte Carlo.

" If I had known that my news was going to shorten

our drive," he grumbled, " I shouldn't have mentioned the fellow at all."

" My friend," she said earnestly, " what you have told me may be of immense benefit for me to know."

" You recognise the man, then? "

" He is probably my aunt's steward," she confided, after a moment's hesitation. " There, you see I am telling you secrets. Do you know whether he played last night? "

" I was only at the Club," Gerald replied. " He did not come there. Is there anything I can do? Would you like me to go and look for him? "

" Yes, you might do that," she said thoughtfully. " When you have dropped me, drive down to the Rooms. If you find him there, touch him on the shoulder. Say that Madame de Ponière awaits him. You will not forget this? "

" I'll drive there at once," Gerald promised.

He set Pauline down, as usual, at the gates of her villa. She scarcely stayed to say good-by, but her smile was more gracious and her manner a little kinder. It was obvious, however, that she was disturbed by his information. Gerald, incurious though he was at most times, felt a growing interest in his mission.

Arrived at the Rooms, he walked straight through to the Cercle Privé, visited each Roulette and *trente et quarante* table, and strolled round the baccarat room. There was no sign here of the man of whom he was in search. He was already on his way out to the Sporting Club when it occurred to him that the Russian might be playing at one of the ordinary tables at the Casino. He turned back and visited them one by one. Towards the end of his quest, he was rewarded. Seated next to the croupier, at the most remote table, with a little crowd of people behind his chair, and with a great pile of notes before him, sat Monsieur Zubin.

The Russian was betting in maximums, apparently on some system, and with varying success. To all appearances, he had not changed his clothes, bathed or shaved since the evening before. There was an untidy growth of beard upon his chin, a bloodshot streak in his eyes; his collar and tie were crumpled; his hair, over-luxuriant at the best of times, was unkempt and disordered. He had a card in his hand, upon which he marked the numbers as they came up, and from which his attention never wandered until the final word of the croupier was spoken, when he turned his attention to the board. Gerald leaned towards the attendant seated behind the croupier's chair, under pretence of handing him a small stake.

" Monsieur gambles? " Gerald remarked, with an inclination of his head towards the man who was the centre of interest.

The attendant turned around with an expressive little nod.

" Yesterday he broke the bank," he whispered. " To-day he can do nothing right."

" He is losing, then? "

The man's grimace was significant. Gerald watched his own stake swept away and crossed to a place behind the Russian's chair. In one of the intervals, he leaned over and touched him on the shoulder. The man took no notice. Gerald whispered in his ear.

" Madame de Ponière awaits you at the Villa."

Zubin for a moment remained perfectly still. When at last he turned around, his face was ghastly. With his strong arm, he pushed back some one who intervened.

" Who are you? " he demanded.

" I am merely a messenger," Gerald replied. " I know no more than that I was asked to give you that word if I saw you at the Casino."

The Russian rose slowly to his feet, left one of the plaques to guard his place, thrust a great pile of notes into his pocket, and led Gerald into a corner.

" You sat next to me last night at Ciro's Grill," he said.

" Quite true," Gerald assented.

" You have been spying on me."

" That is, on the other hand, a falsehood," Gerald replied coldly.

" It is through you that Madame knows I am in Monte Carlo."

" On the contrary," Gerald reminded him, " you yourself wrote a note to her and dispatched it by messenger from Ciro's."

" The note was brought back — Madame was out," the man declared. " It was an accursed accident, that."

" One gathers that you have not been fortunate to-day," Gerald remarked, after a brief silence.

" That is my own affair," was the grim reply. " What I desire to know is how you became acquainted with these ladies to such an extent that they should appoint you as their messenger."

" I do not recognise your right to ask me questions," Gerald asserted, " but, as a matter of fact, my knowledge of them is of the slightest. Actually, I do not know them at all. I happened to have a few minutes' conversation with Mademoiselle de Ponière, and I mentioned your winnings. You will remember that I saw a letter from you to Madame last night."

Monsieur Zubin sat for a moment deep in thought.

" Are you charged to deliver a reply to this message? " he demanded.

" Certainly not," Gerald answered. " I have not the privilege of visiting at the Villa."

" I should think not," the other growled. " I wondered only whether you had been told to take a message to the back door."

" You are a very impertinent fellow," Gerald told him calmly. " You appear to have come from a country where manners have ceased to exist."

The man laughed brutally.

" One puts off manners when one deals with spies and meddlers," he declared. " Get on about your business."

He walked back and took his place at the table. Gerald gazed after him in blank astonishment. Then he heard a little murmur of laughter from the couch behind, and, turning around, found seated there the girl who had been the Russian's other neighbour on the previous night.

" Monsieur grows no more amiable," she remarked, moving her head towards where Zubin had reseated himself. " To-day, one perhaps excuses. Last night he was like all his countrymen — savage, drunken with the lust of gambling."

" And to-day? " Gerald observed.

" To-day he loses all the time," the girl replied. " Sometimes he leaves the table and comes back here and mutters to himself. Then he makes calculations and returns. One wonders sometimes whether he is playing with his own money."

Gerald left the Rooms a few minutes later and strolled out into the Square. He was in some doubt as to what he ought to do. Pauline had absolutely forbidden him to communicate with her in any shape or form, yet he had a conviction that Zubin's exploits in the Casino should be made known to her. He strolled across to the establishment of Madame Lénore. Madame greeted him with a peculiarly knowing smile. He drew her on one side.

" Madame," he said, " you make gowns for Mademoiselle de Ponière."

The smile disappeared from Madame's lips. Her face became impassive.

" It is true, milord," she admitted. " What of it? "

" Just this. You are doubtless in frequent communication with her? "

" Without a doubt," Madame assented. " I shall telephone her within a quarter of an hour. Some lace she desired has just arrived."

" Then you can do me and her a great service," Gerald continued. " I have some slight acquaintance with mademoiselle but I am not permitted to communicate with her. It is important that she should know that the Russian, Zubin, is gambling in the Casino, not in the Cercle Privé, and losing heavily."

" A big man? " Madame asked quickly, — " almost a giant? "

" That is he," Gerald assented.

Madame turned towards the telephone.

" Demand the Villa Violette," she told the operator. " Say that I wish to speak to Mademoiselle de Ponière without delay."

Gerald turned away. Madame laid her fingers upon his arm.

" My congratulations, milord! "

" I don't know what on," Gerald replied, a little ruefully. " I am rather out of luck."

" The little peasant girl," she whispered. " She is

adorable. Such a figure I have never seen, such an air, such simplicity and yet such grace. With her hair done à la Madonne, and those eyes, under milord's tutelage she would turn the heads of half the men in Europe."

Gerald sighed. The memory of the little scene earlier in the day was once more before him.

" You must remember that I have a co-guardian of the strictest principles, Madame," he said, " and besides, that isn't exactly what we are planning for her."

Madame, steeped in the philosophy of her environment, shrugged her shoulders in genuine mystification. Gerald took his leave a little hurriedly, to avoid the comment which he felt was imminent.

CHAPTER XIV

MADAME DE PONIÈRE dismissed the servants with a little wave of the hand and looked thoughtfully for a few moments into the fire of pine logs which had been kindled in the grate. The dinner table at which she and Pauline were seated was piled with dishes of expensive fruits, and there was wine still in their glasses. Nevertheless, Madame de Ponière had not the air of one who has enjoyed her meal.

"Pauline," she said, "Zubin is already four days late."

Pauline made no immediate reply. Her aunt pointed to an escritoire which stood in a corner of the room.

"These people," she continued, "become abusive. Even Lénore has sent an account. You dispatched the telegram?"

"I dispatched the telegram," Pauline assented, "but it was needless. Zubin is here."

"Here in Monte Carlo?" Madame de Ponière demanded quickly.

"I have heard so," Pauline replied. "My information is very scanty, but I understood that he had sent you a letter last night."

The pallor of the older woman's face seemed suddenly deepened. Her eyes glittered ominously.

"Jean spoke of a note that had been brought and taken away," she muttered. "Tell me at once what you know, Pauline?"

" I have no definite information," Pauline reiterated,
" but I understand that he has been seen at the Casino."

Madame de Ponière sat like a woman who has received a shock.   The shadow of fear was upon her face.

" You do not know Zubin," she groaned.   " If he once
smells the atmosphere of that place, it is like a deadly
drug to him.   And he loses!   He always loses! "

She leaned over and struck a bell which stood upon
a table.

" The car in a quarter of an hour," she ordered.
" Pauline, get ready.   We must seek Zubin.   If he has
begun to gamble, he will go on to the end."

They drove first to the Casino, where they explored
only the Cercle Privé.   From there they went to the
Sporting Club, where there was still no sign of him.
Madame de Ponière became more hopeful.

" He is perhaps resting in his hotel," she said, " preparing to visit us."

" He would never come without sending word before-
hand," Pauline reminded her.   " Besides, there are the
ordinary tables at the Casino.   We ought to have
looked there."

Madame de Ponière gave a little shudder.

" One sees too much of them as one passes through,"
she declared.   " The people and the atmosphere are
intolerable."

They sat side by side on one of the settees, two rather
lonely and disheartened women face to face with
tragedy.   Pauline saw Gerald in the distance and determined upon a bold step.

" Aunt," she said, " there is a young man standing
by the easy chair there, whose father lives at the adjoining villa to ours.   He has once or twice offered me
some small courtesies.   He is alone and I am sure he

would be glad to be useful. Let me send him to the Casino."

"Show him to me," Madame de Ponière demanded.

Pauline pointed him out. Her aunt sighed.

"One breaks a cherished tradition," she said, "but it must be done. I leave the matter in your hands."

Gerald and Christopher, strolling round the room, came presently to within a few feet of them. Gerald, bitterly though he resented it, was passing on after one swift glance at Pauline. She leaned over, however, and touched him on the arm.

"Lord Dombey," she said, "my aunt permits me to present you. Lord Dombey — Madame de Ponière."

Gerald, taken by surprise, bore the shock well. He bowed low and murmured a few polite words.

"I am afraid you will think that we are very mercenary," Pauline continued, "but we are going to ask a favour."

"It is granted," Gerald assured her swiftly.

"There is a Russian gentleman in Monte Carlo named Zubin."

"I know him by sight," Gerald declared. "Besides ——"

"Then the rest is easy," Pauline interrupted, with a warning look. "Our request is that you search the Casino for him, and, if he is there, that you bring him to us."

Gerald bowed.

"Mademoiselle," he promised, "if he is there, I will bring him to you within a quarter of an hour."

Gerald, on entering the Casino, made his way at once to the table at the farther end. The seat which had been occupied by Zubin, however, was vacant, though the table itself was crowded. He was on the point of

continuing his search in one of the other rooms, when
he suddenly saw the man of whom he was in search
seated on one of the sofas against the wall. He made
his way thither at once.

" Sir," he said, " I have brought you a message from
Madame de Ponière."

The Russian lifted his head, and for a moment Gerald
was afraid that he had had a stroke. His eyes were
horribly red, the flesh about his cheek bones seemed to
have become drawn tight, and his cheeks to display new
hollows. His hands were trembling. All his truculence
of manner had departed.

" From Madame de Ponière? " he repeated. " Where
is she? "

" She is waiting now in the Sporting Club," Gerald
replied. " I will take you to her if you will accompany
me."

The Russian rose to his feet and the two men left the
place. Many of the bystanders gazed after them, and
Gerald heard something of their whispers.

" I'm afraid you've been having rather a bad time,"
he remarked.

His companion took no notice. He walked, indeed,
like a man in a nightmare. Not only was he unshaven,
but his clothes were creased and tumbled. He was altogether a dishevelled-looking object.

" Might I suggest," Gerald said, as they descended
the steps of the Casino, " that you visit your hotel and
freshen up a little before you come to the Club? "

Zubin seemed suddenly to step down from another
world. He looked vacantly at Gerald for a moment,
at his smoothly brushed hair, his well-cut dinner coat,
his faultless linen. Then, with a little start, he glanced
at himself and shrugged his shoulders ponderously.

" You are right, monsieur. Come this way."

He crossed the street with great strides and entered the Hôtel de Paris. He turned once more to Gerald as he entered the lift.

" A quarter of an hour, monsieur," he said. " I give you my word that I will not keep you longer than twenty minutes."

" I will be waiting here," Gerald promised.

After the departure of the lift, Gerald made his way by means of the private passage to the Sporting Club. Madame de Ponière and her niece were seated where he had left them, the elder lady sipping some coffee, Pauline looking around her with a languid air of half-amused interest. Save for the fact that Madame de Ponière's lips tightened a little as she saw Gerald alone, there was not the slightest indication in their manner or expression that they were confronted in any way with an exceptional situation.

" I have found our friend," he announced. " He is making some alterations to his toilet. I am meeting him in a few minutes and shall bring him here."

" Was he playing? " Pauline enquired.

" Not when I arrived," was the cautious reply.

Madame de Ponière stirred her coffee negligently.

" Had he," she asked, " the air of a man who has been losing? "

" I fear," Gerald admitted, " that he rather gave me that impression."

Pauline smiled up at him.

" It is very good of you to give yourself so much trouble," she said. " My aunt and I are greatly indebted to you. Please do not lose any time in bringing Monsieur Zubin here."

The words were almost a dismissal. Gerald made his

way back through the passage and took a seat in the
lounge of the hotel. Within the time promised, a transformed Monsieur Zubin made his appearance. Gerald
found it difficult to restrain his surprise. His dinner
suit was faultlessly cut, his black pearl studs were
marvellous. He had been carefully shaved and his hair
had been trimmed. He carried white kid gloves in his
hand, a glossy silk hat, and a malacca cane crowned
with malachite. He came over at once to Gerald and
signed to a waiter who was hovering about with a bottle
upon a tray.

"You will give me three minutes," he begged. "I
was interested in a series of numbers, and I forgot to
dine. I have ordered a bottle of wine. You will perhaps join me."

"Very good of you," Gerald replied. "It is rather
between times for me. I'll have a *fine champagne*, if I
may."

Monsieur Zubin bowed gravely and the brandy was
brought. Without turning a hair, he drank two tum-
blerfuls of the wine. Then he turned courteously to his
companion.

"If you have no objection," he proposed, "we will
walk outside to the Sporting Club. The distance is the
same and the air is fresher."

Gerald assented readily, and they started off side by
side. The Russian was walking with his shoulders back,
like a man on parade, and Gerald suddenly felt that his
own stature had become insignificant. All the way his
companion seemed to be reciting to himself in some
foreign tongue, reciting something which now and then
seemed to have the swing of blank verse. As they
reached the steps which led up to the Sporting Club,
he came to a full stop and glanced around.

" Young man," he said, facing Gerald, " you are
probably a little curious about me. This is the truth.
Let those know it who may be interested. I am the
steward of Madame de Ponière and the trustee of as
much as is left of her revenues. I came here ashamed
of their scantiness, and the wild idea of enlarging them
at the tables occurred to me. I have failed. There is
a *voiture* here, you see, by my side, and the commissionaire is there to help you. I apologise for the trouble I am giving. I charge you to deliver the expression
of my undying devotion to Madame and Mademoiselle."

His right hand, which had been fumbling in the
pocket of his dinner coat, shot out like lightning. A
small revolver, flashing in the electric light, was pressed
to his temple. There were two almost simultaneous reports. The last conscious action of the man was to
half throw himself through the door of the carriage.

Rumours were already floating about the Club when
Gerald hurried in, five minutes later. Both women
looked at him in half-fearful enquiry. Gerald was very
grave.

" Madame," he announced, " I bring bad news."

Madame unfurled her black lace fan and fanned herself slowly.

" One hears that a man has shot himself outside," she
said. " It is, perhaps, the man whom I sent you to
seek? "

" It is he," Gerald acknowledged.

Madame de Ponière rose to her feet. She was an
ugly woman whom, up to that moment, Gerald had de-
tested. He found himself now admiring her profoundly.
She leaned a little upon the stick which she carried in
her left hand. Her right she extended towards Gerald.

" If you will give me the support of your arm downstairs, Lord Dombey, I shall be glad," she continued. "I am an old woman, and these shocks become more poignant with the years. Zubin was a faithful servant of my house. I am much affected."

They made their slow progress from the room. Madame held her head high. Mademoiselle was a little paler than usual, but her good night to the commissionaire was as clear and gracious as ever. No signs of any disturbance remained outside, — Monte Carlo knows how to deal with these things. Their automobile was already in attendance, and the two women took their places at once.

"We are much obliged for your assistance, Lord Dombey," Madame declared. "I regret that we should have given you so tragical an errand."

"You will permit me to call, perhaps, at the Villa?" Gerald begged.

"I shall not be receiving for several days," Madame replied. "If you are so gracious as to leave a card, my servants will tell you when I am disposed to see friends."

The car glided off. Madame leaned back with closed eyes. Gerald caught just a faint glimpse of Pauline's profile, ivory pale, a gleam of terror in her eyes, as though she knew that they were passing over the spot where Zubin had died.

CHAPTER XV

It was after dinner at the Villa Acacia, and Lady Mary and Christopher, hardiest of the little gathering, were strolling back and forth on the terrace in the violet darkness. Arc-like, at their feet, stretched the lights of the Bay of Mentone. The whole hillside seemed dotted with little points of fire from the distant villas. Out at sea, sheet lightning sometimes parted the dense clouds and spread a broad, phantasmal glare upon the rocking waves. The two were old enough friends to speak intimately on many topics. They were talking to-night of Gerald.

"Gerald, as a rule," his sister declared, "is almost over-candid about his love affairs. This is certainly the first time I remember him to have been mysterious."

"I don't think he has seen anything of Mademoiselle de Ponière since the tragedy at the Sporting Club," Christopher remarked.

"It isn't for want of trying, then," the girl replied drily. "He's called there every afternoon since. I've been mean enough to watch him up the drive with my glasses, but he hasn't been allowed in once. They must be queer people."

"There was a distinct suggestion at first," Christopher observed, "that they were adventuresses. Their present attitude doesn't seem like it."

Lady Mary leaned over to gather a sprig of the trailing oleander. She was very becomingly dressed in a gown of deep rose taffeta, one which Christopher re-

membered that he had admired on a previous visit.
She had completely lost her slight brusqueness of manner. Her tone and eyes were soft, as though the magic
of the night had had its effect upon her.

"Really," she sighed, "you young men who should
be our greatest comfort are actually our greatest responsibility. First of all you pick up a peasant girl
on the road, over whom you both seem to have lost your
heads more or less, and now Gerald is behaving like a
lunatic about this young foreign woman."

"Has Gerald told you of the latest developments with
regard to Myrtile?" Christopher enquired.

"Good gracious, no!" Mary replied. "Have you
found a post for her, or something?"

"Her father and fiancé turned up," Christopher declared, — "perfect brutes, both of them. We bought
the child between us for five thousand francs."

Lady Mary frowned.

"Exactly what do you mean, Christopher?" she
asked.

"Crudely put, but a statement of fact, nevertheless,"
was the prompt reply. "Her stepfather and this other
man came and made the dickens of a row; Gerald took
the matter in hand and soon discovered that they were
the usual covetous type of grasping peasant. We paid
down five thousand francs between us, and they signed
a paper giving up all claim to her."

"So now she is on your hands permanently," Mary
remarked.

"I imagine so," Christopher acknowledged. "On the
other hand, I do not think that she will be a serious
charge. I have some friends in London who have promised to take her for a nursery governess."

"Are either of you in love with her?" Mary asked,

raising her eyes and looking her companion in the face.

Christopher hesitated for several moments before answering. Mary began to tear into small pieces the sprig of oleander which she was holding. Her face seemed suddenly to have become very white and tired.

" I am sure that Gerald is not," Christopher answered. " As for me — well, that sort of thing is a little out of my line, isn't it? The most serious part of the situation is that I am afraid the child is in love with Gerald."

" She will get over that," Mary said drily. " Most of the girls I know have been in love with Gerald at some time or another. Sooner or later, the wise ones find him out and the butterfly ones flit away somewhere else. It may seem unsisterly, but I am more concerned about you, Christopher, than Gerald."

He passed his arm through hers, an action which their increasing intimacy seemed to render perfectly natural.

" Mary," he began, " you are just the one person in the world to whom I could confess an impulse of folly, and this is, I suppose, the one place I could do it in. I frankly don't understand what you mean by being in love. When I have thought of marriage, it has been in connection with some dear woman friend who would make a home for me and be a companion. Of course, I expected to care for her and all that, but — promise you won't laugh at me? "

" I shall not laugh," Mary promised.

" For the first time in my life, that child has made me think of other things," Christopher acknowledged simply. " I don't know that it amounts to anything, I dare say really it is an unsuspected vein of kindness which she has touched; but there it is. I have an absurd feeling of fondness for her. The idea of her becoming a plaything for Gerald or anybody makes a madman of me."

" And she? "

" Looks upon me as a kind person but an intolerable nuisance. She dreams of nobody but Gerald. If he lifts his little finger, she is his."

" Really! " Mary drawled coldly.

" Please don't judge her too harshly," Christopher begged. " Myrtile is temperamentally incapable of a mean or an immoral action. She is just a child of nature, only instead of being swayed by the lower instincts, she is swayed by the higher ones. She loves Gerald, and nothing else counts with her. She would have thrown herself into the river sooner than have given herself in marriage to the innkeeper. She is equally capable of giving her life and her soul to Gerald, if he requires the sacrifice."

Mary turned her head towards the window.

" I think that father wants his game of backgammon," she observed. " We had better go in, I am afraid. We must talk of this again sometime. Will you go first and say that I shall be there directly? "

Christopher stepped obediently through the window, and Mary passed on to the farther end of the terrace, where the shadows were deeper. For a moment her self-control slipped away. Her fingers gripped the ivy stalks fiercely. There were tears in her eyes, her rather firm but sensitive little mouth quivered passionately. It seemed so many years since Christopher had first represented to her all that she desired in manhood, — a man of character, a worker, a sportsman when the time came, always ambitious, always ready to pit his

brain against others. She had fancied him in Parliament, a Cabinet Minister later in life, perhaps. She
had thought with happiness of the many ways in which
she could further his career; had dreamed with pleasure of playing hostess for him in a joint establishment.
— She had pictured to herself, for weeks before their
arrival, the coming of these two young men, had speculated joyfully as to the reason for Christopher's unexpected holiday. She had told herself that he, too,
had seen the things she had seen, had felt what she had
prayed he might feel. Womanlike, she had taken note
of the signs. She had known that the consummation
of her wish was inevitable, unless something should
come between. And something had most unexpectedly
come between — this peasant girl, this birth of a spurious sentiment — nothing, in a man like Gerald, but very
much to be dreaded in a person of Christopher's poise
and steadfastness. She was a proud young woman, for
all her gracious ways, and, although she refused to find
anything final in his attitude, the pain that she suffered in those few moments was not only of the heart.

Christopher and his host, in the intervals of their
game, talked of the latest suicide. With the usual
amazing secrecy of the local Press, not one word had
appeared in any paper published in the vicinity.

"I feel a great deal of sympathy for our neighbours," Lord Hinterleys remarked. "Old Colonel Hus-
kinson, whom I met on the Terrace this morning, told
me that the man was bringing them money for some
estates he had sold, which were practically their only
means of subsistence."

Gerald looked up from the sofa where he was lying.
He had complained of a bad headache earlier in the
evening.

" I suppose, sometime or other," he said, " the true story of that man will be known everywhere, and his actual connection with the De Ponières. The magistrate or coroner, or whatever he was, knew it this morning, but he wasn't giving anything away."

" There seems to be a great deal of needless secrecy about the matter," his father observed. " You were present in court, I suppose, Gerald? "

" I was fetched by a small army of gendarmes," Gerald told them. " They escorted me there in a carriage, although the court house was only about half a mile away. It was the quaintest scene. They were simply out for hushing the whole thing up in the most extraordinary manner. They summoned us there, but they apparently didn't want anything from us in the shape of evidence. All that they were anxious about was to get rid of us as soon as they could."

Lord Hinterleys had paused in his game.

" This is really a most extraordinary procedure," he declared. " Do you mean to say, Gerald, that no witnesses at all were called? "

" Not a soul," Gerald replied. " The whole affair, from our point of view, was a farce. One was led to believe that he committed suicide for family reasons or because he had an incurable complaint. I saw Pritili, the manager of the hotel, just as I was coming out this evening, and I asked him pointblank who the man really was and whether the story he had told me himself were true. I was interested in knowing, because it was I who had fetched him away from the Casino at the request of the lady whose steward he was supposed to be. Pritili answered me as I have never been answered by a hotel manager in my life. He drew himself up and looked like an archbishop. ' It is one of those things, milord, into which one does not enquire,' he said. So that was an end of me."

Lord Hinterleys picked up his hand. Mary came in from the terrace and seated herself by Gerald's side. The quietness of the evening, however, was almost immediately disturbed. The butler threw open the door, announcing guests.

"The Ladies Victoria and Millicent Cromwell, Mr. James Cromwell, Lady Esseden."

They all trooped in — intimates of the young people of the house.

"We want you to come down to the Club for an hour or two," Lady Victoria, who was always the leading spirit, suggested. "Dad's just paid my dress allowance, and I'm dying to lose it, and Jimmy's going to give us supper and take us to dance somewhere afterwards."

"Added to which," her sister, Lady Millicent, went on, "we have brought you news."

They were all suddenly attentive. Gerald, who had risen to his feet, leaned a little forward.

"News?" Christopher repeated. "From England?"

"No, you idiot!" Lady Victoria declared. "What news should there be from England? There's no polo or cricket or tennis yet, and most of the people we know have already run away with some one, so there's not even scandal left. We know all about the man who committed suicide the other night."

There was a dead silence, a most effective background for Lady Victoria's announcement.

"They tried hard to keep it secret," she said, "but an English journalist discovered the truth. The man's name was Zubin, and he was the steward of two unfortunate ladies who live near you. He had just arrived from Russia with a large sum of money for them, went into the Rooms, gambled with it and lost the lot. They say that it was nearly three million francs and that it was every penny those poor women had in the world."

CHAPTER XVI

CHRISTOPHER and Gerald were taking an early morning stroll and displaying an almost feminine partiality for the shop windows, when the former suddenly felt his friend's hand tighten upon his arm. They had paused to look through the plate-glass window of a jeweller's shop in the Rue de Paris.

"What is it, old chap?" Christopher asked.

Gerald pointed to a pearl necklace which hung in the window.

"You see that?" he exclaimed tragically. "That belonged to Pauline — to Mademoiselle de Ponière. And that marquise ring below — I am perfectly certain her aunt was wearing it. Wait a moment, old fellow."

Gerald entered the shop hastily. A very suave Frenchman came forward to meet him.

"Can you tell me anything about that pearl necklace and the rings below?" Gerald enquired.

"But certainly, sir," the man replied. "One moment."

He unfastened the window and brought out the stand on which the necklace rested. The colour of the pearls was wonderful. They were not large, but they had an almost pink glow.

"I have no doubt monsieur is a judge and I need say little about these pearls," the shopman began. "I would point out to you, however, that they were matched for royalty itself, and the quality of each one is superlative. If monsieur is a purchaser, I could quote him seven thousand pounds, and for that sum there is not such another necklace in the world."

" I recognise the necklace," Gerald admitted. " I might, under certain circumstances, be induced to buy it. I came in, however, to ask you how you obtained possession of it, and the rings below? "

The man's manner changed.

" Monsieur," he said, " I am not able to explain exactly how this jewellery came into our hands. There are certain confidences which, in the interests of our clients, we are forced to respect."

" Quite so," Gerald agreed, " but I can assure you that I am not an impertinent enquirer. This is my name," — he handed the man a card — " and I was an acquaintance of Mademoiselle de Ponière, from whom you must have obtained this necklace. I last saw Madame and Mademoiselle de Ponière under very tragical circumstances, and I understand that they have now left Monte Carlo. I am most anxious to obtain word as to their whereabouts."

" As regards that, milord," the jeweller said, with a measure of increased respect but with no signs of yielding, " I regret that I am unable to help you. The transaction, such as it was, is finished. I was entrusted with no address."

" You would not buy jewellery of such value," Gerald persisted, " unless you knew something of your clients. You can probably tell me whether De Ponière is their real name, and you can at least give me a hint as to where they are to be found."

" I regret deeply that I am entirely powerless in the matter, milord," the man replied.

Gerald held up the pearls and let them slip through his fingers. He remembered something which Pauline had once said to him, — " Pearls are the maidens' children. They love and care for them as such."

" I have reason to surmise," Gerald went on, " that a misfortune has befallen these ladies. If they had confided in me, it would have given me the greatest pleasure to have offered them assistance."

The jeweller smiled inscrutably.

" I fear that it would have been useless, milord," he said. " I have had the privilege of knowing the elder of these ladies for some thirty years, and I supplied the first string of pearls which the younger lady ever wore, at the time of her confirmation. I would willingly have undertaken the payment of such debts as were owing in Monte Carlo, without security, but I should never have had the courage to suggest it. You will see an announcement in the evening paper, milord, that all claims against the ladies will be settled by me on demand."

" If I buy the necklace," Gerald proposed bluntly, " will you tell me how and where to find Mademoiselle de Ponière? "

The jeweller's bow was almost frigid.

" My word is passed to these two ladies, milord. I have no information whatever to give you."

" You cannot even tell me what relation they were to Monsieur Zubin? "

" Monsieur Zubin? " the jeweller repeated, a little vaguely.

" The man who committed suicide a few nights ago outside the Sporting Club."

The jeweller shrugged his shoulders.

" There is no question of relationship, milord. Monsieur Zubin was, I understand, the steward entrusted with the realisation of certain properties be-

longing to Mademoiselle. I do not know whether I
have a right even to say so much," he continued, after
a moment's hesitation, "but it suggests itself that it
was owing to Monsieur Zubin's embezzlements — he is
reported to have lost several millions at the tables here
— that the ladies whom we have been discussing found
themselves temporarily embarrassed."

Gerald laid down the pearls.

"If you care to keep these for me for a week," he
proposed, "until I get the money from London, I will
have them."

The man bowed.

"Milord can take them with him," he said, "or permit me to send them to the hotel. Payment can be as
desired."

"You can send them round to the Hôtel de Paris,"
Gerald directed. "If you are as loyal to all your
clients, you deserve to prosper in your business."

The man bowed lower than ever as he showed Gerald
out.

"Perhaps some day," he said, "it will be my privilege
to explain to milord that loyalty."

"I have committed an extravagance," Gerald confessed, as the two young men continued their stroll.

"You have bought the presents for your supper
party?" Christopher suggested.

"I never thought of them," was the candid reply.
"I have given seven thousand pounds for a pearl necklace."

"Great Scott! Why?"

"Because I was right in my surmise. It was Pauline's necklace, left there so that they could pay their
bills. Madame's rings are there, too. Pretty sort of
adventuresses, Christopher!"

" But what are you going to do with the necklace? "
Christopher, always intensely practical, demanded.

" I am going to keep it until I meet Mademoiselle de
Ponière again," Gerald replied. " Then I shall beg to
be allowed to present it to her."

" Have you found out who she is? "

" I have not, but I have found a loyal and honest
tradesman. If I had asked him another question, I
should have felt a cad."

Christopher looked up towards the hills.

" It's too misty for golf," he said. " Shall we go and
see Myrtile? "

" I suppose so," Gerald agreed, without marked interest. " Any news from your nursery governess
friends? "

" They can't take her for a month or so," Christopher replied. " I don't quite know what to do about it.
I must leave on Thursday week."

Gerald laughed.

"And you daren't trust her here with me, old chap, is
that it? "

" Something like it, I'm afraid," the other admitted
frankly.

Gerald sighed.

" What a Lothario you must think me! " he declared.
"As a matter of fact, Chris, I don't think that the ingénue does attract me very much. I am too young and
unsophisticated myself. It is hardened sinners like
you who are bowled over by rusticity and morals. I
prefer something a little more advanced in the world's
ways."

" Then, for heaven's sake, leave the others alone! "
Christopher enjoined curtly. " We have a difficult task
before us with Myrtile, especially as, for once in her life,

Mary doesn't seem inclined to help us.   Treat the child
sensibly, for heaven's sake."

"What do you mean by 'sensibly', old chap?"

"Well, remember that she has to be a nursery governess and not a Parisian demi-mondaine.   It's idiotic
to take her to these smart restaurants and dancing
places.   It's outside her life.   It gives her false ideas."

"This from the man who took her to the Opera on a
gala night!" Gerald scoffed.

"I took her to the Opera in a small box and in her
ordinary clothes," Christopher retorted.   "I took her
for the sake of the music, and she didn't think of a thing
except the music from the beginning to the end."

"Frankly, you bore me about Myrtile," Gerald declared.   "You ought to have been born in the days of
dear old Oliver Cromwell.   My idea is that girls were
made to live like butterflies, to be happy just in the few
hours when the sun shines."

"You have not even the philosophy of the pagan,"
Christopher retorted.   "You forget that the butterfly
enjoys the supreme advantage of being unencumbered
with a soul."

The street door was suddenly opened in their faces.
They had arrived at Myrtile's lodgings, to find her issuing into the street.   She seemed to look through Christopher at Gerald, who was a pace or two behind.   Her
smile was wonderful.

"I knew that something pleasant was going to happen this morning!" she exclaimed.   "I felt it when I
got up."

"You were quite right," Gerald assured her.   "Something very pleasant is going to happen.   I am going to
take you over to Nice in the car to lunch."

Myrtile clapped her hands.

" Wait one moment," she begged. " I must go and get some different gloves. I'll catch you up before you get to the corner of the street."

The two young men strolled slowly on. There was a serious expression on Christopher's face.

" I am lunching with your people to-day, Gerald — at least I promised to if there was no golf," he observed.

" I heard Mary say so," was the indifferent reply. " Good luck to you ! "

"And you are taking Myrtile to Nice — Mademoiselle de Ponière having left," Christopher continued thoughtfully.

Gerald frowned.

" That was rather my idea," he admitted. " Have you anything against it? "

Christopher passed his hand through his friend's arm. They had reached the end of the street and turned slowly back again.

" Look here, old fellow, don't be shirty," he begged. " You know I'm right. We can only look after this girl decently in one way, and that is by finding her some sort of a situation not too far removed from the way she has been brought up, in which she can earn an honest living. I'm on my way to secure this for her, but if you go turning her head by taking her about to these smart restaurants, and developing her taste for the gaieties of life, you'll only unsettle her terribly and spoil her chances of contentment."

" You've taken her out yourself once or twice," Gerald reminded him.

" I never take her to the very fashionable places," Christopher insisted earnestly, " and I try all the time to impress upon her the necessity of work and the fact that life out here is merely a holiday existence. Take her to Nice, by all means, if you want to, Gerald, but don't turn her head."

Myrtile came down the street towards them. Gerald's face cleared — as he watched her, it was lit with a wave of admiration.

" She is like a piece of floating sunshine," he declared enthusiastically. " Chris, I'm not at all sure that she ought to be a nursery governess. She's going to be beautiful enough to turn the heads of half the men in Europe."

" It will be very largely our responsibility," Christopher said, lowering his voice a little as Myrtile drew near, " whether that beauty is going to be a curse or a happiness to her. Don't you forget that, Gerald — or our bargain."

CHAPTER XVII

GERALD was absolutely amazed as he led Myrtile back to their seat in the palm court of the hotel. They had lunched, wandered about the town, and afterwards made their way back to the hotel lounge, where a Thé Dansant was in progress.

"Why, where on earth did you learn to dance like that, Myrtile?" he demanded.

She laughed softly.

"Learn?" she exclaimed. "Why, there has never been any one to teach me. I have never had a lesson in my life. I just listened to the music and watched the people, and then I saw that it was quite easy. Oh, how I love it!"

"What a pity I can't have you to my supper party to-night!" Gerald sighed.

She leaned towards him. She was still a little out of breath. Her cheeks were pink, her eyes aglow.

"Mayn't I come, please, Gerald?" she begged. "I should be so happy."

Gerald looked doubtful.

"There would be the devil to pay with Christopher," he pointed out. "And, besides, it really isn't the place for you."

"What do you mean?" she persisted.

"Well, it's a Bohemian sort of affair," Gerald explained, a little awkwardly. "The girls aren't all of them just what they should be."

Myrtile laughed again.

"But what does that matter?" she protested. "They will not hurt me or I them. When I am not dancing with you, I can sit alone and talk to no one."

Gerald shook his head.

"Can't be done, little girl," he decided regretfully. "Christopher is quite right when he says I ought not to encourage the taste for that sort of life in you at all. These girls all drink a lot of champagne, and smoke furiously — lead rotten lives, most of them — and their conversation sometimes — well, it wouldn't be fit for you to listen to. Some evening or other I'll have quite a small party — just one or two who I know are all right."

"That isn't what I want," Myrtile declared. "I want to go to the party to-night. You will dance with other girls if I am not there. I don't want you to — not to-day, at any rate. You have danced with me, and it was wonderful."

"I begin to think that I don't want to dance with any one else myself," Gerald confessed, looking at her admiringly. "I'll think it over on the way back."

"Must we start now?" she asked wistfully.

"This moment," Gerald insisted. "I have to dine with the family. It's their last night. They are off to England to-morrow. I tell you what we'll do, though, if you like. We'll take the mountain road."

"Is it longer?"

"About half an hour," he replied. "There won't be nearly so much traffic, though, and I love putting the old 'bus at the hills."

They made their way out to the open space in front of the hotel, where Gerald had left the car, and very soon they were on their way homeward. Driving, for the first half-hour, absorbed Gerald's whole attention, and Myrtile leaned back in the low seat by his side, filled with the joy of their rapid ascent, the smooth, birdlike motion which seemed to be taking them, with scarcely an effort, up into the clouds. Soon all the signs of over-population which spoil the effect of the coast road became blurred and undistinguishable. The natural beauties of that wonderful line of coast reasserted them-selves. Up here in the mountains were no cafés with flamboyant invitations, or jerry-built villas. One had the sensation of being lifted out of the tawdriness and artificiality of a region over-abundant in tourists, a lit-tle over-anxious to display for their benefit its charms. — Once Myrtile turned her head as they were about to round the last corner of the ascent, and looked back-wards. Gerald, with quick comprehension, understood her thoughts and spoke for the first time.

"This is the real road, Myrtile," he said. "It comes straight from Cannes, straight from the gate over which you leaned. The other we only took that night for safety."

Her beautiful eyes sought for his and were rewarded with a momentary glance of sympathy. Gerald was at his best when driving. The slight weakness of his face disappeared in the concentration of watching the road. He drove always with his head a little thrown back, not in any way the action of a poseur, but simply the fixed desire of the born motorist to see as far as possible ahead of him.

"I think," Myrtile whispered, "that this is the real road which leads to happiness. The road down there is tangled and twisted. Here one seems to breathe more wonderfully, to come nearer to the things one feels but does not understand. It is more like the air around the farm, when I used to get up sometimes before the sunrise

and walk through the violet patch and the cypresses to
the gate.   The sun rose at the end of the road."

" You are a quaint child, Myrtile," Gerald reflected.
" I wonder what would have happened to you if we had
not passed along that night."

She shivered.

" I know," she answered.   " I am quite sure that I
know.   I felt it in my heart when I leaned over the gate
and looked to the end of the road.   There was the mystery there towards which I seemed always to have
groped.   That night it was the mystery of life or the
mystery of death.   You came, and it was life."

They were travelling more slowly now, crawling along
the level stretch of ledge-like road at its extreme sum-
mit.   Gerald had never before felt the fascination of
the girl by his side as he felt it in those moments.   He
stretched out his left hand and she gripped it in hers,
tearing off her gloves so that her fingers could clasp
his.

"And since it is life," he asked, " is the mystery passing? "

Her eyes were swimming with the desire of happiness.

" There is no mystery any longer," she told him.   " I
know what lies at the end of the road, where the sun
used to rise.   I know now."

He moved a little uneasily.   The descent was com-
mencing, and he needed his left hand.   There were portents already of the short twilight.   Here and there, an
early light glimmered out amongst the hills.   The air
was cool and crisp.   Gerald, impressionable as ever, felt
the spurious glow of exaltation, spurious because its influence was wholly external.   His face became graver,
his tone was almost stern.

" What we hope you will find there," he said, " is

happiness. Christopher has explained to you about this post in England? "

" Yes," she answered.

" You will like it? "

" No ! "

He rounded a difficult corner and brought the car to a standstill in a wall-encircled arc of the road, a little space thrown out like a bay window, where one may pause for a moment from the strain of driving. Below lay the wonderful bay, the rock of Monaco, the white Casino standing over the dark blue sea. More lights were flashing out now. The blurred landscape seemed to gain in beauty of outline what it lost in colour.

" But you must be happy, Myrtile. We want you to be happy," Gerald declared.

" If you want me to be happy," she whispered, " I shall always be happy because it is you — you ——"

Gerald, a moment ago, had been full of good intentions, of good advice. Myrtile leaned towards him. Her slim body, sweet but throbbing with eagerness, prayed for his embrace. Her left arm stole out towards his shoulder, as though to turn his head.

" Gerald ! " she whispered.

" Myrtile ! " he begged, " you must not ——"

Then all Gerald's good resolutions crumbled for the moment. Her lips were pressed to his, warm and sweet, passionate with the fervour which comes from the soul alone, which takes no count of lesser things than the Heaven where, to the innocent, love only dwells. She rested in his arms, tumultuously happy. Somewhere in the field below was a bonfire of fallen pine boughs, and for years afterwards the smell of burning wood, fragrant and aromatic, brought back to Gerald the memory of those few seconds. — There was a flash of lights below from an approaching automobile. Gerald drew away, pale and a little remorseful. Myrtile's face was like the face of a child who has seen Heaven.

" We must get on," he said hoarsely.

She lay back in her place without moving until they began the last descent into the town.

" May I come to your party to-night, Gerald — now? " she whispered.

" No! "

She laughed quietly to herself. There was no longer any shadow of disappointment in her face.

" But you are very foolish," she remonstrated. " How can you think that it would not be well for me to be where you are? Besides, I want you to dance with me. They are very beautiful young ladies who come to your parties — Christopher showed me some of them at the Opera."

" There is not one of them so beautiful as you," he declared.

She smiled happily.

" Will you think so to-night? " she asked.

" I shall think so all the time — and I shall miss you horribly," he assured her.

" Perhaps you will, perhaps you will not," she replied enigmatically. " You must put me down here. This is my corner."

She jumped lightly down, with only a touch of his fingers for farewell. Gerald, although he had set a stern face against the rush of ideas and anticipations which were crowding into his brain, felt a little pang of disappointment as she left him without further protest. He would never have allowed her to come, he told himself, as he drove slowly off. Yet at that moment he had a vision. He escaped a taxicab by a few inches.

Myrtile waited until Gerald was out of sight. Then she crossed the Square, walked a few steps along the Rue de Paris, paused before the curtained door of Madame Lénore's little establishment, and pushed it open. Madame Lénore herself came forward. There was something sinister, though not unfriendly, in the smile with which she greeted her visitor.

" What can I do for mademoiselle? " she enquired.

" Can I have the clothes for the evening which you showed me when I first came here? " Myrtile asked, a little anxiously.

" But certainly, Mademoiselle," the Frenchwoman answered graciously. " Mademoiselle desires them for this evening? "

" I want to wear them to-night," was the happy reply.

Madame studied the slim figure before her, followed its beautiful lines, yielding her half grudging, half cynical admiration to its undeveloped perfection. Then she studied the girl's face. She had not a doubt in her mind as to what this visit meant. She decided that, if she were properly handled, this peasant child might bring fame even to her establishment.

" There are some other things mademoiselle will require," she said thoughtfully, " and it will be necessary for mademoiselle to have the coiffeur. Mademoiselle will place herself in my hands for the evening? I will promise that there is not a girl in Monte Carlo who will be half so beautiful."

" I want to look as nice as it is possible for me to look," Myrtile confided. " I will do just as you say, Madame."

" Is it a party which mademoiselle desires to attend? "

"A supper party," Myrtile replied. " It is at half-past eleven."

" At the Hôtel de Paris? "

" Yes! "

Madame glanced at the clock.

" If mademoiselle will return at eight o'clock," she said, " I will have a coiffeur here and give him instructions myself. Afterwards, we will dress her. I live here — my assistant and I — on the floor above. It will not incommode us."

" I shall be quite punctual," Myrtile promised. " You are very kind, Madame."

The unwilling admiration shone once more in Madame's beady eyes as Myrtile turned and walked lightly away.

" It is a pity," she sighed, " that the girl is such a fool! "

CHAPTER XVIII

ONCE more Christopher and Lady Mary braved the night air on the terrace of the Villa Acacia. The latter pointed across the gorge to the villa on the other side, a shadowy-looking building, unlit, and without any sign of habitation.

"I wonder what Gerald does without his little play-fellow in the afternoons," she observed.

Christopher frowned.

"I know what he did this afternoon. He took Myrtile over to Nice."

"Myrtile?" Lady Mary repeated coldly. "Your little protégée?"

"Yes," Christopher assented.

"The young lady you purchased from a sordid step-father and an amorous suitor," Lady Mary continued, the irony of her tone merging almost into bitterness. "You young men will end by getting into trouble with the police or your own consciences."

"I am not in the least afraid of either contingency," Christopher assured her.

"Then why do you look so disturbed every time the girl's name is mentioned?" Lady Mary asked him, pointblank.

They were passing one of the long, high windows. Christopher paused for a moment to look inside. Gerald and his father were playing chess, — Gerald slim, handsome, obviously a little bored with the game; his father keenly interested by a somewhat audacious move which had just been made.

"If I do," Christopher said, "as I tried to explain to you before, it is not on my own account."

Lady Mary laughed.

"You can't imagine that Gerald is likely to find her dangerous!" she scoffed. "Why, he was head over ears in love with that strange girl over at the Villa Violette yesterday, and, besides, Gerald isn't vicious — you know that."

"Gerald is very weak sometimes," Christopher said bluntly. "He has a man's conscience where men are concerned, but with regard to women — well, he sees things differently. He has been terribly spoilt, of course, and in this particular instance the trouble is that the child fancies herself in love with him."

"In love with Gerald!   How ridiculous!"

"You don't quite appreciate her, if you don't mind my saying so," Christopher declared, a little timidly. "She is extraordinarily ignorant and she is also extraordinarily innocent. All her life she has been starved for kindness and beauty. I don't think there was ever a human being in the world who needed help and counsel more than she does to-day."

"Shall I remove her from temptation?" Mary enquired, after a moment's reflection. "My maid has just broken it to me that she is going to stay here and get married. Shall I take your protégée back to England in her place?"

"If only you would!" Christopher exclaimed eagerly. "You needn't keep her. My cousin is going to find a place for her as nursery governess, but she isn't quite ready yet."

Lady Mary considered the matter, leaning over the

balcony, her head a little thrown back as though to enjoy the perfume of the pines. Her profile was luminously sweet against the dark background, but there was rather a tired droop at the corners of her lips. Her thoughts wandered for a moment from the subject of discussion.

" I wonder whether I am glad to go home," she ruminated.

" We shall miss you," Christopher declared.

She turned her head and looked at him.

" Will you? "

" Immensely," he assured her. " I shall miss our tennis more than anything. To tell you the truth," he went on, " except for the tennis and the rather amazing golf, I don't think Monte Carlo appeals to me very much."

" You are no gambler," she observed.

" I haven't the faintest inclination towards it," he confessed. " I hate the things in life which I cannot control."

" Isn't that a little rash? " she ventured. " You might have to hate your own affections."

He was silent for a moment. She watched him curiously.

" I don't think I am the sort of person," he said, " who would be likely to be led very far by his affections alone. — What about the child, Mary? "

" I will take her if you wish it," she decided. " She must be at the station at eight o'clock. You know that we have to make an early start. There will be nothing for her to do. Janet has packed and will arrange all my things for the journey."

Christopher drew a long breath of relief.

" You are a dear! " he exclaimed enthusiastically.

"You can't imagine what a weight this is off my mind."

"I am doing it for your sake," Lady Mary told him. "I do not like the child. I disapprove most strongly of the whole situation. However, I will do what I have promised. We are going straight to Hinterleys. She can remain there until your cousin is ready for her."

Gerald came strolling out to them, pausing on the way to light a cigarette. The game of chess was over and his father was buried in the *Times*, which had just been brought in.

"What are you two conspiring about?" he enquired.

"I have been saying good-by to your sister," Christopher replied.

Gerald passed his arm around her affectionately.

"We shall miss you, dear," he said.

"I think I am really rather sorry to go," Mary confessed. "Father is getting quite restless, though. He never cares to stay in one place too long."

Gerald glanced at his watch.

"I must be off," he announced. "I've a few of my frivolous friends coming in to supper after the Opera. Are you coming, Christopher?"

"I don't think so, if you don't mind, Gerald," was the apologetic reply. "I dance very badly, and none of those little lady friends of yours seems to understand my French. I shall stay and talk to your father for half an hour and then walk down."

For some unaccountable reason, Gerald felt relieved. He took his leave of his father and sister, started up his car, and drove through the scented darkness back to the hotel. All the time he was conscious of a little quiver of excitement for which he could not account. The Villa Violette, at which he gazed as he turned out of the avenue, was dark and empty. He thought of Pauline and sighed. The ghost in the empty seat by his side faded away. He was for a single moment a man, angry with himself, bitterly regretful.

"I was a cad to kiss her like that," he muttered. "All the same, a child has no right to such lips."

Gerald was met in the hall of the hotel by Charles, the *maître d'hôtel* to whom he had left the arrangements for his supper party.

"If milord will be so kind as to ascend with me," the latter suggested, "I can show him the preparations I have made."

Gerald nodded and ascended to the first floor. The man threw open the door of a large apartment with smoothly polished floor. A round table, arranged for sixteen, stood in the middle of the room under a glittering chandelier. A heavily laden sideboard stood in a recess. At the farther end, on a slightly raised dais, three musicians were seated, looking through their music.

"This is the most convenient suite for milord," Charles explained, "because the door at the left-hand there communicates with milord's own suite of apartments, where his friends, if they like, can leave their hats and coats. I shall serve the supper myself. Everything will be as commanded. The supper table can be moved into a corner of the room at any time desired, — as soon, in fact, as milord cares to start dancing. Monsieur Léon presents his compliments, and, although he has no desire to impose anything in the way of restrictions, he begs that the party may finish at half-past three, in order to avoid complaints."

Gerald nodded and dismissed the man. He stood for a moment in the centre of the waxed floor, his hands be-

hind him and a freshly lit cigarette between his lips.
The sight of these preparations for the night's festivi-
ties had left him curiously unmoved.   He could picture
the whole affair, — a little cosmopolitan crowd of gig-
gling, shrieking girls, half French, half Russian, with a
dash, here and there, of the Egyptian and the Italian.
It was a surge of femininity with which the room would
presently be assailed, and he was conscious of a sudden
sense of revulsion.   Nadine, with her pale cheeks, her
eyes half green, half yellow, like the eyes of a cat, her
alluring smile.   Somehow or other she would find her
way to his side, she would whisper to him in corners,
brazenly ignoring the fact that she was the guest of the
American whose yacht was moored in the harbour, but
who had gone to Paris for a week.   Then there were
Chlotilde and Phrynette, Parisians to the rosy tips of
their fingers, more blatant still in their desires, frank
and unashamed of the silken net they trolled.   It was,
after all, a dull game to play.   The finesse of refusal
had never seemed so flat, the ignominy of consent so re-
pulsive.   He moved impatiently to the window and stood
looking across the strip of garden to the bay.   The
violinist behind was playing something very softly, nothing to do with the dance, a little fragment of music
made for himself.   Gerald leaned towards the cool darkness.   The music helped him to a momentary escape.
He thought of Pauline, cold as the snows, proud and
indifferent, yet with the charm of hidden things in her
clear eyes and delicate aloofness.   Her indifference had
hurt — how much he realised when he thought of the
coming evening.   And then, like a flash, his mood
changed.   There was the other type, as beautiful in its
way, as serene, as wonderful in its strange, virginal passion, the lips that had clung to his with the frank offer

of supreme, unselfish love. — Christopher was right. There was no pleasure amongst the herds.

He turned away, and, crossing the room, opened the door leading into his own suite. A wondrous — an amazing — vision confronted him. For a moment he was aghast. Myrtile, transformed as though by the wand of an artist, her gown, simple and unadorned, retentive of all the grace of her girlhood, yet exquisitely suggestive of the woman to come, — Myrtile, her hair drooped low on either side of her oval face, a robed lily, unspoilt and untarnished by the cunning fingers which had produced a veritable triumph. Her bosom was rising and falling quickly, her lips were parted. Then she began to laugh softly. Everything was right with the world. Gerald's look of transfixed admiration told her all that she needed to know.

CHAPTER XIX

" WILL I do? " Myrtile asked demurely.

" You are wonderful! " Gerald exclaimed. " But — what does it mean? "

" I have come to your party," Myrtile announced, " and even Monsieur Christopher shall not send me away. I went to Madame Lénore. She dressed me and she had my hair arranged. It was so droll. When I looked in the glass I scarcely knew myself. You are pleased? "

" I am more than pleased," Gerald answered, taking her hand. " But about this party. I am not sure ——"

" You don't want me? " she whispered.

He could no longer resist the invitation of her lips. After a moment, however, she sprang away. The violinist in the room beyond had commenced a waltz. She dragged Gerald through the open door and gave a little cry of delight when she saw the room.

" Dance with me," she begged, " just you and I, all alone. Dance with me, Gerald! "

They moved off to the music. The violinist smiled with pleasure. The other instruments took up the strain. Myrtile was as light as a feather in her partner's arms, her feet flashed or lingered upon the floor like flecks of sunlight upon a wave-stirred sea. She closed her eyes, half fainting with the joy of the music, the smooth floor, Gerald's arms. Presently he stopped. He was unaccountably out of breath. He took one of the gold-foiled bottles from the sideboard, opened it and filled two glasses with the foaming wine. Myrtile's eyes shone like stars as she drank.

"Oh, I am happy!" she murmured. "This is wonderful! Promise, Gerald, that you will never send me away. Promise?"

There was a shriek of voices as the room was invaded. Nadine came through the door which led from his own suite.

"Gerald," she cried, "there is a cloak already upon your bed! I am on fire with jealousy. Who is your early guest? — Ah! A thousand pardons!"

Gerald's movement had disclosed Myrtile. Nadine, daringly, almost shamelessly dressed, raised her bare arms.

"Heaven!" she exclaimed. "Gerald has robbed a convent!"

Some men followed, accompanied by a little crowd of girls. Every one was curious about Myrtile. She shook hands shyly with those whom Gerald presented to her. When they asked for her name, however, he shook his head.

"Mademoiselle is our guest for this evening," he announced. "She is not, alas! of our world. Let us call her Mademoiselle X."

"Mademoiselle the Spirit, rather!" a Frenchman exclaimed. "I think that you have dragged her down from the skies. Present me, Gerald, or I shall be your enemy for life."

"The Marquis Chantelaine," Gerald murmured, "Mademoiselle X. The Marquis is a shameless fellow, Myrtile, and you must not believe a word he says."

"I am shameless or not according to my surroundings," the Frenchman declared. "No one could look into the eyes of Mademoiselle and speak other than the truth."

Chlotilde pouted.

" Is no one going to say nice things to us others? " she complained. " Gerald, you ought to have warned us. I would have worn my new gown. It is exactly the colour of the sky. Even my maid declared that I, too, slipped down from heaven."

There was a little chorus of laughter. Cocktails were brought in and cigarettes lit. Every one gathered around and talked to Myrtile. She answered them naturally enough, but every now and then with embarrassment.

" Mademoiselle X may be asked no questions," Gerald insisted. " Where she comes from I shall not tell any of you. Whither she goes after to-night, you will none of you know."

" Mademoiselle is of the *haut monde*, perhaps? " Nadine whispered maliciously, under her breath.

" Mademoiselle belongs to a world we are none of us privileged to enter," Gerald answered. " It is the one favour I ask, as your host. Please accept my guest as a butterfly, born this evening, passing away to-morrow."

" Oh, là, là! " Chlotilde exclaimed. " We are all like that. Give me another cocktail, Charles. I have not had a drink all the evening, and my sylph dance was twice encored."

They made their way presently to the supper table. Myrtile sat at Gerald's right hand, and next her, on the other side, was the Marquis de Chantelaine. Any form of tête-à-tête conversation, however, was impossible from the first. They all seemed to be talking together at the top of their voices in an almost incomprehensible argot, a jumble of personal quips and sallies. Myrtile listened sympathetically but understood little. Occasionally she laughed when the others laughed, but as a matter of fact she needed nothing to complete her happiness. She was next to Gerald, who whispered every now and then little words of encouragement in her ear. The Marquis, too, murmured occasional compliments, but he was man of the world enough partially to understand the situation, and he restrained his natural instincts towards unbridled gallantry. Presently Chlotilde jumped up and danced. Phrynette followed suit and executed a wonderful *pas seul*. There was a good deal of boisterous applause. Myrtile felt the colour burning in her cheeks. She glanced towards Gerald. He was laughing, so it must be all right. Nevertheless, she was relieved when at last Phrynette sat down.

"I will show you," Nadine suggested, "how they dance in Algiers."

There was a little chorus of applause. Gerald alone for a moment looked doubtful. He glanced towards Myrtile at his side.

"Don't overdo it, Nadine," he begged.

Nadine laughed subtly.

"Is it for your ingénue you fear, or yourself?" she asked. "Very well, I will give you both something to think about."

She danced at first with all the quivering grace of restrained but passionate movements. Myrtile watched her with fascinated eyes. Then she suddenly broke loose. Myrtile looked down at her plate and gripped Gerald's hand.

"Remember I warned you, dear," he whispered. "Don't watch."

"Mademoiselle would perhaps care for a little

stroll upon the balcony? " the Marquis whispered in her ear.

Myrtile shook her head.

" Thank you," she murmured, " I do not wish to leave Gerald. As for the dancing, it is foolish of me but I have never seen anything like it. It never seemed to me possible that women could do such things. That is because I have not lived in the world. I shall progress."

The dance came to an end amidst uproarious applause. Nadine, dishevelled and breathless, pirouetted towards the door leading to Gerald's suite.

" I shall go into your bedroom and make myself tidy," she called out. " You can come and fetch me when you want me," she added, looking over her shoulder at her host.

The corks began to fly faster still. Presently, couples stood up and danced. Then, indeed, happiness began for Myrtile. She danced with Gerald again and again, danced to music which was indeed of the best, for Gerald was somewhat of an epicure in such matters, until she forgot the loud voices, the haze of cigarette smoke, the slightly unsteady condition of one or two of the guests. To her, so long as it was Gerald's arm which controlled her, it was all beautiful. By degrees she seemed to slip into her place, however incongruous it might be, in the little company. The first impulse of resentment against her presence, shown most clearly by Nadine after her prolonged but useless wait before Gerald's looking-glass, soon passed away. She was accepted as one of the kaleidoscopic pictures of Monte Carlo flirtations. She had come, and there was an end of it. There were other hosts besides Gerald, other Englishmen crowding all the time into the place. The very singleness of her devotion made her to some extent a rival to be accepted philosophically. She at least made not the slightest response to the advances which were offered her freely enough by the other men of the party.

It seemed incredible that four o'clock had arrived when Louis presented himself with many apologies. There was a ball that night at the Carlton, however, so every one was resigned. They invaded Gerald's rooms for their coats and wraps. Myrtile remained talking with the Marquis, with whom she had been dancing. Her body was still swaying a little to the rhythm of the music.

" So this is your first night, Mademoiselle? " her companion said softly. " I shall hope that we may meet many more times."

" If you are a friend of Gerald's, I hope that we may," Myrtile replied.

" You have enjoyed yourself, on the whole? " he asked, looking at her curiously.

Her ears were straining for Gerald's voice. She could hear all the time the shrill laughter of Nadine and her friends.

" I have enjoyed the dancing," she said.

" But not the dancing of Mademoiselle Nadine? "

Her cheeks were suddenly hot. There was a look of trouble in her eyes which he had noticed before and wondered at.

" No, I did not like that," she acknowledged. " I cannot believe that Gerald liked it, really. It was not beautiful."

" She is very famous," the Marquis remarked.

" It was not beautiful," Myrtile repeated. " It frightened me a little."

The Frenchman, a little intrigued, smiled.

" I begin to believe," he said, " that you are really as young as you look."

" I am eighteen," she told him.

" For that moment I was not thinking of your actual years," he explained. " How long have you known Lord Dombey? "

" Gerald? " she queried. " Only a very short time. I have never danced with him before to-day."

" It seems easy to believe," he said, " that you slipped down from the skies, only nowadays Heaven does not part with its children so easily. Tell me, where did you come from, really? "

"A little farm on the other side of the mountains," she said. " Gerald and Monsieur Christopher brought me here. Monsieur Christopher wants me to go to England, but I hope that Gerald will not let me go."

" But what shall you do if you stay here? " he asked.

" Gerald will take care of me," she answered. " I shall be very happy if he lets me stay."

He looked at her thoughtfully. He was inclined to be a disbeliever, the accepted pose towards women at his age, but a little flicker of genuine feeling disturbed for a moment his placid and cultivated cynicism.

" I am not at all sure," he said, " if you are what you seem to be, that it would not be better if you went to England."

They all came trooping out. Myrtile got up to fetch her own cloak, but Gerald detained her. She stood by his side, bidding good night to his guests with him. The Marquis frowned slightly as he made his adieux. The look in his eyes haunted her for a moment as he turned away. Then she was conscious of a curious sense of disturbance. Throughout the dancing she had been soothed into a state of ecstatic happiness. Suddenly there was a change. She was alone with Gerald and he was looking at her strangely. Two of the musicians were packing up their music. Once more the violinist was playing softly, as though to himself.

" You have been happy, Myrtile? " Gerald asked, and his voice seemed to come from a long way off.

" Wonderfully," she answered. " I — there is my cloak."

She moved towards the open door leading into Gerald's suite. She seemed suddenly torn by a strange medley of sensations and memories. She saw Nadine pass through it, dishevelled and indecent, with that backward glance at Gerald which, even to her ignorance, seemed ugly. She heard the voices of all of them laughing stridently. Little half-understood sentences puzzled her. She passed into the sitting room. Gerald followed, closing the door. The sound of the music came more quietly. Myrtile felt suddenly faint.

" You are tired! " Gerald exclaimed, bending anxiously over her.

She put her arms around his neck like a child.

" Gerald," she whispered, " take care of me. I am afraid. Be good to me, Gerald."

Their lips met, but there was something absent from the warm joy of that first kiss. Side by side with her happiness came the feeling of discordant music all around her. Rank perfumes seemed to hang in the air. A ribbon from one of Nadine's discarded garments lay upon the sofa. Yet when Gerald leaned towards her and his eyes sought for hers, a strange content seemed to creep like a flood over all these other things.

The door of the sitting room was suddenly opened and closed. Christopher stood there, a little breathless, as though he had run up the stairs, pale, and with a look in his eyes from which both Gerald and Myrtile quailed, — Gerald with fuller understanding. His arms dropped. He was nearer fear than ever before in his life. Christopher spoke with marvellous calmness.

" Gerald," he said, " were you thinking of breaking your trust? "

" Yes! " Gerald answered hoarsely. " Drop this Don Quixote business, Christopher. I'm sick of it."

Christopher came a step nearer.

" Myrtile is coming back to her lodgings with me," he announced. " She is going to England to-morrow morning. Your sister has promised to take her."

" But it is impossible! " Myrtile cried passionately.

" It is arranged," Christopher declared. " I went to your rooms to-night, Myrtile, to tell you. I received Annette's lying message. I was told that you were in bed and asleep. I left a note. Then, for the first time since I have been here, I went to the Club and stayed late. I heard your guests downstairs speak of your good fortune, Gerald."

Gerald laid his hand upon Myrtile's wrist.

" Well," he said, " what are you going to do about it? "

" I am going to take Myrtile home," Christopher insisted.

" I refuse to let her go," Gerald declared.

Christopher looked for a moment away at Myrtile. She clung to Gerald like a frightened child.

" Listen," Christopher went on, " you and I have been friends all our lives, Gerald. We know one another pretty well. You know of me that I am a man of my word. I know of you that, though you are selfish and worship pleasure, you are white enough when the hour strikes. The hour has struck, Gerald. Let me take Myrtile home."

"Myrtile shall choose," Gerald proposed.

"Myrtile shall do nothing of the sort," was the prompt reply. "You might as well ask her to choose the right path through a strange city. Gerald, old chap, don't take this hardly. I am not here to sling abuse at you. And Myrtile — just doesn't understand. Thank God I was in time! — Myrtile, take your cloak."

She clung to Gerald's arm, looking anxiously into his face. Something else discordant had come into the room, something unbeautiful, something to be feared. She looked from one to the other of the two men. Gerald's fist was clenched. For all his calm, there was a subtle threat in Christopher's attitude.

"I don't want to quarrel," Christopher went on. "Don't let it come to that, Gerald, but you see it is inevitable that Myrtile should leave with me to-night. I shall not go without her. You know what that means."

"I am to remember, I suppose," Gerald said thickly, "that you were the Varsity boxing champion?"

"Please don't," Christopher begged. "Myrtile must come. I can't always be in the way. To-night I am. To-night, at any rate, you have a reprieve. — Myrtile!"

She stooped for her cloak. Christopher arranged it around her shoulders. His fingers shivered at the touch of the filmy laciness, as though he loathed it.

"You are ready, Myrtile?" he asked.

She looked once more at Gerald. He seemed so far away. And was it her fancy, or was there something in his face which she had seen in the faces of those others? — He lit a cigarette almost ostentatiously.

"You had better go, Myrtile," he said. "Christopher has the whip hand of us. We can't have a row here."

"Good-by, Gerald," she faltered. "It isn't my fault."

"Of course not," Gerald answered. "We are all a little overstrung, I think. Good-by, little one!"

He kissed her almost carelessly and nodded to Christopher. The two left the room. The music had ceased.

They walked through the empty streets in silence. When they arrived within a few yards of Myrtile's lodgings, Christopher slackened his pace. Myrtile was crying quietly.

"Myrtile," he begged, "please listen to me."

"I am listening," she told him drearily.

"This morning at eight o'clock I shall be here to take you to the station. Please leave behind the clothes you are wearing, and I will return them to Madame Lénore. You will go to London, and Lady Mary will take care of you. Lady Mary is Gerald's sister. Do you understand?"

"Yes," she faltered.

"Please don't think of me as an executioner," Christopher went on, with a note of unusual feeling in his tone. "Love is a very wonderful thing, Myrtile, but it is also a very dangerous paradise. If you care for Gerald, and he cares for you, believe me, some day, you will belong to one another and you will be happy, but the love which brings happiness is not of a moment's growth. It is not a matter of feeling only. To-day you love Gerald with your whole soul. Gerald has simply a little affection for you. You are a whim to him, a child whose softness and prettiness attracts him. The kingdom of love is a wonderful place, but no two

people who are in the position of you and Gerald can
enter it by the lower gates. If you are faithful, remember this. A year or two of life will bring womanhood
to you, and you will understand just what was lacking
to-night, just what, in a corner of your heart, Myrtile,
I believe that you guessed was lacking. That something would have poisoned even your wonderful happiness. You must wait, dear. Nothing in the world will
keep you and Gerald apart if your love for one another
becomes the love that endures."

Myrtile crept away without a word. For an hour
Christopher waited, unseen, at the darkened corner of
the street. He waited until he saw the light go out in
Myrtile's room. Then he went back to the hotel,
changed his clothes and rested for a couple of hours.
When he returned to her room, she was waiting for him,
dressed in her little blue serge suit, pale, mutely pathetic. Christopher carried her small bag and they
made their way to the station.

" Myrtile," he said, as they stood together, watching
the train come round the bay, " this morning I think
that you are hating me. You think me very cruel. Try
and not judge me for a year."

" I think that you mean well," she sighed, " but you
do not understand."

Christopher put money into her purse and took her
up to where Lady Mary was standing with her little
array of dependents. She spoke a few kindly words to
Myrtile, who answered her politely but without any
trace of feeling in her tone. Myrtile sat down on one
of the trunks and looked steadily across at the sleeping
white-fronted hotel. Christopher and Lady Mary
walked for a moment apart.

" I don't know why I am doing this thing for you,"

Mary said. " If you want to know the truth, I dislike
the young woman intensely."

" If you can't feel that you are doing it for my sake,"
Christopher replied, " think that you are doing it for
Gerald's."

Lady Mary stared at him for a moment, and Christopher fancied that he could read in her somewhat
haughty look some trace of that patrician superstition
which claimed for its people the bodies and souls of
their satellites. — The train thundered in.

" You will come and see me in London? " she asked, a
little softened.

" Directly I return," he promised. " I shan't forget
this, Mary," he added, a little awkwardly. " You've
been a brick."

She smiled, curiously gratified at his hesitating
words. Christopher leaned towards Myrtile.

" Good-by, Myrtile," he said.

She removed her eyes from the window for a moment.

" Good-by, Christopher," she answered — and looked
back again at the white building, with its irregular front
and close-drawn curtains. Behind one of them Gerald
was sleeping. With a cloud of black smoke and a succession of hoarse, sobbing pants, the long train steamed
slowly out of the station.

BOOK TWO

BOOK TWO

CHAPTER I

GERALD had been lunching at the Hyde Park Hotel and was on his way to pay a call in Curzon Street. Hence his progress through the sun-baked and dusty park at three o'clock on a Saturday afternoon in August. Christopher, who had been his fellow guest, caught him up just as he had reached the shelter of the trees. The two young men were apparently still on the same friendly terms. No one but themselves realised the slight cloud which had never wholly passed away from between them since the night in Gerald's sitting room at the Hôtel de Paris, eighteen months ago.

" Couldn't get near you at lunch," Christopher remarked. " What a squash! "

" Hideous! " Gerald agreed.

" Every one all right at Hinterleys? " Christopher enquired.

" Haven't heard for over a week. Aren't they rather expecting you down there? "

" I'm going to-morrow. Can't take you, I suppose? " Gerald shook his head.

" I can't stand Hinterleys when there's nothing to do," he confided. " I shall be there on the 31st. all right."

" You're not going to stay in town till then? "

" I'm off to Bourne End this afternoon," was the unenthusiastic reply. " I shall probably stay there a day or two. I ought to have gone up to Scotland this week, but I have put it off until the end of September. The Governor forgives a good deal, but he wouldn't forgive me if I weren't at Hinterleys for the 1st."

Christopher took his friend's arm lightly. He had made several attempts to break through the slight restraint that existed between them, and Gerald's appearance these days rather troubled him. He was thinner, his eyes were restless, his manner a little nervous. He was still fit enough, for he had had a great season at polo, and had played cricket half a dozen times for his county with almost startling success. Yet he had not the appearance of being the spoilt child of fortune that he certainly was.

"I wonder you don't get fed up with that Bourne End crowd," Christopher remarked.

"I very nearly am," Gerald confessed. "They were much more amusing in the old days, before they took up marriage as a hobby. Now the most flagrant little hussy begins to talk about her people in the country and St. George's, Hanover Square, if you hold her fingers. It's all the fault of these callow youths — Christopher — Great Heavens!"

They had passed the Achilles Statue and were making towards Stanhope Gate. The crowd here seemed more spiritless than ever. There was a sprinkling of ladies' maids, sitting demurely alone, waiting patiently for the coming of romance; a few young men of doubtful types, a certain number of loafers pure and simple, and a few reasonable people, driven out by the craving for air which had some of the qualities of freshness. In chairs a little way back and apart from the others, two women, dressed in plain black, were seated. One was elderly, the other young. Both were weary, both sat there with the air of wishing to avoid observation. To Christopher they were entirely unfamiliar. His whole attention was absorbed by Gerald's strange demeanour. Gerald's long fingers had gripped his arm almost painfully. For the first time for many months, there was real feeling in his face.

"It's Pauline!" he exclaimed. "Wait for me, Chris."

Without hesitation, Gerald turned and threaded his way among the chairs. The two women watched his approach, the older one with stolid indifference, Pauline apparently with some faint resentment. Gerald, however, in these last few seconds had become a very determined person. He stood before them with his hat in his hand. His bow was lower than is customary amongst English people. His manner could scarcely have been more respectful if he had been paying his homage at Buckingham Palace.

"May I be permitted to recall myself to the recollection of Madame de Ponière?" he begged.

The woman looked at him with unrecognising eyes. The last eighteen months had dealt hardly with her. The flesh had sagged a little from her cheek bones, her mouth had become bitter, her throat was thin, her eyes cold and glassy.

"You do not succeed in doing so, monsieur," she said coldly.

Pauline intervened. There was some faint note of courtesy in her manner, nothing whatever of kindliness.

"This young gentleman," she explained to her aunt, — "Lord Dombey, I believe his name is — was kind enough to be of assistance to us at Monte Carlo, on the night when Zubin met with his unfortunate accident."

Madame de Ponière inclined her head.

" I trust that we tendered our thanks on that occasion," she observed icily.

Gerald held his ground. Pauline was paler than ever, and thin, but perhaps he fancied that there was a shade of encouragement in those soft, weary eyes.

" Madame," he said, " there was some slight previous acquaintance between your niece and myself, some trifling service I had been able to render which gave me the right to perform this further one. It gives me great pleasure to see you again in my own country."

The older woman laughed hardly.

" It is difficult to believe," she scoffed, " that the sight of us could give pleasure to any one; apart from which fact," she added rapidly, " it is not our wish to make or renew acquaintances whilst we are here."

" Madame," Gerald replied, " that was your attitude in Monte Carlo, an attitude which I may say occasioned me the deepest regret. I venture to hope that I may be able to induce you to modify it."

" And why should I? " she asked, almost insolently.

" Because I have the sincerest and most profound admiration for mademoiselle," Gerald declared stoutly, " and because, in my own country, there is the possibility that I may be of service to you."

Madame de Ponière opened a plain pair of lorgnettes and looked for a moment at Gerald.

" For an Englishman," she remarked coolly, " you seem to have some manners. Who is this, Pauline? "

There was the faintest possible indication of a smile on Pauline's lips.

" His name is Lord Dombey," she answered demurely. " He is the son of the Earl of Hinterleys."

" Dear me! " Madame de Ponière murmured.

"The Earl of Hinterleys," Pauline continued, "is one of the lesser English noblemen."

Notwithstanding his anxiety, Gerald's sense of humour was touched. If only his father could have been standing by his side to assist in the conversation with these two shabbily dressed ladies!

"Our titles are, at any rate, not unduly modern," he pleaded deprecatingly. "Besides, is this of any real consequence?"

"What precisely do you want of us?" the older lady asked, after a slight hesitation.

"The privilege of renewing my acquaintance with you both," Gerald replied.

"You have done so," Madame de Ponière reminded him.

"With permission to pay my respects at your London residence," he urged.

"We do not receive in London," was the curt reply.

"I trust," Gerald persisted, "that you will make an exception in my favour."

Pauline suddenly intervened. There was a shade of hauteur in her manner, but some frankness.

"My dear aunt," she said, "there are certain things which it is impossible to conceal. My aunt and I," she went on, addressing Gerald, "are living in some impossible rooms in an impossible hotel in South Kensington. I see no reason, however, why we should not receive you there, if you are in earnest in your desire to call. We are without acquaintances in this city."

Madame de Ponière closed her lorgnettes with a little snap.

"We are staying at Number 28, Erriston Gardens, South Kensington," she said. "I believe they call the place the Erriston Gardens Hotel."

"If you will permit me," Gerald suggested, "I will bring my sister to call upon you when she is in town. In the meantime, may I venture upon a daring suggestion? You are without acquaintances in town; so, for these few days, am I. Will you do me the great honour of dining at Ranelagh to-night with me? We shall escape this insufferable heat and be able to listen to music out of doors."

"I regret that it is impossible, sir," Madame de Ponière replied.

Gerald was naturally quick-witted. There were many little things he had already noted.

"Mademoiselle," he said, turning to Pauline, "I beg you to intercede with your aunt. I do not invite you to one of the established restaurants. The great charm of Ranelagh is its informality. The people who have been playing tennis and golf stay on to dine, with some trifling change in their attire. I myself should have to ask you to excuse my remaining in morning dress. It is a convention of the place."

"Milord Dombey doubts our wardrobe," Pauline remarked, with a faint smile. "No," she went on hastily, "please do not think we are offended. I think your discretion is admirable. And, aunt, I beg of you, let us accept Lord Dombey's invitation. Think how much we are suffering from the heat. Think of our stuffy room, our unspeakable dinner! In short, I insist."

"If you will allow me, I will call for you at a quarter to eight," Gerald proposed, turning to Madame de Ponière.

Madame de Ponière hesitated for another moment. Perhaps it was something in the almost boyish quality of Gerald's eagerness which decided her. This Englishman was at any rate no *boulevardier*.

"We will await you at that hour," she replied. "I trust," she added, after a moment's pause, "that you will not consider my hesitation in any way discourteous. There are reasons which make it difficult for my niece and myself to accept hospitality."

Gerald bowed low, and, acting on a momentary impulse, raised Madame's fingers to his lips. She yielded them naturally enough, but with a little glance around, almost of fear. Mademoiselle also extended her finger tips. He took his leave and was received by Christopher, who was waiting for him, with a gaze almost of astonishment. Gerald was holding himself differently, his eyes were filled with a lustre which they had lacked for months, he was smiling again in his old manner.

"My dear fellow," Christopher exclaimed, "what on earth has happened?"

"That old devil has recognised my existence at last," Gerald declared. "I had almost to force myself upon her. Chris, they're dining with me to-night!"

"Before you say another word," Christopher enjoined, "I want you to look at the man on that seat by the side of the tree. Look at him carefully, please."

The two young men slackened their pace. The person whom Christopher had indicated was a man of medium height, dressed, notwithstanding the heat of the day, in sombre black clothes, and wearing a black bowler hat. He was dark, and he was, or affected to be, reading a book. His complexion was sallow and he wore a slight black moustache. His hair was unusually long and even covered a portion of his ears.

"Well, I see him," Gerald admitted. "Not much to look at. Looks like one of the chaps who go in for this tub-thumping up at the far end."

"He came from that way," Christopher said, "but

the reason I am pointing him out to you is because he
appeared to recognise your two friends at the same instant that you did. He was walking down between that
last row of chairs. Directly he saw them, however, he
stood quite still for a moment. He seemed almost as
knocked over as you were. Then he slunk back into
that chair and he has been watching them ever since."

Gerald attached no undue importance to the affair.

"I'll tell them about it this evening, if I can remember," he promised. — "Chris, did you ever know such
luck! She is more wonderful than ever. No wonder I
could never get the feeling of her out of my blood, the
thought of her from my brain! Her eyes — Chris, did
you ever see such eyes in your life!"

"Kind of hazel, aren't they?" Christopher hazarded.

"You   ass!"   Gerald   declared   contemptuously.
"They're brown — the most glorious shade of brown I
ever saw. I'm going to call for them in South Kensington at a quarter to eight, Chris. We're going to dine
at Ranelagh."

"So you told me," Christopher observed, smiling.
"What about Bourne End?"

Gerald's radiant happiness was not for a moment
disturbed. He took Christopher's arm.

"Bourne End," he confided, "has, allegorically
speaking, vanished into the blue horizon. Chris, I know
now what has been the matter with me all these months.
I knew it directly I saw her sitting there, tired and miserable, under the trees. I came up against the real
thing and never knew it. I am in love with Pauline!"

CHAPTER II

PAULINE leaned back in her chair with a little murmur of content. Through the drooping branches of the great plane tree was a fascinating little vista of scarlet-clad orchestra, of the terrace with its curving rows of lights, the little groups of people sitting about, the waiters in their quaint liveries. And beyond, the smooth lawn, the picturesque front of the house; up above, the deep blue sky, pierced here and there with an early star. Even the little murmur of conversation seemed to blend with the strains of the music. A breeze rippled in the tree tops. After the heat of London, it was a wonderful respite.

" You are very kind," she murmured to Gerald, " to bring us here."

" I was very fortunate to meet you," he declared. " Don't you think, after all the discouragement I have received, I was very brave to come and beard your aunt? "

" Not so very," she answered. " We were two defenceless women, very sad and weary with life."

" I wish," Gerald said deliberately, " that you would tell me more about yourselves."

Pauline glanced across at her aunt, who was leaning back in her chair, also with the appearance of deep content, her eyes closed, her air of isolation complete.

" My aunt does not approve of such questions," she said quietly.

" We speak in English," Gerald reminded her, " and your aunt does not understand."

" My aunt understands English better than you would believe," Pauline replied. " There is the fact, also, that I have confidence in her. I believe that she knows what is best."

" The best thing for you," Gerald said firmly, " is to believe in me."

She looked at him with a slight smile. Her face, however, remained unsoftened.

" Really? And why should I believe in you? And what is there to believe? "

" That I am deeply interested," Gerald replied promptly, " in everything that concerns you; that I wish to be your friend; that I wish ——"

She stopped him with a little gesture instinctively mandatory.

" Neither my aunt nor I," she interrupted, " are in a position to accept more than the simplest acts of good will from any one. I have tried to make that clear to you."

" You have," Gerald admitted, " but before I accept your decision finally, I shall expect some further explanation."

" We do not belong to your world," Pauline said. " We are what you call, I think, adventuresses."

" Of a unique type, then," Gerald declared, smiling. " It is not the usual action of such people, having met with a great loss, as you did at Monte Carlo, to sell their jewellery to pay their bills, and leave without owing a penny."

" You are well informed," Pauline remarked coldly.

" I saw your pearl necklace in Desfordes', the jeweller's."

"I cannot believe that Desfordes ——" Pauline began, in some agitation.

"The man told me nothing," Gerald interrupted. "I recognised the necklace and I bought it."

"You bought my necklace?" she repeated incredulously.

"Hoping," Gerald ventured, "that some day it would be my privilege to return it to you."

She was distinctly taken aback.

"You are apparently a rich young man, Lord Dombey, as well as an impertinent one," she said. "Are you often subject to these whims?"

"I am well off," Gerald replied, "that is to say that I have an income apart from my allowance. For the rest, I have never done anything of the sort before, because I have never felt the same inclination."

"I thought that you were rather by way of being the support of the ladies of the ballet at Monte Carlo," she observed. "Did you not entertain them at supper and that sort of thing?"

"I entertained them at supper occasionally," Gerald admitted, "but that is the extent of my acquaintance with them."

"Then there was a child whom you and your friend found at a mountain farm — she became your ward, did she not? — a pretty child, with large, affectionate eyes?"

"My family has relieved me of my responsibility in that direction," Gerald replied. "She is living down at Hinterleys with my people. My father will allow no one else to read to him, my sister is devoted to her, and my friend is in love with her."

"I still do not understand what made you buy my pearls," Pauline remarked, after a moment's thoughtful silence, " or under what possible conditions you contemplated returning them to me."

" I bought them because I am in love with you," Gerald declared.

She turned her head and studied him deliberately. She was still lounging in her chair, but she gave him the impression that she was looking down at him.

" That," she said quietly, " is a style of conversation which you must keep for your dancing ladies or your village maidens."

" It happens to be the truth," he insisted doggedly.

Once more she looked at him, still puzzled, but this time a little more leniently. His dark eyes were aglow. He was obviously in earnest.

" You must forgive me if I find your methods a little unusual," she said. " Do I understand that you are proposing an alliance? "

" I ask you to do me the honour of becoming my wife," Gerald replied.

Pauline turned to her aunt.

"Aunt," she said in French, " Lord Dombey desires to marry me. He has just told me so most eloquently."

Madame de Ponière's expression was, for her, almost tolerant.

" Never mind, my dear," she rejoined, " he is a very amiable young man and he has given us an excellent dinner."

Pauline turned back to Gerald, smiling.

" You see, my aunt is quite reasonable about the matter," she remarked. " Order some more cigarettes, will you? And some coffee, I think."

Gerald obeyed promptly. Then he leaned forward.

" Madame de Ponière," he said, " do I understand

that I have your permission to pay my addresses to your niece? "

" You must not be foolish," she replied soothingly. " We are exceedingly obliged to you for giving us dinner in this charming place. It is really quite a revelation to me. The *suprême de volaille* reminded me — but that is not of any import."

" Mademoiselle de Ponière," Gerald continued, appealing to Pauline, " will you be my wife? "

" Monsieur Lord Dombey," was the prompt but not unkindly reply, " I will not."

" Then may I become your suitor," he pleaded, " hoping that you will change your mind when you find that I am very much in earnest? "

" It appears to me," she answered, " that the office would be a thankless one."

" I am content to take my chance," Gerald pronounced. " I can command all the usual resources which might make life more endurable for you. My personal devotion you are already assured of."

" You had better not tempt us too far," Pauline warned him, a little bitterly. " The good folk at Monte Carlo were only guessing when they called us adventuresses, but we are down on our luck just now — we might accept your offer."

" I will take my risk," Gerald declared eagerly. " You have given me no encouragement. You have no responsibility. As for the rest, we are all adventurers or adventuresses, more or less. I am in quest of happiness, and I have met no one else except you who could give it to me."

There was a touch of real feeling in her eyes as she glanced towards him, feeling, however, composed of varying elements, — some curiosity, a tinge of scorn, an iota of compassion. She shrugged her shoulders slightly beneath her wrap of black lace.

"How long do you remain in London, Lord Dombey?" she enquired.

"As long as I can be of service to you," was the quick reply. "I was going down to Hinterleys soon, for want of something better to do. A day's visit there will suffice. I shall remain at your service."

"I am in love with another man," Pauline assured him.

Gerald considered the matter for a moment.

"I do not believe it," he declared.

Pauline sighed.

"Nevertheless, it is true," she reiterated. "He is very bad-tempered, and if he knows that I am accepting all these attentions from another man, he will certainly quarrel with you."

"I will risk it," Gerald decided.

"How am I to get rid of this persistent young man?" Pauline asked her aunt.

Madame de Ponière had a great deal to say about the subject in a rapid undertone. When she had finished, Pauline turned back to her companion.

"My aunt was very much against a renewal of our acquaintance," she told him, "but, as she justly remarks, one must live. This evening has turned our heads a little — a return to the fleshpots, you know, and that sort of thing. You shall be my suitor if you will, Lord Dombey, but of one thing you may be very sure — I shall never marry you."

"There is another thing of which you may be equally sure," Gerald rejoined. "I shall never leave off trying to persuade you to."

"Gallant but pig-headed," Pauline murmured.

"You can judge of my aunt's newly found tolerance when I tell you that she permits us to walk in the rose garden. I want to see whether those delphiniums are really as blue as they seem to be."

Gerald sprang eagerly to his feet and they moved off together across the lawn. He was obliged continually to half pause, to return the greetings of his many friends. Pauline walked steadily on, looking neither to the right nor to the left, composed and stately, her clothes, although they were not in the very latest style, individual and obviously the creation of an artist. People put their heads together and whispered. The same question must have been asked a score of times before they left the little crowd behind them, but no one knew, no one could even hazard a surmise as to whom Gerald's companion might be.

The walk in the rose gardens, although Gerald welcomed with intense satisfaction this new phase in his relations with Pauline, was in some ways a disappointment. Pauline looked around her all the time with serene pleasure. She was fond of flowers, she knew them all by name, and paused often to admire some wonderfully fine bloom. She acceded without demur to his suggestion that they should take one of the small boats moored against the bridge and lay back amongst the cushions whilst he lazily sculled round the small stretch of water. On the far side of the island he let the boat drift and laid the oar across his knees.

"Pauline," he said, leaning a little forward, "you are adorable."

"I suppose it goes without saying that you should find me so," she answered composedly. "I suppose, also, that I must permit you the privilege of my Christian name. On the other hand, do not try to get on too quickly, will you? I must warn you that you have reached the extreme limit of my complaisance."

His eyes flashed for a moment. He was much too spoilt to regard her indifference as anything more than part of the game. It was a duel between the two, the result of which he scarcely doubted, but with his usual impetuosity he resented delay.

"You will accept me some day," he said. "Why not now? We could spend the honeymoon in Paris and go on to the Italian lakes. Or we could be married at the Embassy in Paris, if you liked. Enthoven, the first secretary, is my cousin, and would see things through for us."

"You are taking base advantage of this lonely spot," she murmured, dipping her hand in the water. "I have told you that I am in love with another man."

"You will forget him in a week," Gerald assured her. "I am a most companionable person."

"I have no doubt that you have given many people the opportunity of finding you so," she replied drily. "However, I am not prepared just yet for such an experiment."

"Pauline, do you like me a little?" he asked earnestly.

She looked him in the eyes.

"Not very much," she admitted frankly. "You see, the nicer part of me — the part with which I should care — is numb — numbed with misfortune. The most that I can say is that if you are very kind, I may change — to some extent. Personally, I think it hopeless."

"You wouldn't consider, I suppose," he suggested, "telling me your history now that we are on a slightly different footing?"

" Nothing would induce me to do anything of the sort," she replied. " I think that we have left my aunt alone quite long enough."

He took up the scull and dug it into the still, stagnant water. He did not speak again until they reached the landing stage.

" Where is this other man? " he asked, as he handed her out.

She thought for several moments before she answered. Then she turned towards him with the air of one who has arrived at a decision.

" The other man," she declared, " is my brother. He is in prison, condemned to what you call, I believe, penal servitude."

CHAPTER III

Lord Hinterleys leaned back in his chair and prepared to enjoy his greatest treat during the day, — his one glass of vintage port.

" So you did not go to Scotland after all, Gerald? " he remarked, on the evening of the latter's arrival at Hinterleys.

" No, I didn't go, sir," Gerald replied. " Some old friends of mine turned up in town. I have been spending a good deal of time with them."

" I would have preferred hearing that you had been on the moors," his father observed, with a glance at his son's pallid face and careworn expression. " London in August always seems to me intolerable."

" It was certainly very hot," Gerald admitted. " I was on the river a great deal of the time, though."

There was a short silence. Lord Hinterleys was, as a rule, a reserved man, and he very much disliked the task which he had set himself. He dallied with it for a few moments, looking through the high window, across the terrace to the gardens below. His face softened as he glanced at the two girlish figures seated under the cedar tree, where coffee was being served.

" You have been guilty, I suppose, Gerald," he said drily, " of the usual number of indiscretions, but one action of yours which threatened to come under that heading, I shall always remember with gratitude. Myrtile is the most wonderful child who ever came to brighten a somewhat dull household."

"I am glad you approve of her, sir," Gerald replied indifferently.

"The more I study her," Lord Hinterleys went on earnestly, "the more she fills me with amazement. It seems as though she must be some sort of a spiritual changeling. I have always been, as you know, rather a stickler for race. Myrtile is one of those marvellous exceptions which upset all argument. She is an aristocrat to the finger tips in every way, small or great, that counts. It seems as though it were absolutely impossible for her to do an ungracious or ungraceful thing. She has destroyed every prejudice I ever possessed."

Gerald was interested at last. It was many years since he had known his father so enthusiastic.

"I am very glad you kept her here, sir," he remarked.

"I am more than glad — I am thankful," was the fervent reply. "I look forward with a pleasure which I can scarcely describe to the hours she gives up for my entertainment. When I think that nothing but an outbreak of scarlet fever in the household to which she was bound was responsible for her staying here long enough for us to appreciate her, I can never feel sufficiently thankful. To watch her development, too, during the last year, has been like watching a beautiful flower."

"She's made a conquest of you, at any rate, dad," Gerald remarked. "I thought myself that she looked perfectly sweet to-night at dinner time."

"She has made a conquest of me to an extent which I should never have believed possible," Lord Hinterleys admitted, glancing across at his son. "I have had an elderly man's desire, Gerald, to welcome home to Hinterleys the woman whom you might decide to choose for a wife. I have kept a little list in my mind of the young women at present known to Society, whom it would give me pleasure to see here. I have never for one second contemplated the addition to that list of an unknown person. And yet ——"

"There is no question of anything of that sort between Myrtile and me, sir," Gerald declared, breaking a somewhat embarrassed pause.

Lord Hinterleys sipped his port and looked once more out of the window. Gerald, a little startled by his father's unexpected suggestion, was suddenly conscious of that one wild moment after his supper party at the Hôtel de Paris, of Christopher's stern figure, of that strange medley of sensations, the flare of passion which seemed to have perished in the shame of Christopher's triumph. He, too, looked out of the window. Myrtile had been a child then. She was a woman now, more wonderful, more gracious, just as completely virginal. Yet to him she existed at that moment only as the picture of something that had passed.

"I am afraid," his father said, a little sadly, "that Myrtile does not look at it in quite the same way. However, that is nothing. It may be only a sort of hero-worship with her. It was you, I understand, who took the initiative in bringing her away from her home. Her indifference to your sex is a little abnormal for her years. Doubtless it will pass when the right man arrives. I envy that man more than any other living."

Lord Hinterleys slowly finished his wine. Gerald produced his cigarette case.

"You are ready, sir?" he asked. "Will you take my arm?"

"Not for a moment," was the quiet reply. "You perceive, from my references to Myrtile, that I am in a confidential frame of mind. I shall go even further to prove it."

"You won't mind my cigarette, sir?"

"Not in the least. — Gerald, I do not, as a rule, interfere in such matters, as you know, but I take a certain natural interest, I think, in your associates and your affairs generally. It has come to my knowledge through various channels that you have spent the greater part of the last month with two ladies bearing a French name — an aunt and a niece, I believe — both unknown to English Society."

"That is true, sir," Gerald admitted.

"Furthermore," Lord Hinterleys continued, "although again I am a little outside my province, I must confess that I was somewhat disturbed to hear from Mr. Bendover that you had offered for sale a portion of the Lutsall property and were considering a mortgage upon Rhysalls."

"I do not know why Mr. Bendover should have troubled you with these details," Gerald said, a little uneasily, "but in the main they are correct."

"I make you an allowance, as you know," his father continued, "as my only son and the heir to Hinterleys, of five thousand a year, which I can well afford to do. You have yourself something like the same amount, I believe. You occupy a portion of Hinterleys House in town, and you have the use of my servants there. Your polo ponies, by express arrangement, have always been charged to my own stable expenses. You must forgive my feeling some surprise, therefore, at the fact that you have found it necessary to raise these large sums of money."

Gerald was silent for a moment, conscious of and inwardly resenting his father's anxious scrutiny. Something of the bitterness which he was feeling showed itself, perhaps, in his tone.

"I needed the money, dad," he said. "It will probably all come back to me, or its value."

"If the necessity is occasioned by your losses at cards or on the turf," Lord Hinterleys continued, "I should prefer making you some advance myself, to having you part with land which belonged to your great-grandmother, or executing a mortgage upon any part of your property."

"I have needed the money for quite a different purpose," Gerald explained, "a purpose which precluded my applying to you. There are other people involved."

"I see," Lord Hinterleys concluded drily. "We will leave the matter where it is, then, for the present. — If you will give me your arm now, we will take our coffee in the gardens."

"Sorry, dad, to seem mysterious and uncommunicative, and that sort of thing," Gerald apologised, with an attempt at levity. "I'm not quite off my head, I can assure you."

"You have never presented yourself to my mind, Gerald," his father admitted, "as being a likely tool for the adventurers or harpies of the world. I shall continue to believe that you are able to take care of yourself, although I am bound to say that I regret your lack of confidence."

"I shall be in a position to tell you the whole story very shortly," Gerald promised. "The element of secrecy about it at present has nothing to do with me."

They made their way through the window, on to the terrace, down the steps and across the lawn to the cedar tree. Myrtile was standing behind the coffee tray, and Gerald, remembering his father's recent words, gazed at her with a new, though somewhat languid interest. She was wearing a simple frock of grey muslin, her hair was parted in the middle and drooped low over her ears. The thinness of a year ago had given place to the slender perfection of early womanhood. She had the air of being wholly and gracefully at her ease, yet the sweetness of her smile, a certain ever-present but unobtrusive desire to please, seemed like the hallmarks of her constant but unexpressed gratitude. Lady Mary, sunburnt and amiable, lolled in a hammock, with a cigarette between her teeth. There was a telegram upon her knee. She seemed content with life.

" Have you heard the news? " she asked. " Christopher has been invited to stand for West Leeds. It is a certain seat and he has accepted. He is coming down to-morrow afternoon."

" Good old Chris! " Gerald murmured. " Though what on earth he wants to spend half his time pottering about the House of Commons for, I can't imagine."

" Your friend Christopher Bent," Lord Hinterleys observed, " finds his pleasures, without a doubt, somewhat interfered with by the possession of some out-of-date principles. He will be very welcome here. — My coffee and the evening paper, if you please, Myrtile."

Myrtile's attention had momentarily wandered. Her eyes were fixed upon Gerald, who was looking paler and more tired than ever in the clear evening twilight.

" You found it hot in the city? " she asked softly, as she poured out the coffee.

He frowned impatiently. There is nothing which irritates a selfish man more than the evidences of an affection which he does not covet.

" If it was, I don't deserve any sympathy," he replied. " I was only there because it amused me."

He threw himself into a chair, declined coffee with unnecessary abruptness, and asked for brandy. Myrtile, with a little pain at her heart, no infrequent visitor there, took her place apart from the others, near Lord Hinterleys, and, spreading out the newspaper, commenced her evening task.

CHAPTER IV

THE world seemed a very good place to Lady Mary as, from the depths of her chair under the cedar tree on the following afternoon, she watched Christopher, conducted as far as the terrace by the butler, descend the steps lightly and move across the lawn towards her. He had been away for a holiday earlier in the summer and was still healthily tanned. His grey tweeds became him. He walked with the dignity and assurance of a man whose life is being worthily lived. It was a long way across the lawn, and the girl who waited for his coming had time for a crowd of pleasant thoughts as she watched the approach of the man on whom she had set her heart. Everything that he did and had done in life appealed to her. She even appreciated now the reticence which he had shown in their many conversations, the absence of any indications of more than ordinary interest in her. He had sentiment enough, — that was proved by the tenderness for Myrtile to which he had confessed that night at Monte Carlo, a night which she had always remembered as one of the unhappiest of her life. She had long since been convinced, both by his manner and Myrtile's, that the tenderness, such as it had been, had become merged in a purely fraternal and kindly regard. Of his reticence towards herself she thought nothing. He was possessed, as she well knew, of a very high sense of honour, and she had always felt that, however greatly she might have desired to hear his declaration, he would say nothing until he had passed definitely out of the somewhat miscellaneous category of rising young men into the position of one whose future is assured. To-day he was the youngest K. C., and a seat in Parliament was almost within his reach. She thought of her own fortune with a deep sense of pleasure. It was larger than he imagined, larger than any one else except herself and her father knew. Christopher would be free to make the best of himself, free for all time from any shadow of financial worry. How well he looked, how strong and eager! She held out both her hands as he drew near, and her smile of welcome made her for a moment radiantly beautiful.

"How delightful to see you, Christopher!" she exclaimed. "And what wonderful news! It's just what you wanted, isn't it, and just what we all wanted for you."

He took her hands and stood smiling down at her. Her heart was beginning to beat more quickly. She hoped that he would suggest walking in the gardens.

"It is a wonderful stroke of fortune, isn't it?" he agreed. "It all came about through going down to help Andrew Hodgson at the Darlington election. I knew I'd got on pretty well with the speech-making down there, but I never thought it would lead to this."

He did not sit down, nor did he suggest the gardens. He had looked around for a moment, almost as though disappointed to find her alone. Still her heart did not misgive her. She thought him a little nervous, and she smiled tolerantly.

"You were a dear to telegraph to me at once," she said. "I can't tell you how interested and flattered I was."

" I wanted you all to know," he declared, looking around once more. " How is every one? "

" In excellent health, thank you," she answered. " Father is having his usual afternoon sleep. Gerald has been here, but, as I dare say you know, he went away this morning. We must talk about him later, Christopher. I am rather worried — but that can wait. Will you sit down, or would you like to see how wonderful the gardens are? "

He looked at her a little apologetically, yet without the slightest idea of how great an apology was needed.

" I wondered," he said, " if I could see Myrtile."

" Myrtile? " Mary repeated.

He assented a little sheepishly, yet with a rather engaging smile.

" I wanted to see her and tell her about it," he confided. " She won't understand just what it means, perhaps, but she's so much more of a woman now."

His voice seemed to come from a long way off. It seemed all part of a horrible nightmare, something unreal, some black thought, the figment of a nocturnal fancy. — Then she was conscious of his standing before her, waiting, expectant, with the eagerness of a lover in his eyes.

" Myrtile went down to gather some roses," she told him. " You will find her at the end of the pergola."

He was gone almost before the words had left her lips, gone with some sort of mumbled excuse, unconscious of the tragedy he had created, clumsily oblivious of the fierce struggle which had kept her calm and collected. She turned her head and watched him go, watched his long, eager footsteps, saw his tall figure stoop as he entered the pergola. Her fingers tore at the sides of her chair. She looked at the distance between her and the terrace steps. If only she could escape! Her limbs for the time seemed powerless. She sat there with all the healthy colour drained from her cheeks, her fixed eyes seeing nothing but the ruin of her confident hopes. There were three old ladies in the family of Hinterleys — one her father's sister, the others a little more distantly related — prim beings, full of the weaknesses and prejudices evolved by their unlived lives. She remembered now how she had shrunk, even in her school days, from the thought of ever finding herself in a similar situation. But she was suddenly face to face with it now. She could see herself growing old, marching down the avenues of time, preserving in a certain measure, perhaps, her dignity, but growing day by day a little more jealous and narrow, a little more captious of the happiness of others. There was only one Christopher, and he was there at the bottom of the pergola with Myrtile. Even in her bitterness she did not blame him for a moment. There were a hundred different ways in which she might have misunderstood him. She had made the foolish mistake of many ignorant young women. She had mistaken companionship, and the desire for companionship, on his part, for the subtler and rarer gift which she herself had been so ready to offer. Christopher, she remembered, had even warned her, more than a year ago, at the villa in Monte Carlo that night when they had paced the terrace together. She had refused to take him seriously, and he had never once reverted to the subject. It had seemed to her, indeed, that he had almost avoided Myrtile during his visits to Hinterleys, and she had commended him for his discretion. Myrtile was sweet and full of charm, but what use could she be as a wife to an ambitious man like Christopher? How

she herself could have helped with her sympathy, her
social influence, her tact, to say nothing of her great
fortune! It was amazing what follies a man could com-
mit for the sake of a fancy! She could call it nothing
else.

Presently she rose calmly to her feet and walked towards the house. Soon it swallowed her up, the key
was turned in the door of her room, the long minutes
that passed were her own. She never counted them
then, she never dwelt on them afterwards. The period
of her agony was, in fact, short enough. Her pride
came to her rescue. When her maid tapped on the
door she had already bathed her eyes, and there remained nothing to denote her suffering but a little tired
look about her mouth and a slight weariness of gait.
She opened the door at once.

"Mr. Bent is obliged to go back to town almost immediately, your ladyship," the maid announced. "He
has asked specially whether he could see you for a moment."

"Tell Mr. Bent that I shall be down in five minutes,"
her mistress enjoined.

The maid departed, and Mary turned once more
anxiously to the mirror. This was a trial which she
had scarcely expected. Her fingers passed over her
face, anxious to smooth out its lines. Her lips moved,
as though she were uttering a prayer. She was, indeed, appealing to herself, to the strength and pride
of her young womanhood. When she entered the library
where Christopher was waiting for her, she knew that
she was free from all trace of disturbance.

"Christopher, you don't mean that you are going to
leave us at once?" she protested. "And where is
Myrtile? I expected to see you both together."

" I left Myrtile where I found her," Christopher answered, a little harshly. " Will you keep my secret, please, Mary, and forget my visit? "

" Forget your visit? " she repeated wonderingly.

" Myrtile does not care for me," Christopher explained, " not in the way I want her to. It is the same with her now as from that first moment. I thought it was a fancy of which she might have been cured. I find it is nothing of the sort."

At that moment Mary hated herself, hated the joy which swelled up in her heart, hated the sudden passionate rush of blood through all her veins, the sense of grotesque, immeasurable relief. She hated the lying words she spoke.

" Oh, Christopher, I am so sorry!" she said. " I do not understand, but I am very, very sorry."

" Myrtile loves Gerald," he continued. " She will love him all her days. She is one of those strange creatures who will never change, to whom love is just one final thing for good or for evil. She loved Gerald when she stepped into the car and we carried her with us along the road around the end of which she had woven all her dreams. She cares for him so much that I am not sure whether, at the bottom of her pure heart, she does not hate me because I once kept them apart."

She laid her hand upon his arm. That sense of sickening joy had gone. She was a woman again, feeling nothing but sorrow for the suffering of her man.

" Christopher dear," she begged, " Myrtile will see the truth in time. Gerald cares nothing for her, nothing for anybody except himself and his own pleasures. She will understand this presently. Remember, although she has grown so sensible and so gracious in her attitude towards life, she is really only a child."

" In one way she will always be a child," he answered
sadly. " Her love will last her time, whether Gerald
ever returns it or not."

" There is still your work," she went on, " great, wonderful work waiting for you. And your friends. Don't
take this so hardly, Christopher."

He looked down at her with a very forced smile.

" Oh, I shall get over it," he assured her. " I am
not the first man who has had to face this sort of thing.
It is odd, though, that it should have happened to me.
Whatever thoughts I may have had in the past about
marriage were so different."

" Isn't it just possible, perhaps," she ventured, " that
those other thoughts were the wisest? "

" Wisdom has so little to do with life, really," he
answered drearily. " I should have planned it differ-
ently if I could. — Well, I had to see you, Mary.
You've been perfectly sweet, as I knew you would be.
I want to get off without seeing a soul now, if I can.
You won't mind? "

" Of course not! You wouldn't like me to speak to
Myrtile? "

" Absolutely useless," he replied. " She was really
shocked when she knew why I had come. I believe it
seems to her a trifle irreligious to discuss the possibility
of her caring for any one except Gerald. No, I'm not
going to encourage any false hopes, Mary. I've had my
answer and there's an end of it. What I want to do is
to get away."

" That you can do and shall," she assented. " I did
so want to hear about Leeds, but that must be another
time. You won't keep away from us because of this,
Christopher? "

" Of course not," he promised half-heartedly. " I'll

write, if I may. There are heaps of things I want to tell you. You won't mind?"

She smiled and let him open the door, taking him by a devious way to the courtyard where his car was still standing.

"There," she directed, "you can go out by the south drive, across the deer park, and you won't meet a soul."

He held her hand tightly for a moment at parting.

"God bless you, Mary!" he said. "You're a wonderful pal."

"Thank you," she answered simply.

CHAPTER V

" WELL, thank heavens you haven't forgotten how to hold your gun straight!" Lord Hinterleys remarked, a few days later, laying his hand affectionately upon his son's shoulder. " It is always a treat to see you shoot, Gerald. I used to fancy myself when I was your age, but I could never have touched your performance to-day."

" You mustn't forget the difference in the guns, dad," Gerald reminded him, " and the powder. You were pretty useful yourself at those last two drives."

Lord Hinterleys mounted his pony.

" I brought down a beautiful high one at Smith's corner," he admitted. — " Are you sure, you people, that you wouldn't like to have a car sent down? I shall be home in ten minutes or a quarter of an hour, and Oliver could be here with the shooting brake whilst you are having a cup of tea with Mrs. Amos."

No one, it appeared, was tired. Gerald shouldered his gun and passed his arm through Myrtile's.

" Come along," he invited, " we'll go home through the forty-acre wood. It isn't more than a mile. It seems to me we've been standing about all day."

" I should like it very much," Myrtile assented joyfully.

" We are all coming presently," Mary remarked. " Amos is just making up the bag. Dad wants the exact figures. Don't you want some tea, Myrtile? Lady Hadley and I are going to have some."

Myrtile shook her head.

"I do not care for tea very much, as you know," she said, " and I should like to walk with Gerald."

" Showing thereby your good taste, my child," Gerald observed, as they strolled off, " and also a wise regard for your digestion."

" One sees so little of you nowadays," Myrtile sighed. "You are all the time in London."

" You're not going to lecture me?"

" That would not be for me," she said gravely. " If you think it well to be there, it is well. I am only glad that you are here to-day. It has made your father so happy."

They crossed the meadow and entered the little wood. The path here was so narrow that Gerald took Myrtile's arm again. He was quite unconscious that at his touch she shivered with emotion.

" Myrtile," he confided, " I saw Chris yesterday."

" Yes?"

" Poor old chap," Gerald went on, " he looked absolutely done in. I made him come and have some dinner with me. I don't think he meant to tell me, but it all came out in time. He told me about his visit here."

She walked on, her head uplifted, her face a little tense.

" Yes?" she murmured.

" I'd no idea," Gerald continued, " that he was seriously in love with you, Myrtile. He's such a sober sort of chap really — no lady friends, you know, or anything of that sort. When he takes a fancy to any one, it's a serious affair."

" He is not like you, Gerald," she said quietly.

" You're quite right, he isn't," Gerald acknowledged frankly. " We all have our different hobbies. I candidly admit that the society of your sex has been one of mine. Christopher has never been like that, though. You are his first love, Myrtile."

" It is a great pity," she declared.

" You used to seem very fond of him," Gerald hazarded, " and he certainly looked after you jolly well at Monte Carlo."

" Do you mean," Myrtile asked calmly, " when he came to your room in the Hôtel de Paris, after the supper party? "

Gerald was completely taken aback. She had turned and was looking at him with her large, serious eyes. She was deliberately forcing upon him the memory of an episode which he had slurred over in his mind.

" I wasn't thinking of that altogether," he replied, with a certain rare awkwardness. "All the same ———"

" All the same, what, please? " she insisted, after a moment's pause. " I should like you to finish your sentence."

" Well, from old Chris's point of view, he was doing the chivalrous thing, and all that," Gerald explained clumsily. " He must have thought, of course, that I was going to be a perfect brute."

" Were you not? " she asked.

He was amazed at her coolness. She, whose purity seemed rather to increase with her larger knowledge of the world, seemed to be forcing him to speak of those very ugly moments.

" I am afraid that I can't say what would have happened," he admitted. " I was very much attracted by you, and you hadn't the faintest idea what it all meant. So, you see, you do owe him a very great debt of gratitude, Myrtile."

" I do not think so," she replied.

Gerald was more startled than ever. Her deliberate speech seemed to him almost a challenge.

"You are about the only person in the world who would say that," he observed.

"Perhaps so," she admitted. "Perhaps, too, I am the only one who is in a position to know."

Gerald was poignantly interested. He looked down at her face, calm and serious. There was no added colour in her cheeks, no sign of any confusion.

"You mean that you are sorry that Christopher interfered? That you would have risked my forgetting — all that I ought to have remembered?"

"I am sorry that Christopher interfered," she said distinctly. "At that moment I loved you, and I did not know that it was wicked for me to love you. If afterwards you had got tired of me, as you would have done, then I should have killed myself when I understood. But I should have been happy first."

"But aren't you happy now?" he asked.

"I am very contented," she answered, "and I am very, very grateful. I think that no one in the world has ever received such wonderful kindness as I have. But happiness, it seems to me, is a thing apart. It is a great and a wonderful and a rare gift. I do not think that very many people possess it, although they think they do. I should have possessed it, for however short a time, if Christopher had not interfered."

Gerald was staggered. It seemed to him that this girl, walking so sedately by his side, had suddenly become his monitress; was trying to explain to him, as though he were a pupil, great and elemental things.

"Myrtile," he declared, "you surprise me very much. I never dreamed that you would feel like that. Supposing, then, I were to say to you — 'Come away from here with me to-morrow; come up to London and be my companion there'?"

"You could not do that," she said simply. "You could not offer me so terrible and so ugly an insult. Surely you understand that then I did not know that you did not love me?"

"I see," he murmured.

"I loved you," she went on, her eyes lifted a little to the interlacing boughs of the trees under which they were passing, "when you came like a prince to the gate where I stood shaking with terror, and laughed at my fears. I loved you when you pointed to the end of the road and promised to take me there. I loved you in those first few moments, and just as it seemed to me then that I had loved you before I was born, so I know that I shall love you after I die. That is just the kind of wisdom which even children have. Where I was simple and ignorant was that I did not understand that love could be one-sided. I thought that love belonged to two people. Now I know very differently."

"Myrtile ——" he began.

She checked him gravely.

"To-day," she continued, "there is more for me to say than for you, because I am rather glad that you should understand. Only you must not talk to me about Christopher. I am very sorry, but I think that he is foolish. I was a peasant child and I knew nothing. But a wise, clever man like Christopher should understand. It seems to me absurd that he should think it possible that I might love him. It is so absurd that I do not believe his love is a real thing. I think that he will soon forget."

"What is to become of you, then, Myrtile?" Gerald demanded.

She looked up at him with a smile.

"What happens to all those others," she asked, "who go through life as I shall go through it? They are very content. Very many pleasant things come their way. They are spared a great deal of suffering. So it will be with me. Now that we have had this talk, Gerald, I can speak to you, perhaps, a little more frankly. I watch you so closely that I see things which others might not notice. You were without actual happiness before because you did not understand what happiness was. Now you are unhappy. That is so sad."

"Yes," Gerald admitted, "I am unhappy."

"There is some one for whom you care?"

He had no idea of evading the issue. He replied at once, simply and directly.

"It is Mademoiselle de Ponière, whom I met at Monte Carlo, and who used to go out with me in the car. I have met her again."

"And yet you are not happy?"

"I am not happy," Gerald acknowledged, "because I have not the least idea whether she cares for me or not. She is very mysterious. She has troubles which she will not let me share."

It seemed to him that Myrtile smiled. They were out of the wood now and crossing the park.

"All that you tell me is very strange," she confessed. "I do not pretend to understand it. One hears, Gerald, that in your way you have cared for very many women. That is rather a pity, but, if it is true, you perhaps do not know your own mind. Are you sure that you love this young lady?"

"I only know that she makes me feel and suffer as no one else in the world has ever done," he answered a little drearily.

They were approaching the house now. Myrtile laid her fingers timidly upon his arm.

" It seems to me, Gerald," she said, with a rather pathetic smile, " that we have changed rôles. You asked me to walk home with you that you might talk to me about Christopher, and now we have finished all that and it is your own affairs only which remain."

" There is nothing about my affairs which even lends itself to discussion," Gerald sighed.

" Not at present," Myrtile assented, " but in the end there must come happiness, because where there is love there is always happiness. — May I say one word more? "

" Go ahead," he answered.

" It is of your father. Why is he so troubled about you? "

Gerald frowned.

" I am afraid, Myrtile," he said, " that that is a matter which I cannot altogether explain to you."

" Perhaps you are right," she admitted. " I must dare to say this, though, because, you see, I am with your father many hours in the day, and he is not so strong as he was and so he shows his mind more easily. Something about you is worrying him. That is not right, is it? "

Gerald was silent for a moment. A telegraph boy, who had been riding down the drive which curved through the park, seeing them, had dismounted from his bicycle and was crossing the turf towards them with an orange-coloured envelope in his hand. Gerald took it from him, tore it open, and read the few lines which it contained. Then he gave the boy a coin and dismissed him. He looked once more at the message.

" It is good news? " Myrtile enquired gravely.

"Good enough," Gerald answered. "I have been living in a miserable state of uncertainty. Now it will all be cleared up."

"There will be no more trouble, then?"

"I cannot say that," he replied, "but at least there will be action. Next week will see the beginning of the elucidation. I leave for Russia on Tuesday."

CHAPTER VI

THE change in Pauline's manner, when Gerald was
ushered by an untidy-looking waiter into her sitting
room on the following afternoon, was almost electrify-
ing. In place of her usual languid greeting, she sprang
lightly to her feet and gave him both her hands. The
slight sullenness had all gone from her face. There
was no living person just then who would not have
found her beautiful.

" You received my telegram? " she demanded eagerly.

" And I came to you at once," was the prompt reply.

She drew him down to her side upon the sofa. Her
manner and tone displayed an animation entirely new
to her.

" Reusser returned the night before last," she said.
" He seems to have had a comparatively easy journey,
and he reports conditions over there very much more
lenient in many ways. He had no difficulty in landing,
or in making his way wherever he wished to go. On
the other hand, the stories he brings back as to the
distress and misery everywhere are simply shocking.
The country bleeds to death. There are few trains
running, no order, no discipline, despotic and arbitrary
police surveillance everywhere. But there is also cor-
ruption. People, especially the official classes, are looking everywhere for the means to live. A merchant who
was imprisoned only a month or so ago on a charge of
murder, to which he actually pleaded ' Guilty ', was set

free the day before Reusser left. It cost him little more than five thousand roubles."

" Did this man Reusser discover where your brother was? " Gerald asked.

" For ten thousand roubles," she answered, " he could have searched every police register in Russia. Paul is at the Fortress of St. Maria, at a small town called Sokar, about three hundred miles south of Petrograd. It is a bad journey, of course, but the place is accessible. The Governor of the prison is a Major Krossneys. He is half an Austrian and half a Pole. When he is sober, he is simply greedy. When he is drunk, he is reckless. He is to be managed with ease, but always it is to be remembered that Paul is his chief prisoner. If Paul were to escape," she went on thoughtfully, " he would, without a doubt, lose his post, certainly his promotion; he might even have to flee the country. To buy him would probably cost a sum of money sufficient to support him for the rest of his life. There are still people who would tear Paul to pieces if they knew who he was."

" This Major Krossneys," Gerald enquired, " does he speak French? "

" Fortunately, yes," was the eager assent. " Tell me, Gerald, what do you think of it all? "

" Just this," he replied. " I shall sail on Tuesday. There is a steamer from Hull. In less than two months I will bring your brother back."

Her eyes shone. She seemed to be trembling in every limb. There was ecstasy in her face, passion on her quivering lips. Yet even as he drew a little nearer to her, Gerald was drearily conscious that she had almost forgotten his presence. It was the thought of her brother which had wrought this transformation.

"If I bring him back to you, Pauline ——" he began.
She suddenly seized him by the shoulders.

"Bring him back!" she interrupted passionately.
"I make no bargain. I give no promise — you should
know better than to ask for any such. All that I can
tell you is that I would give my soul to see him again."

Gerald clenched his hands almost in pain.

"Pauline," he pleaded, "for heaven's sake, soften
just a little. You keep me all the time in torment.
Paul shall be set free — I swear it. If it costs me my
fortune, my liberty, even my life, he shall be set free.
But I'm doing it for love of you. My love is choking
me. Soften for one moment. Remember what you will
be to me some day. Give me at least a memory to take
with me."

She laid her hand upon his. It seemed to him that
it was as cold as the snows. Her eyes looked into his.
They were soft and beautiful, full of colour and sweetness, yet they looked him through as though he were a
denizen of some other world.

"When I give, I give all," she said. "You do not
understand the people of my race. We cannot give in
driblets — a kiss here, a caress there, the promise of
more to-morrow. God never made us Russians like
that. When I give, it will be the full glory of love.
Bring Paul back to me and you may know what that
can mean."

Gerald rose to his feet.

"I should go to my task a stronger man," he complained, a little bitterly, "if you could throw me the
dole one might give to a beggar."

She gave him her finger tips. She was standing by
his side, so near that the desire to hold her in his arms
and take from her lips the one kiss he craved was al-

most irresistible. At that moment he almost hated her.

" Haven't you even the grace to pretend? " he muttered.

She laughed, wringing her fingers slightly as though his lips had seared them.

" You have been spoilt," she murmured. " The women you have played with have been your too willing slaves. A trifle of homage, a trifle of philandering, a few shadowy caresses — that is all you have known of love. — Wait! "

Gerald spent that afternoon in the City, the next few days in making restless preparations for his absence from London. On the afternoon of the last day, he was permitted to see Reusser, and he recognised in him at once the man whom he had seen watching over Madame de Ponière and her niece in Hyde Park. The meeting took place in the sitting room of the South Kensington hotel. Reusser, who leaned heavily upon two sticks, was brought thither by a tall youth, his son, who waited for him outside the door. He was as thin as a skeleton, his cheeks were sunken, and every now and then his voice seemed to die away.

" It is my first day out of the hospital," he told Gerald apologetically. " I caught cold on the way back, and my lungs are not good. Please ask what questions you desire. I am subject to attacks of weakness."

" I understand," Gerald said, " that you reached Sokar? "

" I reached it," he admitted, " but, alas! I was powerless to act. I took with me every penny of money we could scrape together, but by the time I reached the city I was penniless. I lodged at the house of a saddler, whose name you will find in the book I have given you. He took me to look at the fortress. He showed me the room where the brother of Mademoiselle lies. He told me much about Major Krossneys, the commandant of the fortress. But of what avail was it? We had not enough money between us to pay for a bottle of wine."

"How do you propose," Gerald enquired, "that I approach Krossneys?"

"The way is arranged," Reusser replied eagerly. "There is a woman living in the town, half German, half English. Her name is Elsa Francks. To-day Krossneys is her slave. You go first to her. Her address is in the little book you have. She speaks English and French, besides her own language; even some Russian. Talk to her frankly. She will bring you to Krossneys. There is one thing, though. You must go as an American. No one will do anything to help you, although they are all greedy for money, if they think that you are English. It will be quite easy, that. There are many Americans in Russia, prospecting. There is a great oil field on the plains south of Kreussner. Some say there is oil there; others deny it. That is how your bribes must be worked. You will buy property. It will be worth nothing. You will find that Krossneys has land to sell; so has Elsa."

"I understand," Gerald said.

"You leave to-morrow?"

"At ten o'clock from King's Cross," Gerald assented. "The boat leaves at night."

Reusser raised his right hand.

"The Father of God speed you!" he said. "Speed is very necessary. The Government has kept that young man alive, hoping that some day he would be useful as a bribe or a hostage, but there are still many fanatics in Russia, haters of his race, who would tear him limb from limb if they knew."

" I shall be in Petrograd in a fortnight," Gerald declared, " and at Sokar, I hope, a few days later."

Reusser once more raised his hand and muttered inaudible words. Nevertheless, though his strength seemed departed, he tried to kneel when Pauline came into the room. She raised him to his feet and called to his son.

" All is well," she said, dismissing them. " Take care of your strength, Reusser. You must be one of the first to welcome him."

The man bowed his head and prayed silently. Then his son led him away.

Gerald also rose to his feet. He had nerved himself for this interview.

" I shall have the pleasure of wishing Madame farewell? " he asked.

" My aunt sends you her excuses and her prayers," Pauline replied. " She is too agitated to risk a meeting. You do not quite know what this means to us."

" I know," Gerald said, " what its results may mean to me."

She looked at him a little sadly.

" My unhappy country," she sighed, " is to-day only a furnace of woe and suffering, yet in the jumble of it there are a few millions still who would kneel through the night and pray for you, if they knew your mission. I bid you farewell, Gerald, and every throb of my body will live with you. I have sworn that no word of love shall pass my lips, nor any feeling of love linger in my heart, so long as my brother lies in that fortress. But I am here. I would give you anything that would speed you on your journey. It is for you to choose."

She stood perfectly passive, her arms hanging by her
sides.   Her eyes looked sadly into his, her lips were
composed and still.   For a moment the fires burned in
his blood.   He took a quick step forward.   She waited,
unmoved, yet without shrinking.   So they faced one
another for a moment.   She extended her hand.   Gerald
seized it, then dropped it.

"I   shall   do   my   best," he   promised   hoarsely.
"Good-by!"

She listened to his departing footsteps; she even
moved to the window, watched him leave the hotel and
step into his waiting automobile.   He was well enough
to look at, good-looking as ever in his slim, lithe way,
and with his fine carriage.   Nevertheless, there was
neither love nor pride in her eyes as she watched him.
There was something else, which seemed to point back
down the avenues of the history of her family, something, perhaps, which had sounded the knell of their
doom, generations before.   It was there in her lips, in
her eyes, spelled out in her fixed stare, — the cruelty of
a race whose heart is given only to passion.

CHAPTER VII

CHRISTOPHER was warmly welcomed at Hinterleys when he made his promised appearance there, about a fortnight after Gerald's departure. He would have preferred postponing his visit altogether but for Gerald's urgent request, made on the night before he had started for abroad. It all seemed very natural, however. Myrtile welcomed him without a shade of embarrassment, Lady Mary with her usual delightful friendliness, and Lord Hinterleys with more than his usual hospitality.

"Any news from the traveller?" Christopher asked, as they sat round the fire in the hall, before going up to change.

"Just a telegram yesterday from Petrograd," Mary replied, — "'Arrived safely. Love.'"

"Satisfactory so far as it goes," Christopher remarked.

"So far as it goes," Lord Hinterleys grumbled, "but what on earth Gerald wants to go over to that barbarous country for, at this time of the year, I can't possibly imagine. Who are these friends of his, Bent? Do you know anything about them?"

"Very little," Christopher admitted. "I gather that they are Russian *emigrées*, but really I don't know a thing more about them. Gerald seems to have made their acquaintance at Monte Carlo, when they were occupying the next villa to yours."

"I saw them out driving once or twice," Lord Hinter-

leys ruminated. " The girl was beautiful and looked
well-born. The aunt might have been any one."

" I think there is no doubt that they are aristocrats,"
Christopher pronounced.

" Wasn't there something rather strange about the
way they left Monte Carlo? " Mary enquired, from the
depths of her easy-chair.

" Strange but not discreditable," he hastened to assure her. " Their steward had brought them out a
large sum of money, which appears to have been all
that they possessed in the world, and instead of handing it over, he gambled at the tables, lost it and committed suicide. The two women apparently sold all
their jewellery, scrupulously paid their debts and disappeared. I believe Gerald discovered them living at a
cheap hotel in South Kensington."

" Don't like the type," Lord Hinterleys muttered.

" The girl is very attractive," Myrtile ventured. " I
used to see her driving sometimes with Gerald."

" All the same, I can't see why Gerald wants to go
mixing himself up in their affairs," his father observed
pettishly, " especially in the middle of the shooting season."

" He expects to be back before you shoot the cov-
erts," Mary reminded him. " I don't know the reason
for his journey to Russia any more than you do, but I
don't imagine he'll want to stop there any longer than
he can help."

" I should think not," Lord Hinterleys grumbled, —
" a country of madmen and anarchists. I expect he's
there on some fool's errand."

" I shouldn't be surprised," Mary declared, laying
down the book which she had been studying at intervals, " if Gerald didn't know perfectly well what he was

doing — if he hadn't, in fact, stumbled upon some sort of a romance. The only time I have ever seen these two women, except in the distance at Monte Carlo, was at Ranelagh on a quiet day after the season was over; I expect Gerald had given them vouchers. They were walking about the gardens, and I was with Susan Armitage. Lord Armitage, as you know, was on the Staff at Petrograd in the old days. We met them crossing the lawn and I heard Susan give a little exclamation. Then she stopped quite short and stood almost to attention, looking steadfastly at the girl. I am perfectly certain that she was going to curtsey. I could see it in her eye. And I am perfectly certain, too, that this Madame de Ponière and her niece knew who she was. They took not the slightest notice, however, so Susan unbent and came along."

"But surely you asked her who they were?" Lord Hinterleys enquired.

"Of course I did," Mary assented. "Susan, however, was exceedingly mysterious. Since Jack began to fancy himself a diplomatist, she apes all his little ways. 'I may be mistaken, my dear,' she said. 'In any case, the ladies did not desire to be recognised.' I pressed her hard, but she wouldn't even tell me who she thought they were. Before that I had asked Gerald if he would like me to go and see them, but he told me they were in great trouble and were not receiving anybody at present."

"This is all very well and charitable and that sort of thing," her father remarked, "but I don't quite see why Gerald should have had to raise thirty thousand pounds within the last few weeks."

"Frankly, I cannot think that these two women are responsible for it," Mary declared. "Gerald told me, the day before he left, that they were still living in that poky little South Kensington place."

" Young men are much better married, anyway," Lord Hinterleys growled. " Why don't you get married, Christopher? You could afford to, and a man like you, with a political future, needs a wife."

Christopher smiled imperturbably.

" Give me time, sir," he begged. " It's different with Gerald. He has the estates, and very little else to think about."

" Gerald's an ass," was the irritable reply. " He's too fond of women to understand them, or even to realise when he comes across the right thing."

" Gerald may have his faults," his sister observed, " but at least he has spared us the usual musical comedy infliction. There goes the gong. Christopher, come into my room for a moment and I'll show you those photographs."

They trooped up the great oak staircase, and Mary led their guest into her own little boudoir. She closed the door carefully behind them.

" Christopher," she said, " I am so glad you came. Honestly, I am anxious about Gerald. He came to see you, didn't he, the night before he sailed? "

" He did," was the cautious admission.

" He must have told you a little more than he told us," she went on.

" Very little," Christopher assured her. " He mumbled something about Russia being an uncertain country just now, and got me round to his rooms to witness his will. Of course, I don't think there was any secret that he was going over on business connected with these two new friends of his. What that business is, though, I haven't the slightest idea."

" Honest? "

" Honest! If I were to make a guess, I should say he was going over to see if he could do anything about their estates, if they have any. On the other hand, if he'd been doing that, I should have expected him to have taken a lawyer."

" Gerald in matters of business," his sister sighed, " is a perfect idiot. I hope he isn't going to get himself into trouble."

" Well, they can't eat him," Christopher declared consolingly, " and they seem to have left off murdering people, at any rate for the present. Besides, they have common sense enough to know that molesting Englishmen is an expensive amusement, even in Russia."

" You're a dear, cheering-up sort of person," Mary said gratefully. " And, Christopher, I haven't had an opportunity of saying so before, but I am still very sorry."

" Thank you, Mary."

" You'll have another try, I suppose? You're a tenacious person."

He shook his head.

" Never," he answered firmly. " Myrtile is a strange little creature, but she was cast in the mould of all good women. She loves Gerald, and so long as she lives she will never love anybody else."

" And Gerald ——" Mary murmured.

" Gerald will never love any one," Christopher interrupted, " not unless something changes him — trouble or some great disaster. It's quite hopeless, Mary, and I know it. I have sealed the chamber down tight, and here I am, as you see, very much as usual."

She pressed his arm.

" Dear old Christopher! — You'll find you're in the

oak room at the end of the corridor, as usual. How-
son, Gerald's servant, is down here doing nothing. He
will look after you. After dinner you must tell me
about the election. I am so interested, and so is dad,
when he can spare a moment from thinking about his
pheasants. He is certain to insist upon Myrtile's reading to him after dinner, and you and I will knock the
balls about in the billiard room."

Christopher would have been less than human if he
had not realised the pleasure of having a very charming
and attractive young woman, who was also his hostess,
keenly interested in the one subject which was just then
absorbing the whole of his time and attention. Mary
knew a great deal about politics, and her shrewd com-
ments were not only sympathetic but at times fairly
helpful. They were left undisturbed throughout the
whole of the evening in the billiard room, and Christopher was surprised at the ease with which he forgot
that slim, frail figure with the haunting eyes and
tremulous smile, who had sat opposite him at dinner.
There is something about inevitability which sets its
mark upon all enterprise and sensation. He knew perfectly well that Myrtile would never alter. She was as
far removed from him as though she had become a
beautiful picture or an exquisite piece of statuary. The
conviction itself had a certain soothing effect. No man
was ever known to sigh his heart out for the unattain-
able. With the merest chance of some alteration in
her feelings, he would have been a persistent and un-
changing lover. There was no chance, and he knew it.
The disappointment was there, a dull pain in his heart
whenever he thought of certain chambers in the building of that house of his future. But it was a pain of
the past, a pain from which frequent escape was at

least possible. He found the coming of the footman with whisky and soda that night unwelcome and surprising.

" Eleven o'clock! " he exclaimed. " Why, what has become of the evening? "

" Flatterer! " she laughed. " Never mind, I was just thinking the same myself. One game of billiards, and then to bed. You'll have a long day to-morrow, for you're walking in the morning, at any rate, and dad always relies upon you to do the outsides. — Here's Myrtile come to wish us good night."

" Haven't you people played yet? " Myrtile enquired, looking at the unused table in surprise.

" Not yet," Christopher replied. " Lady Mary and I have been talking politics."

Myrtile made a little grimace.

" Politics! " she sighed. " Lord Hinterleys has tried to explain English politics to me, but I think that I am stupid. I do not think that I have ever heard of anything quite so dull. — Good night to you both. I am going to bed."

She waved her hand and disappeared. Mary looked after her thoughtfully.

" Sometimes," she said, " Myrtile presents herself to one as a problem. I wonder whether it is really for their happiness to transplant any one."

" Don't you think that Myrtile is happy? " Christopher asked.

Mary shook her head.

" No girl is really happy without love in her life," she declared. " You can realise for yourself how little chance Myrtile has of ever being rewarded for her devotion."

He frowned.

"Poor child!" he said. "But aren't you a little sweeping, Mary? There are lots of girls who seem to get everything they want in life, and to be perfectly happy without a man — without caring for any one in particular, that is. Yourself, for instance?"

Mary selected a cue with great care.

"I suppose I am an exception," she admitted. "Come along, I'll play you one fifty up before I go to bed."

CHAPTER VIII

GERALD, worn out with long and comfortless travel, pulled the long, iron bell outside the closed door of Elsa Francks' house in Sokar, with a sense of relief that the first part of his quest was accomplished. The street was one which formerly had been possessed of some pretensions. The houses were tall, solidly built, and had apparently been occupied by a wealthy class of merchant. They were now mostly let out in tenements. Exactly opposite where Gerald stood waiting, men and women — shrunken-looking creatures, most of them — were continually passing in and out of a broad entrance, from which the gates had been done away with altogether, with sacks or baskets of partly finished boots, and the sound of fitful hammering seemed to denote a factory devoid of machinery. In the centre of the road were some rusty rails, around which some grass was growing, — the remains of an electric car service. Most of the houses seemed empty or over-full, — locked and barred, with broken window frames and closed shutters, or converted into tenement houses. The long street, full of holes and strewn with all manner of refuse, ended in a steep hill. Way beyond it, the so-called fortress, a sinister, grey building of many stories, glittered in the afternoon sun.

The door in front of which Gerald was standing was suddenly opened. A dark-visaged, corpulent woman, dressed apparently in nothing but a petticoat and shawl, thrust out her head. Gerald handed her a card,

on which, through the friendly offices of the hotel porter, was inscribed his desire to see Madame Francks.
The woman turned it over, looked Gerald up and down
with wide-mouthed astonishment, and finally motioned
him to enter. As soon as he had done so and stepped
into the little cobbled courtyard, she drew the bolt and
muttered something which he understood as an invitation to follow her. She pushed open a heavy door on
the right, and they ascended a gloomy staircase. The
atmosphere was close, almost stifling. There seemed to
be no window, or any means of giving light or ventilation. Arrived on the first floor, she threw open the
door of a room and departed, with a wholly incomprehensible grunt. Outside, she began to shout, apparently through the door of another apartment. There
was a vigorous duet, the other voice shriller but scarcely
more pleasant. Then there was silence, followed by
the sound of some one moving about in the adjoining
room.

Gerald took a seat upon a couch, upholstered in
stained purple velvet, over which several soiled cover-
ings of imitation lace had been thrown. The room itself
was large and lofty, but scantily furnished. There was
a huge undecorated stove in one corner, which, notwithstanding the heat of the day, already exuded fumes of
burning coke. The polished floor was innocent of any
rug or carpet, and covered with stains and fragments of
cigarettes and cigars. There was a piano, littered with
soiled and torn copies of music, in a distant corner, a
small gramophone with black enamel mouthpiece, blis-
tered by the continual heat of the room. The walls
were hung with the faded remains of some former attempt at decoration. The windows were covered with a
sort of wire netting, which kept out alike light and air.

There was everywhere an odour of stale tobacco smoke, mingled with a strange smell of cheap incense or crude perfume of some sort.   Gerald, exceedingly sensitive to surroundings, felt a momentary faintness as he sat and waited for the woman whom he had come to visit.   He began to fidget in his place.   He walked up and down. He was even meditating an attack upon one of the window fastenings, when he was aware of the sound of heavy footsteps outside.   The door was opened.   A woman entered and came towards him with an enquiring expression upon her face.

It seemed to Gerald that the newcomer alone was needed to complete the squalour of his surroundings. She was a big woman, coarsely built, and with indications of obesity.   She wore a dressing gown of some red material, trimmed with soiled white fur and fastened round her waist with a girdle.   Her hair was a bright yellow, abundant but badly arranged.   It lay in loose coils upon the top of her head, fastened with some flamboyant ornament.   Her features were not ill-shaped, but were partly concealed under a thick coating of powder.   She had eyes of a peculiarly light blue shade, large and saucer-like when she first entered the room, but with a habit of narrowing at intervals.   She spoke in English, with a strong German accent.

" You wish to see me, sir?   I am Elsa Francks."

Gerald rose to his feet and bowed.

" Madame," he said, " I have found my way here under the name of Harmon P. Cross.   I have told every one that I am an American, looking for an opportunity to invest money.   That story is not true.   It is my wish, if you will allow me, to be perfectly candid with you."

" You can sit down," she invited, regarding Gerald

with suspicion not unmixed with favour. " I will hear
what you have to say."

She threw herself in a lump at the far end of the
sofa, and pointed to a battered horsehair easy-chair.

" Bring that to the side of me," she continued. " I
do not hear very well and it is some time since I listened
to English.   Tell me what you want? "

" I have a further confession to make," Gerald began.
" I am an Englishman."

" There are Englishmen and Englishmen," she said
indulgently.   " Some are different from others.   You
are not like those whom our officers have had to correct
in the streets and cafés of Berlin.   Now what is your
business, please? "

" It is very difficult to state," Gerald admitted
frankly, " and I am only emboldened to approach you
because in these difficult times, and in Russia especially,
one needs money.   If you will do me a service, I can
find you a great deal of money."

Gerald's methods had at any rate succeeded in exciting the interest of the woman he had come to visit.   Her
becarmined lips were parted; her pale eyes were filled
with the light of cupidity.

" There is not much we would not do for money, nowadays, over here," she declared, laughing hardly.
" You are a very interesting man.   Go on."

" Major Ivan Krossneys is a friend of yours," Gerald
said.

" Ho, ho! " the woman laughed.   " So you dabble in
politics, eh?   Never mind, Krossneys is my friend.
What of it? "

" He is the Governor of the fortress here," Gerald
went on.   " He has a great number of prisoners under
his care."

" One hundred and thirty-seven," Elsa Francks replied promptly. " I see some of them exercising when I am at the fortress. What he keeps them alive for, I cannot imagine. They crawl about the yard like lice. What about these prisoners? "

Gerald moved his chair a little nearer. The woman smiled at him graciously.

" If one of them should escape," he remarked significantly, " there would be a great deal of money."

" What do you call a great deal of money? " she asked.

" I do not bargain," Gerald replied. " I know very well that the escape of a prisoner is a serious thing. I have at my disposal the sum of ten thousand pounds."

The woman started so that she nearly rolled off the sofa. She sat suddenly upright. She was too stupefied for emotion.

" Ten thousand pounds? " she almost shrieked. " Why, it is two million roubles! Ivan Krossneys would sell you his whole batch of prisoners for that, and throw the fortress in! Why, if it rested with me," she went on, " you could have Krossneys as well, for a quarter of that. Talk sense, please! There is not an Englishman there. Of that I am certain."

" The prisoner whose liberty I desire to buy," Gerald confided, " is a Russian. I do not know under what name he passes, but his number is twenty-nine."

Elsa Francks rose to her feet, opened the door and shouted to her maid in Russian. Then she took up a battered telephone instrument.

" I will speak with the Major," she said. " I am the only civilian in the town with a telephone. It is a great favour. You can wait whilst I speak with him."

There was a good deal of delay before she was connected, and a further delay before the person with whom she desired to speak arrived. In time, however, the conversation was finished, apparently to her satisfaction. She set down the instrument.

"The Governor is on his way down," she announced triumphantly. "Come, we will see to this little affair quickly. You can remain."

The maid entered the room, carrying a tray on which were bottles of beer and glasses. The woman eyed them with satisfaction.

"You are not Russian," she said, "so I do not offer you the samovar. Beer every one drinks — the English especially. That is so, is it not?"

"That is so," Gerald admitted. "I shall drink to your good health, Madame."

"You may call me Elsa," she invited graciously, coming over to his side with a glass in her hand. "We will drink to the success of our enterprise."

Gerald accepted the glass and exchanged courteous amenities with his hostess. She eyed him with growing favour.

"It is a pity that you are not staying longer," she observed. "We might become friends. Who knows?"

"In that case," Gerald replied gallantly, "I might have to quarrel with Major Krossneys, and that would not do at all."

She snapped her pudgy fingers. A man who had ten thousand pounds to dispose of! What was Krossneys!

"Do you think," she scoffed, "that I shall stay here with him if I can get hold of half that sum you spoke of? Not I! I shall choose a different companion. I shall go to Monte Carlo. I shall never enter this accursed country again. Even to think of leaving it makes me giddy with happiness. It will be you who will be my deliverer. Let us drink again together."

"Perhaps," Gerald suggested, "the Governor will not give up his prisoner."

Her exclamation of contempt was almost a shout. The very idea, while she scouted it as ridiculous, seemed to infuriate her.

"Give him up? Of course he will give him up!" she declared. "If he refused — why, I would take him by the beard — I would kill him!"

Her eyes were lit with cruelty. The snarl of an animal of prey twisted her lips. Then she burst into a fit of laughter.

"Why do I make myself furious?" she exclaimed. "Why, Ivan would sell every one of his hundred and thirty-seven prisoners for a tenth part of the money you speak of! Come, let us be gay. I will put something on the gramophone. You shall dance with me, yes?"

"What about His Excellency the Governor?" Gerald asked.

The woman made a little grimace.

"You are perhaps right," she acquiesced. "One must wait — wait until everything is arranged. After that I shall snap my fingers at Ivan. He wearies me, and he is an old man. Will you take me out of the country, my friend? We might go into Poland — I have friends at Warsaw."

There were heavy steps outside. She held up her hand as though to warn him.

"It is the Governor," she announced. "It is Ivan Krossneys who arrives. Mind, he is very jealous. Be careful."

Gerald, with all his nerves on edge, was yet able to

indulge for a moment in a grim smile. The door was opened. The maid poked her head in and muttered something unintelligible. Close behind her entered the Governor of the fortress.

CHAPTER IX

THE Governor was a large, corpulent, untidy-looking man in an ill-fitting uniform, with coarse features and a straggling beard. He clicked his heels together and made some pretence at a military salute, as Elsa introduced her visitor. She whispered a word or two apart with him in Russian, and then continued in French, which she spoke apparently with less ease than English.

" This gentleman," she declared, " has a great affair of business to discuss with you. He was sent here by a friend of mine whose name I may not give. He is an Englishman pretending to be an American, but that makes for little. He is entrusted with a great sum of money for a certain purpose."

Into the Governor's eyes flashed for a moment some reflection of the cupidity which had gleamed in the woman's. Money was scarce in Russia; pay was small and irregular in coming. The thought of money whetted his interest.

" Let me hear what this gentleman has to say," he invited.

" I have come with a very bold proposition," Gerald began, " but it is one which I hope you will consider carefully. You have many prisoners in your fortress who are detained largely through misfortune. There are many there whose offences are trivial, who will probably be released shortly in any case, and who might just as well be free as remain a charge upon the Government."

"You seem to know a great deal about my prisoners," the Governor remarked ungraciously. "Many of them are criminals of the worst order."

"It is not one of these whom I wish to discuss with you," Gerald assured him. "It happens that you have a young man there who is not of the criminal class at all. He has very wealthy friends."

"Ha!" the Governor exclaimed. "How wealthy?"

The woman broke into the conversation. She gripped her friend by the arm.

"Ivan," she cried, "it is incredible! Do you know the sum which monsieur speaks of? It takes one's breath away! He speaks of ten thousand pounds! It is two million roubles! What do you think of that?"

"Holy mother of God!" Krossneys muttered. "A prisoner of mine?"

"A prisoner of yours," Gerald repeated. "I will be quite frank with you, sir. I speak, I know, to a man of honour, but I will ask you to remember that this young man is unconvicted of any crime, and that the Government by whom he was sent to you is tottering. This is not a bribe which I am offering you. It is the price of an act of justice. The money is to be paid in cash."

Krossneys was showing now as much agitation as the woman had displayed. Mingled with his emotion, however, was a fear, signs of which were at once manifested in the anxiety which distorted his face, the eagerness of his demand.

"The number?" he cried. "Tell me the name or the number of the prisoner you desire?"

"Number twenty-nine," Gerald replied.

The Governor struck the table with his clenched fist, so that the glasses rattled.

"A million devils curse and blast you both!" he
shouted.

He kicked a footstool which was close at hand across
the room.   Then he flung himself into an easy-chair and
sat there with his arms crossed, glowering at Elsa.   The
woman gazed at him as though he had suddenly gone
mad.

"Are you out of your senses, Ivan?" she asked.
"Twenty-nine or thirty-nine — what does it matter?
Is not one prisoner like another?   Who comes to
visit them?   Who knows which cell is empty?
Bah!"

"So you thought you were rich for life, did you,
Elsa?" the man in the chair muttered.   "Well, you
can just rid yourself of the idea.   And as for you, sir,"
he went on, with a malicious glance at Gerald, " you
may think yourself fortunate if you leave this country
as easily as you entered it."

The woman drew a little nearer to him.   There was
the look of a wild animal in her face.

"Listen, Ivan!" she cried.   "Are you mad?   It is a
fortune which this man carries in his hand!   What is
there amongst the scum that infests your prisons of account against that?   You terrify me.   The money is
for us, to be divided.   Cash, Ivan!   Money to spend —
to-morrow — the next day — every day!"

"You fool!" the Governor retorted.   "Of what use
is money when your feet dangle in the air and your neck
is broken?   That for you, and a dozen rifle bullets in
my heart!   You are a bold man who came to Russia on
such a mission," he added, glowering at Gerald.

She turned to her visitor.

"What does this madman mean?" she demanded.
"Who is this prisoner whose freedom you seek?"

" I do not know," Gerald replied. " I am only an emissary."

The Governor sat up in his chair.

" I will tell you," he declared hoarsely. " Number twenty-nine is all the fortress records say of him, but his name is Paul, Grand Duke of Volostok, Prince of Tamboff, hereditary Grand Duke and Ruler of all the provinces of the Dvina, nephew of Nicholas, the late Tsar, head of the House of Romanoff, — himself, if the people changed their fancy to-morrow, Tsar of all the Russias! There, my woman, now you know the secret of my fortress! You can guess where we might be if I traded with this lunatic! "

The woman flopped upon the sofa. She was pale through all her rouge and powder. Her yellow hair had broken loose from its band of ribbon. Her dressing gown had fallen away a little from her ample bust. She sat breathing heavily for several moments. Gerald, of the three, was the only one who kept his head.

"All that makes for nothing," he said calmly. " You excite yourself greatly for nothing. The Romanoff dynasty is past. There will never be another Tsar in Russia. This young man has rich friends and they want him out of the country. I should think your Government would be glad to be rid of him."

Gerald's words were not without their effect, especially upon the woman.

"After all," she muttered, " this man speaks sense. Who cares about Grand Dukes, nowadays? There are plenty of them who have already escaped. What does one more or less matter? "

" But this one — I have told you who he is! " the man growled.

The woman was beginning to pluck up spirit. She scoffed at him openly.

"When the people of Russia want the days of Tsardom back again," she said, "they will find one of the brood fast enough. But that day will not come yet. This young man in your fortress is of no account. You are a fool, Ivan. You cannot see the truth. You have not thought to yourself what ten thousand pounds may mean."

Krossneys sat back in his chair, biting his finger nails.

"Who are you?" he demanded suddenly. "And where does this money come from?"

"My name is Dombey," Gerald replied. "I have admitted to Madame Francks that I am an Englishman. This money has been collected in London by friends and relatives of the young man. The desire for his release has not the slightest political significance."

"And what the devil excuse can I make for letting him go?"

"I should put one of your less important prisoners into his cell and say nothing about it," Gerald suggested.

"There is an inspector of State prisons," Krossneys muttered. "He does not often come, but who knows when he might take it into his head to pay us a visit?"

"The last time he was here," Elsa Francks reminded him, "you met him at the station and took him to the hotel. Afterwards, you brought him on here and he was so drunk that he had to stay for two days. He did not even go near the fortress. Your papers and books were brought down here for him to sign."

"It is true," Krossneys assented, "yet next time another man might come. And again, how will this number twenty-nine get safely out of Russia?"

" Think less of these difficulties and more of what one could do with ten thousand pounds," the woman insisted. " You are not asked, Ivan, to run a risk for nothing. I say that it is worth it."

" For you, yes," Krossneys sneered, " because you risk nothing and you have the spending of the money. For me it is different. I have an official position. I am Governor of the fortress; I wear the uniform of the Russian Republic."

Elsa Francks laughed loudly and scornfully. She pointed jeeringly at Krossneys.

" Uniform of the Russian Republic! " she exclaimed. "A pity they didn't make it to fit you! Official position, indeed! What do you get out of it, I should like to know? Would you not starve if it were not for the contributions of the prisoners themselves? "

" It is true," Krossneys assented gloomily. " It is a dog's life."

"And a dog's country to live it in! " the woman proclaimed. " Listen to me, Ivan."

She sat upon the arm of his chair and talked to him in Russian. Soon it was evident that he was yielding. She fetched him beer and then spirits of some sort from a cupboard. Once or twice she turned and winked stealthily at Gerald. At last she turned towards him in triumph.

" It is arranged," she announced.

" Not so fast," Krossneys intervened. " Let us hear how this money is to be paid? "

" In cash," Gerald replied. " I have drafts upon your own banks."

" Well, well," Krossneys muttered, " the money is right enough, then. At ten o'clock to-morrow morning," he went on, " present yourself at the fortress.

Enquire for me. I shall give you an audience. The affair may be concluded at once. Get back to your hotel now and be careful not to speak of your real business."

Gerald rose blithely to his feet. The idea of leaving the horrible atmosphere of that room was undiluted joy to him. He bowed to the Governor. Elsa took him to the door and, under pretext of calling the servant, passed out with him into the passage.

" You can come back later if you like to talk with me again," she whispered. " Be careful, though, for he is very jealous."

She shouted something to the Russian maid and stepped back into the room with a meaning smile. Gerald put money into the hand of the woman who opened the postern gate and stepped into the street with a gasp of relief. The clear air was wonderful. He drew in great gulps of it as he made his way along the uneven pavements, stared at by every passer-by. He could scarcely believe that his task was coming so easily to an end. If all went well, in twenty-four hours he might be on his way back to England.

CHAPTER X

GERALD, after a weary climb out of the town, stood at last, at the appointed hour on the following morning, before the rusty iron gates of the fortress. Untidy and neglected though the whole place seemed, there was still something sinister about the various crude precautions against the escape of a prisoner. For a quarter of a mile, on the outside of the walls, not in themselves formidable, everything in the shape of trees, shrubs or dwellings had been razed to the ground, and every fifty paces around the walls, on the top of a buttress, was mounted a machine gun, from which an iron ladder led to the ground. The walls themselves were about eight feet high, of stone covered with white plaster. The fortress itself was built of a kind of grey-coloured brick, a square, solid building, with a curiously unexpected pointed top. The barred windows were no more than slits. The space of open ground by which the main building was surrounded was inches deep in dust.

A porter in stained and ill-fitting uniform admitted Gerald to the building, escorted him across the yard, and passed him on to a duplicate of himself, to whom Gerald once more presented the card which had obtained him admittance. He was led down a stone passage, which had apparently neither been cleaned nor swept for months, into a lofty but bare apartment at the farther end. Krossneys, who was sitting before a wooden table, apparently expecting him, dismissed the attendant and motioned Gerald to sit down. He looked at his visitor in unfriendly fashion.

"Why did you not come to me direct instead of going to Elsa Francks?" he demanded.

Gerald was not unprepared for the question.

"I knew your reputation as a soldier and a man of honour," he replied. "I feared that unless this matter was put to you in the proper light, tactfully, as a woman can put it, you would have nothing to say to me."

The Governor grunted.

"It was a mistake," he declared sourly. "The woman is greedy. She will demand her full share of the money. It is scarcely justice."

"I am sorry," Gerald said. "I acted as I was advised."

"Supposing I accede," Krossneys went on, after a short pause, "how do you propose to get Number Twenty-nine out of the country?"

"I was hoping," Gerald admitted, "that you might have been able to help with some suggestion."

The Governor stroked his beard.

"Suggestions," he muttered, "are worth money."

Gerald acquiesced.

"I have not command of much more than the amount I spoke of," he said, "but if you can show me how to get our friend safely out of the country, I will add a thousand pounds to your share."

"Which sum," the Governor insisted quickly, "will not be mentioned to Elsa Francks and will belong to me alone."

"Agreed," Gerald acquiesced.

"Show me your papers," the Governor demanded.

Gerald produced them without hesitation, — his passport, an urgent letter of recommendation by the one statesman who was in good odour in both countries,

banker's drafts, which needed only his signature to pro-
duce a never-ending flow of cash. The Governor's eyes
glittered as he turned them over in his hand. It was
horrible that a share of these treasures must go to the
woman! She was well enough under his thumb, the
slave of his command, but with money in her pocket —
they were neither of them in their first youth, but, so
far as looks went, in his eyes she still had charm — if
she were independent of him, all sorts of things might
happen. He threw down the documents with a little
oath. The passport, however, he kept in his hand.
His manner, as he looked at Gerald, changed. He became almost servile.

"You, too, are an aristocrat, then," he remarked.

"I am of the English aristocracy," Gerald admitted.
"I have another passport in my pocket, which pro-
claims me an American citizen."

The Governor nodded. He pushed a box of black
cigars across to his visitor. The latter contented himself, however, with accepting a cigarette. Then he
touched a bell. The attendant brought in beer, which
was poured into two glasses. As soon as they were
alone, Krossneys motioned Gerald to draw his chair
close to the desk.

"Now here is my scheme," he said. "Number Twenty-nine is of your height and build. You shall see him
for yourself and judge. Number One Hundred and One,
also a young man, died yesterday afternoon of malarial
fever. His death has not yet been officially reported.
Very good! I take you to the cell of Number Twenty-
nine. You exchange clothes with him. You give him
your American passport. You go in with me to his
cell. He comes out with me. You remain."

"The devil I do!" Gerald muttered.

" Do not be a fool! " the Governor exclaimed impatiently. " I beg your pardon, Excellency," he added a moment later, as he remembered his visitor's identity. " Your stay there will not be long. I shall explain in a moment. I drive Number Twenty-nine to a small station on the line, eleven miles off. I take leave of him there. He is an American who has bought my oil concessions. The station is in the middle of the district. My presence with him will remove all suspicions and prevent their examining the passport too closely. He will travel through to Petrograd. There, I take it, you have made arrangements."

" I have a ship waiting," Gerald replied.

" That is my scheme, then."

" So far, I approve of it," Gerald declared, " but what about me? "

" You will bore yourself for twenty-four hours," the Governor replied. " I will see, though, that you have beer and newspapers. If you will, Elsa can come and see you."

" For heaven's sake, no! " Gerald begged. " I mean," he added hastily, " I shall need no society. I am very tired. I shall sleep."

"As you will," the Governor acquiesced. " In the morning, Number One Hundred and One — I should say his remains — will be carried secretly down to your cell. You will be moved up to the cell of Number One Hundred and One. I shall at once report the death of Number Twenty-nine. He will be buried in the cemetery here before intervention is possible. Now the question comes how to dispose of you."

" I was getting interested in that myself," Gerald admitted.

" Number One Hundred and One's time was up," the

Governor explained. "He could have gone home last week if he had been strong enough. I have his papers of release here, signed by myself. To-morrow morning early, I shall provide you with suitable clothing, and I shall drive you to the railway station. I myself have leave of absence in my pocket, granted to me a fortnight ago, but, to be honest with you, I have not used it because I have had no money with which to enjoy myself. I shall travel with you myself to Petrograd. You will have acted as my clerk in the prison, and I take some interest in you. In my company you are absolutely secure. No one will venture even a question. Arrived at Petrograd, I will drive with you to the docks, you shall take me on board your ship, and we will drink a bottle of champagne together. — What do you think of my plan?"

"Capital!" Gerald replied.

"I will conduct you now," the Governor announced, "to Number Twenty-nine. We will lock ourselves in his cell. You shall explain the scheme to him and change clothes. I will bring pen and ink with me, also the deeds which will put Harmon P. Cross in possession of my oil properties. You shall pay over the drafts. After that you must be patient."

"I am ready," Gerald declared, rising to his feet.

Krossneys unlocked a drawer and took out a bunch of keys which shone like silver, — the only clean thing, it seemed to Gerald, that he had seen in the prison. They tramped up two flights of stone steps.

"I am a humane man," the Governor said, "and it does not please me to turn my prisoners into vermin. I have cells underground, without light or air, which were used by my predecessors. I have had them blocked up. You will find it not so terrible here."

They had reached a long, whitewashed passage with arched roof. The Governor dismissed the attendant who had followed them, inserted the key into the lock of the door over which " 29 " was painted in black letters, and entered himself, motioning Gerald to follow him.

In the sudden sombre twilight of the cell, Gerald's first impressions were that a man opposite had hanged himself against the wall. At their entrance, however, the figure dropped to the ground, releasing his clutch of the rusty bars to which he had been clinging. A tall, thin young man, with sunken cheeks, long, unkempt hair, and eyes a little more than ordinarily bright, stood gazing at them. His clothes seemed to be the remains of a prison uniform. The trousers, always too short, had worn away at the bottom of the legs, and he wore neither socks nor shoes. He stared at the two men — at Gerald especially — in wonder, but remained silent.

" You speak English? " Gerald enquired.

Number Twenty-nine shook his head.

" I speak French better," he replied.

" What were you doing when we came in? " the Governor asked.

Number Twenty-nine smiled wanly.

" For an hour every day," he told them, " sometimes for more, I spring till I catch those bars, and I hang on until I am tired. I can always see the sky; sometimes, if I am feeling strong, I can lift myself so that I see a little of the country."

" Well, you have something better to do now," the Governor declared. " You were a man when you were brought in. I have seen you play a man's part. Remember, if you faint or do anything foolish, you spoil

everything. Set your teeth and take off your clothes.
You are going to be set at liberty."

Number Twenty-nine scarcely faltered.

"I am to be shot, I suppose," he said coolly. "I
trust that your warders are better marksmen than they
are soldiers."

"There is a long story," Gerald intervened, "of
which the Governor will tell you as much as he chooses.
I am an Englishman, sent here by relatives of yours. I
have been able to arrange for your freedom. In a few
days' time, you will be steaming for England."

"Cut it short," the Governor interrupted. "I will
do all the explaining."

Gerald took a letter from his pocketbook.

"Read that letter," he invited. "It is from Pauline.
She is my friend. I am Lord Dombey, an Englishman.
We shall meet at Petrograd later. On the steamer I
will explain everything. Meanwhile, take off your
clothes. You will have to wear mine for a couple of
days."

The young man took off his coat almost mechani-
cally. His shirt was ragged. He had apparently no
underclothes. His fingers began to shake.

"I cannot," he faltered.

"But it is necessary," Gerald assured him. "See, I
am half undressed myself."

He took off his coat and waistcoat. At the sight of
his silk underclothes, the other man began suddenly to
sob.

"I — I have had no water here for a fortnight," he
groaned.

Gerald looked him in the eyes.

"We've done campaigning, both of us," he said. "I
read of you when you led your regiment into Germany.

I was in a trench myself for five days at a stretch. Those things don't really matter. Five days was quite long enough there in the mud. We didn't worry about soap then. Get on with it, please."

Number Twenty-nine closed his eyes as he shed his last garments. Then he drew on Gerald's. Presently the Governor laughed.

"Upon my word," he declared, "it is better than I thought. I have ordered the barber into the next cell. He is a prisoner himself, so there is not much chance of his blabbing. Come along. We will be back in five minutes," he added, turning to Gerald. "In time to take your orders for lunch, eh? Give you time to settle down."

They passed out. Gerald felt a queer sense of loneliness as the door closed behind him. He looked around him half fearfully. Everything was worse than he had feared. The floor was of concrete, and there was not a single article of furniture of any description in the room except a straw mattress already full of holes. The floor had apparently not been swept for weeks. While he sat there, however, there was the click of a key in the door and a burly Russian entered. Without a word he commenced some effort at cleansing the place. When he had finished, he threw in a rug and disappeared. Gerald breathed a little more freely. Then he heard footsteps outside again. The Governor and Number Twenty-nine entered, the latter curiously changed in appearance.

"By all the Saints," the Governor chuckled, "I never realised that the barber was so wonderful a person! This little scheme of mine marches well. Now, then, for your share."

He handed a fountain pen to Gerald, who endorsed

the drafts he had brought, wrote out a further cheque for a thousand pounds, and handed them, together with his American passport, to Krossneys. The latter thrust a document into Number Twenty-nine's pocket.

"You may not know it," he said, "but you are now the owner of five hundred acres of forest where oil may some day be found."

He roared with laughter. Neither of the young men moved a muscle.

"Now, listen, both of you," he went on, "the only automobile in the town awaits me outside. We depart in a minute. Say your farewells, you two. At one o'clock to-morrow morning," he concluded, turning to Gerald, "you will be moved into cell '101,' and later you will go to attend your own funeral. From now until one or perhaps half-past one to-morrow morning, you will have to make the best of it. I will come and superintend your removal myself and let you know that all is well."

"I shall try to sleep until then," Gerald announced. "I am very tired."

"You shall have a little meal in my office in the intervals of being changed," the Governor promised him. "I shall lock the door and no one will know. — Now, Mr. Harmon P. Cross, please, American speculator who has bought my oil fields, come with me. I am going to drive you to the train."

Number Twenty-nine held out both his hands to his deliverer. There was a simple dignity in his few words.

"Sir," he said, "I know nothing of you, but my life will not be long enough for me to express my gratitude. The day after to-morrow ——"

"The day after to-morrow there will be much for us to talk about," Gerald interrupted. "What I have

done, I have done joyfully. So far, it has been much
easier than I expected."

The Governor and his charge took their leave. The
door closed behind them. Gerald heard their footsteps
die away on the paved floor. He threw himself down on
the mattress and tried to sleep. It was an impossible
task but there was plenty to think about. — At one
o'clock the same burly Russian entered, bearing a bowl
of something which was half stew, half soup. Gerald
smelt it, looked at it, and set it in a distant corner of
the room. Then he walked back and forth, counting
how many paces it took him from wall to wall. Presently, with a throb of joy, he remembered his cigarette
case. He smoked two cigarettes. Afterwards, he
dozed for a little time. Towards evening, he amused
himself trying to make his predecessor's daily jump.
It was not until the seventh attempt that he succeeded,
and then the rust of the bars cut so deeply into his
palms that he let go almost at once. At eight o'clock,
the Russian appeared again with a bowl of soup similar
to the last. Gerald waved it away.

" Not hungry? " the man asked in German.

Gerald shook his head. Somehow or other, it was a
relief to find that he was not shut out altogether from
communication with the outside world.

" You speak German, eh? " he asked.

The man shook his head.

" Few words."

" Bring me something better to eat," Gerald begged.
" Can't I have some beer? "

The man held out his hand and Gerald filled it with
silver. He disappeared and returned presently with
two bottles of beer concealed in his baggy trousers, and
a loaf of bread.

"Not understand this," he said, shaking his head. "Where Number Twenty-nine gone?"

Gerald shook his head.

"Better ask no questions until the Governor comes back," he enjoined.

"No fear talk," the man declared with a laugh. "Governor given me twenty marks. If talk, I get twenty lashes instead. Good night!"

He departed finally, closing and locking the door behind him. Gerald ate some bread hungrily and drank the beer. Then for a time he dozed. When he woke up and looked at his watch, it was twelve o'clock. Very soon he would begin to expect the Governor. He sat up on the mattress with his back to the wall. Between twelve and one o'clock he looked at his watch twenty times. One o'clock came and passed; half-past one. Then he rose to his feet and began pacing the cell restlessly. Two o'clock came; half-past. He held his watch in his hand now, to save himself the continual dragging it out from his pocket. Every few minutes he stopped to listen. The great fortress apparently slept. There was no sound anywhere. Only time went on. Three o'clock arrived and passed — four! — five! Presently streaks of daylight began to appear. At six o'clock at last there were footsteps outside. The warder entered once more. This time he carried a jug of hot liquid.

"Tea," he announced, "from kitchen. Give me something."

Gerald gave him more silver. The tea was the colour of straw and water, but the faint smell of it was refreshing.

"Where is the Governor?" he asked.

The warder shook his head.

"Not ask questions," he begged. "Governor not here."

Gerald pulled himself together and dismissed the man. He drank the tea slowly. Once more he sat down on the mattress. The room now was a little lighter. He could see as far as the opposite wall. He sat down and waited. Every nerve in his body seemed tingling. He tried to keep his mind off the subject of what could have happened to detain the Governor, to turn his thoughts back to England. — He suddenly found himself by the roadside, watching the mending of the puncture, looking impatiently along the white ribbon of road which led to Cannes, and, beyond, to Monte Carlo, where the lights were burning and the violins were playing their pagan overture. He saw Myrtile's pale, terrified face gleaming out against the background of the cypress trees, heard her pathetic story throbbing in the pine-sweetened stillness. He remembered their drive. All those things seemed part of another world. He remembered those few furious moments when Christopher had taken her from his arms. A faint feeling of shame crept over him as he sat there, huddled up. Then, with a rush, came the memory which swept everything else out of his mind. He saw Pauline, felt the disturbance of her presence, remembered the slow ebbing away of her pride, her first few kind words, the half-spoken promise. What was there about her, he wondered vaguely, which had brought him, with all his experience, so completely to her feet? She had shown him no kindness. She had not even been gracious. He had read dislike in her eyes more often than any other feeling. There remained, too, the pitiless truth that all the favours he had won from her he had bought, indirectly if not directly. Yet there she was, ruling over his life, the one sweet, dominant figure, for whose sake he sat in these miserable clothes, a forgotten figure, — perhaps, even, in danger. — He took out his watch with trembling fingers. It was ten o'clock. His thoughts mocked him now. He could find no escape by means of them. He could think of nothing but the present. Something had gone wrong with their plans. What would it mean for him? Not a soul in the world knew where he was. If he had a name at all here, it was the name of the man whom the people of Russia had once threatened to tear limb from limb.

At last there came a little stir, an unaccustomed sound of voices. Presently he heard footsteps outside, the key turned in the lock. His heart turned sick with disappointment — it was the warder alone! Gerald dug his hand once more into his pocket. This time he brought out a note. For some reason or other he was terrified. Even the stolid features of his visitor seemed disturbed.

" Where is the Governor? " Gerald demanded. " See, there is this note if you will go and fetch him."

The man returned to the door and shook it to be sure that it was fastened. Then he came back to Gerald.

"A strange thing has happened," he said. " There is a German woman in the town. Last night the Governor spent at her house. They were both drunk. They quarrelled. Elsa killed him. The Governor is dead."

CHAPTER XI

THE telegram was brought in to Lady Mary as she sat alone in her little sitting room, in the hours between tea and the dressing bell, — hours which, so far as possible, especially during the last few months, she tried to keep to herself. It had been handed in at a branch office in the north of London and contained the news for which she had been waiting:

Elected majority two thousand heartiest thanks for good wishes.

CHRISTOPHER.

Her first impulse was one of genuine pleasure. She started to her feet, meaning to take it to her father, who was with Myrtile in the library. Then she stopped short and slowly resumed her seat. That little orange-coloured form might have meant so much more, so much food for her ambitions, her natural and proper ambitions for the man she loved. It might have been such a pledge for the interest of their life together, such a wonderful life, brimful of movement and colour in which she, too, might well hope to take a part. In her quiet way, she had for years looked upon her marriage with Christopher, sooner or later, as a certainty. Without the slightest desire in any way to mislead her, Christopher had subconsciously encouraged the idea. She knew perfectly well that, as soon as his position was a little more

assured, he had intended to ask her to be his wife.   It
was one of those pleasant yet wonderful arrangements
which seemed to develop automatically.   Christopher
was well born, his friends were her friends, his disposition accorded with hers.   She could never have married
an idle man.   Christopher had many a worthy ambition.
She was precisely the wife to further them.   Her money
and her social influence would save him years of fruitless
labour.   He could leave the Bar whenever he liked, and
turn his whole attention to politics. — And now the
dream had crumbled.   This slip of paper was nothing
but a friendly message, telling her of the success of a
friend with whose career she had no intimate concern.
Her disposition was too kindly not to feel a certain
amount of pleasure at his success, but that very pleasure brought its shadow of personal grief.   She sat looking into the fire, twisting the little slip of paper in her
hands.   She knew very well that she was cursed with
that one terrible and self-mortifying virtue, the unalter-
able fidelity of the woman who permits in her mind the
thought of one man only and who can never replace him.
The very thought of marriage with any one but Christopher was revolting.   It seemed to her, as she sat
there, that she was doomed to a career of lovelessness
and inutility.   She might labour in good works till her
hair was streaked with grey and her face lined, and she
knew very well the fruitlessness of all that she would
accomplish.   The best work of a woman, as she well
knew, is the work done for the man she loves.

It was perhaps natural that her thoughts should turn
to Myrtile.   She wondered for a moment, slowly and
painfully, at the instinct which had warned her of coming trouble when the two young men had told her of
their adventure.   She had felt it when first she had

seen the frightened child, whose unspoken appeal for
protection had met with so cold a response from her.
She had been conscious of a cruelty wholly foreign to
her nature, in those days at Monte Carlo, whenever the
name of Myrtile was mentioned. She had puzzled Christopher and her brother alike by her lack of sympathy.
Well, she was punished now. The child had justified all
that she had felt. She had robbed her, unconsciously
and unwillingly, of the greatest thing in life. As she
sat there, the telegram crumpled up in her fingers, all
that old hardness came back to her. It seemed to her
a bitter thing that this unknown child should have been
brought into the august household in which her own serene days had been spent, to rob her, the benefactress,
of the crown of her life, to draw the sunshine from her
days and send her down to a joyless grave. For a moment she was on the verge of a passion. She hated
Myrtile, hated the sight of her gentle movements, the
thought of her and all to do with her. She rose to her
feet with an unaccustomed fire in her eyes and swung
round — to find that the slight noise which had disturbed her meditations had been caused by the entrance
of Myrtile herself.

There are moments when revelation is self-illumina-
tive. This was one of them. Myrtile, gazing almost in
terror into the face of her benefactress, knew that she
was hated, and, with an extraordinary insight, she knew
why. She saw the crumpled up telegraph form; she
guessed at everything which had lain unspoken between
them. She closed the door firmly behind her, came
across to Lady Mary's chair, fell on her knees and
struggled with her sobs.

"I know! I know!" she cried. "I am very miserable!"

Mary looked at her coldly and critically. All the natural impulses of her heart seemed dried up. Even her pride refused to come to her aid. The truth lay naked between the two.

"I was a fool not to realise what bringing you here meant," she said. "It is too late now. Here is the telegram. Christopher is elected."

Myrtile brushed it away. It was a thing of no account.

"I care nothing for Christopher and you know it," she declared passionately. "I do not care whether he is elected or not. Nothing about him makes any difference to me, or ever will."

Myrtile was speaking the truth. To Mary it seemed amazing, but she knew that it was the truth.

"It is only a fancy which Christopher has for me," Myrtile went on. "It will pass — oh, I am sure that it will pass! Deep down in his heart I know that there is another feeling."

"There was," Mary agreed. "But for your coming, he would have known it himself before now."

Myrtile shook with the pain of it.

"But for my coming!" she repeated. "And I have prayed that I might bring a little happiness to you who have been so good to me!"

Her anguish was apparent. There was something almost unearthly in the sorrow which shone out of her eyes. Mary's heart began to fail her. Her fingers rested on the top of the other girl's head. A gleam of coming kindness shone mistily in her eyes.

"It wasn't your fault," she said.

"It is my fault that I am alive!" Myrtile moaned. "But listen, please. I have my plans. I am going away."

"What good would that do?" Mary asked doubtfully.

"It would do great good," Myrtile declared. "I shall remove myself altogether. Christopher's fancy will pass. And besides — I must go."

"My father would never spare you," Mary said, ashamed of the joy with which the thought filled her.

"I have thought of everything," Myrtile insisted. "Lord Hinterleys has been very kind to me, but he will forget. If he chooses to see me sometimes, it will be possible. Let me tell you, please. I have a plan. Only yesterday I heard from the curé. He is back again in the valley. He is at the church there now. He says, if I need ever to go back, I can teach at the school. All my people have gone away many, many miles. My stepfather has a larger farm. I shall go back. I should never have come away."

Mary looked at her searchingly. All the suffering in the world seemed to be quivering in Myrtile's sensitive face. She leaned a little forward towards the kneeling girl.

"Myrtile," she whispered, "there is pain in your heart, too."

"Oh, God knows it!" Myrtile sobbed. "There will be for ever and ever. It is for my own sake that I must leave. I thought that love was a toy, and I laughed to find it in my heart. And now I know that it is a torment. I want to go back along the road I have come and hide."

"We have both been a little foolish," Mary said kindly. "You looked out into life, expecting to find happiness, just as children go into the meadows to pick flowers. And I, too, forgot that happiness only comes when it is earned. — Now let us try and be sensible. I think that yours is a very good idea. We shall miss you very much here, but perhaps it will be best for you to go away for a little time."

" I must go," Myrtile insisted fervently.

" But teaching? "

" There is no need for me to teach," Myrtile declared. " This letter that I have from the curé, it was written to tell me that my mother's brother, who went to Geneva many years ago, has died and left me some money. An *avocat* at Toulon has it for me. It is quite a great deal. I thought that I would buy a small farm and work in the fields there, work and work until I got brown and hard and grew like those other peasant girls there, lumps of the earth to which they stoop all the time. In a way I used to love the farm," she went on, " when I was alone — those first few mornings when the fields began to show purple with the budding violets, and the still evenings when the cypress trees looked as though they had come out of a box of children's toys — and the colours the sunset used to draw out of the mountains, the magentas and purples, and the pink glow coming in such unexpected places."

" Why, you're positively homesick!" Mary exclaimed.

" No, I am not homesick," Myrtile assured her gravely, " but I am like an animal that has been hurt and wants to limp back to its home. A little time ago it was different. Every fibre of me longed for escape, to be where life was. Now I would like to go where I can forget it."

Mary sighed.

" Fortunately," she said, " you are very young. You will learn soon that there are many men of Gerald's type, and that they are not to be taken too seriously. They have the trick of making you believe what they want you to believe, and they use it because they must. They are never quite honest. They are never quite bad. They certainly are not worth a broken heart. — Now we must take this message down to my father and send a reply. He does not altogether approve of Christopher's politics, but he will be glad to know that he is elected. Afterwards, I will talk to him about you. I shall have to be very eloquent, for I know he will hate your going."

"If it could be before Gerald comes back," Myrtile pleaded.

Mary had even more trouble with her father than she had expected. At the first mention of Gerald's name in connection with Myrtile's desire to return to France, he stiffened.

"Mary," he insisted, "I shall require you to tell me the exact truth as to this matter."

"I will do so," Mary promised.

"How much blame is to be attached to Gerald, and precisely what are his relations with Myrtile?" Lord Hinterleys asked sternly.

"Gerald is to blame only for thoughtlessness," she assured him. "He is a born philanderer, just as Myrtile was born to be a ready victim. Myrtile loves him, and I am afraid she will never care for any one else. Other women have to bear their hurts, though, and I dare say she will get over it."

"Gerald is a fool," his father declared. "Marrying in one's own class is well enough in an ordinary way, but — well, there isn't another woman like Myrtile in the world. Gerald is an ass not to realise it instead of going to Russia, risking his life and liberty for the sake of this Russian girl. I don't like Russians — never did. You are a person of common sense, Mary. If you say

Myrtile must go, go she must, but I'd much rather Gerald came to his senses and married her."

"Men are rather difficult in that way," Mary rejoined, a little bitterly.

CHAPTER XII

THE butler made his announcement to his mistress a little doubtfully.

" There is a person here, your ladyship, who desires to see you."

" What sort of a person? " Lady Mary enquired.

The butler coughed.

"A woman, your ladyship. She struck me as being some sort of a foreigner. She assured me that her business was urgent. I have shown her into the morning room."

Mary rose to her feet at once.

"A foreigner? " she repeated, with suddenly aroused interest. " Perhaps she has news of Lord Dombey."

Nevertheless, when she entered the little room where Elsa Francks was waiting, it scarcely seemed likely that news of so fastidious a person as her brother could come from such a source. Her doubts, however, were soon set at rest.

"Are you Lord Dombey's sister? " the woman asked bluntly, without offering to move from her chair.

" I am," Lady Mary acknowledged at once. " Have you brought news of him? "

" I have brought him home," was the unexpected reply.

" You? " Lady Mary exclaimed.

The woman laughed coarsely.

" Yes, me! " she declared. " I have saved his life a dozen times over, as I dare say he will tell you some day. Even now I do not know why."

" But where is he? " Lady Mary demanded.

" He is safe in the Charing Cross Hospital," the woman replied, " and if you want to know all about him, you will give me some wine quickly."

Mary, scarcely conscious of what she did, rang the bell. This woman was certainly the strangest visitor who had ever penetrated the portals of Hinterleys House. She seemed larger and coarser than ever. Her clothes were showy, but unbrushed and crumpled as though she had slept in them for nights; her hair was yellow but untidy. The rouge and powder were distributed upon her face in ungainly daubs. She breathed an atmosphere of stale scent. Notwithstanding all these things, she had news of Gerald, Gerald who for seven months had been lost! Lady Mary waited eagerly for the butler, who entered the room, full of the confident anticipation that he would be asked to remove this incongruous visitor.

" This lady would like some wine," Lady Mary announced. " Do tell me what you would prefer? " she added, turning towards her guest.

" Champagne, if you have it," was the prompt reply.

" Bring champagne, Richards," his mistress directed. " Perhaps you had better tell his lordship. This lady has brought us news of Lord Dombey."

The woman held out her hand.

" Don't bring any lordships here," she begged. " I will tell my story to you, ma'am. I am very near hysterics myself. To reach here from Sokar has taken us a month. We tried at seven places on the frontier before we could get into Poland."

" Poland? " Mary exclaimed. " But here is the wine. Do, please, help yourself."

The woman was served with champagne and dry biscuits, which latter she scornfully rejected. She drank three glasses of champagne, however. Then she filled a fourth glass for herself and began to talk.

"How much do you know of your brother's visit to Russia?" she asked.

"Only that he went there on some mysterious errand at the instigation of two ladies, who are, I believe, Russians."

"One of them was called Pauline — his sweetheart, eh?"

"I suppose so," Mary admitted.

"Well, here is my story," Elsa Francks said, draining the contents of her glass and refilling it. "Remember it, for I shall never tell it again. It is a story I would like to forget."

"I will certainly remember it," Mary promised.

"Twelve months ago I went to live at Sokar," Elsa Francks began. "It is a miserable place, but I went there to be near my friend Ivan Krossneys, the Governor of the fortress. In that fortress was confined a man whom your brother went to Russia to rescue. He came to me to ask me to help him bribe the Governor. That was in the month of October last year. He was a very different person then, and I thought that I liked him very much."

The woman sipped her champagne. The warmth of the room, and the wine, had moistened her face. A little streak of rouge had spread upon her left cheek. There were black lines under her eyes. Her voice, however, was stronger.

"He offered a great deal of money and I agreed to help. I sent for Ivan and, although he made difficulties, he was easy to persuade. It was all arranged. The prisoner — Number Twenty-nine, we called him —

walked out of the fortress in your brother's clothes and
with his American passport. Your brother was to take
his place for twenty-four hours. Then he was to leave
the prison in the funeral coach of another prisoner who
had died."

" This was seven months ago," Mary faltered.

The woman wiped her lips, shivered at the sight of
the colour upon her handkerchief, closed her eyes for a
moment and recovered herself.

" That seven months," she said deliberately, " has
seemed like seven years, and each year like a lifetime in
hell! — Listen. I go on with the story. Your brother
entered the fortress as arranged, changed clothes with
Number Twenty-nine, who walked out of the place and
came, without doubt, to London. Your brother was to
spend that night in the fortress. Krossneys came down
to me. We were both excited. It was a great sum of
money which we had been paid, and life in Russia is a
horrible burden. We drank a great deal of wine. The
more we drank, the more quarrelsome Ivan became. He
resented having to part with so large a share of the
money to me. We quarrelled. Once or twice we made
it up. Then Ivan's anger flared out again. In the
end, he declared that he would take away a part of my
share. We had a struggle. Somehow or other, his revolver went off. He went backwards with a groan. He
was dead."

The woman dabbed at her face. Mary could find no
word of any sort. Her visitor's eyes seemed fixed in a
rigid stare. It was as though she were living through
the scene again.

" The police came," she went on. " I was arrested.
I told my story. There were no witnesses. After four
days they had to let me go. The moment I was free I

went to the fortress. Ivan's deputy was taking his place. He was a man of a different type, a politician, a Bolshevist from conviction. Every time he mentioned Number Twenty-nine, he spat. I had much trouble with him."

" Go on," Mary begged, glancing at the clock.

" You need not worry about your brother," Elsa Francks said. " He will not know you when you go to see him. He has forgotten most things. — This man's name was Ahrensein. I told him the whole truth. I am quite sure that if he had come into charge of the prison whilst the real Number Twenty-nine had been there, he would have found some excuse for having him shot within twenty-four hours. He even told me so. He was furious at the trick which had been played, — ' But,' he declared, ' the Englishman who has put himself in Number Twenty-nine's place shall suffer for him!' I was allowed to see your brother. He had got over the first shock of what had happened and I found him full of courage. We discussed several plans for his escape, which, however, we never carried into effect. I do not believe that any one could have bought the life of Number Twenty-nine from Ahrensein for a million pounds. With your brother, however, it was different. In the end, I made over to him one of your brother's drafts — one I took back from Ivan Krossneys after he was dead — cashed one of the smaller ones, and one dark night we drove away from the fortress."

" But this is all so long ago! " Mary exclaimed wonderingly.

The woman nodded.

" We were in the train for Petrograd," she went on, " when I had a message from Ahrensein, telling me that he was superseded. His successor had arrived, and was holding an enquiry into the escape of Number Twenty-nine. He advised me not to go near Petrograd. We left the train just as a company of soldiers from the fortress arrived on the platform. The train was held up and searched. We took a carriage and drove away, anywhere, away into the plains. We had money but nothing else. We bought the carriage and horses, bought the driver, body and soul. Driving by night, resting the horses and hiding ourselves by day, we travelled a hundred miles southeastwards."

"You must tell me the rest another time," Lady Mary suggested.

"What I am going to tell you, I shall tell you now or never," Elsa Francks answered fiercely. "It won't be much, I can promise you. When I leave this house, the story of these months is coming out of my mind, whether I have to dull it by drink, or even cut it out of my brain. — We were always in danger, always being tracked. We went short distances by train. Sometimes we hired carriages. We even travelled for the whole of one day in an electric car which crawled between two small towns. Seven times we tried to cross the frontier into Poland, and each time we were turned back. Once they had heard of us and we were placed under arrest. Your brother shot two of the guard and we escaped. After that it was life or death with us. We were passed across the frontier at last in a spot where the war zone had been. We were scarcely in Poland before half a regiment of Russians was after us. We were in Poland, however. We left them fighting. We heard afterwards that the Russians who had crossed the frontier were wiped out. — We got across Poland, somehow or other, into Germany. The rest was all discomfort and misery, but most of the danger was past.

Your brother fell ill in Warsaw. Since then he has
been dazed and weak, with a high temperature, and with
fits of unconsciousness. How I got him here, I don't
know. We arrived at Fenchurch Street this morning.
I drove to Charing Cross Hospital and they took him
at once. He was shouting like a madman. Then I
drove here."

She poured out the last glass of wine from the bottle
and drank it. Then she rose to her feet.

"It is a wonderful story, this!" Mary exclaimed.
"You must not go away yet, or, if you do, you must
come back again. My father will want to thank you."

"I do not want thanks," the woman scoffed. "I
started out on this adventure because your brother had
paid a great sum of money and because I had a fancy
for him. I have lost that fancy, but I made up my
mind that I would bring your brother home, and I have
done it. I do not wish for any further payment. I
have spent your brother's money freely, but I have
enough left to give me all that I need in life. I do not
like England and I am going away to-day. Is there
any further question you wish to ask?"

"None that I can think of for the moment," Lady
Mary admitted. "I think that it was very wonderful
of you to run all these risks. You might have left my
brother there and gone away with the money."

"I very nearly did," the woman confessed bluntly.
"Many a time, on the way home, I wished that I had
done it. Your brother has a fine courage at times, but
he is a weakling in the ugly places of life. Often when
I dragged him along through the mud, and he had to
sleep on a stone floor, with coarse food to eat, and no
wine, he would rather have come out into the open and
fought for his life and ended it. I dare say, when he

recovers, he will be grateful to me. There have been many times when he has hated me. — Now I will go."

She rose to her feet, dabbed more powder on her face and looked at her hostess a little defiantly. Lady Mary rang the bell. Then she held out her hand.

"Thank you very much for bringing Gerald home," she said.

Elsa Francks laughed hardly. She refused the hand.

"You have no need for gratitude," she said. "I started on the job because I had a fancy for your brother. When I lost that, I went on because I am an obstinate woman. As for recompense, I still have a fortune, but I am glad that these months are over. You can tell your brother that I took Krossneys' share of the money as well as my own. When he comes to think it over, I think he will say I earned it."

She followed the butler out of the room. Mary watched her from the window with fascinated eyes, saw her hail a passing taxicab with her outstretched umbrella, watched her fling herself into it, put up her feet on the opposite seat and light a cigarette. She had the air of a woman who has accomplished a great task.

Lady Mary rang the bell.

"The car at once, Richards," she ordered. "Lord Dombey is in London. I am going to fetch him home."

CHAPTER XIII

CHRISTOPHER had taken his seat — had already, indeed, made his maiden speech — when Gerald left the nursing home into which he had been moved from the hospital. The doctors, however, were far from satisfied with his condition. He was still thin, listless in manner, with long periods of absent-mindedness. He seemed, in a way, to have lost self-control. Mary, as they drove home together to Hinterleys House, made up her mind to break the long silence which had existed between them on the subject of Pauline.

"Gerald," she asked, "have you seen or heard anything of the De Ponières?"

Gerald turned and looked at her out of his hollow eyes.

"Nothing," he confessed. "I wrote from the nursing home six times. I have had no reply. They must have left the hotel in South Kensington."

"Would you like me to try and find out?"

"It doesn't matter," he answered. "I have made up my mind to go there myself this afternoon."

"May I come with you?" she begged.

"If you like," he answered half-heartedly. "They won't be there, though. I am just hoping that I may hear of them."

The hope, however, was not realised. Madame and Mademoiselle had left the hotel many months ago, and had left no address behind. The hall porter, encouraged to tell what he knew by Gerald's liberal tip, showed a great sheaf of letters which he had been unable to forward.

" Can't understand their leaving no address, sir," he confided. " They paid their accounts well and regular, gave notice in the usual way, and just drove off. I asked if they wouldn't leave an address in case there should be any letters, but the young lady replied that she would call round for them when she was in town again."

"And she hasn't been here since? " Lady Mary enquired.

" Never a sign of her," the hall porter replied.

Gerald handed the man his card.

" It will be worth a five-pound note to you at any time if you should discover their address," he said.

" I'll let you know within ten minutes, if I can get hold of it, sir," the man promised. " I've a sort of an idea, though, that we shan't set eyes on those two ladies again. The manageress," he went on, dropping his voice to a confidential whisper, " wasn't too sorry to see them go."

" Why? " Gerald asked.

" Well, she don't like foreigners, to start with," he explained, " besides which we were always getting queer sorts of people here asking about them. Might have been detectives or anything. I'm not saying a word against them — they always paid their way right and generously — but there was a queer lot of people watching them all the time."

Gerald and his sister drove away from the hotel in silence.

" You are disappointed?" Mary asked him anxiously.

" I thought they might have left a message for me," he admitted.

" You'll come down to Hinterleys to-morrow? "

He shook his head.

" I must find her," he announced, in a tone curiously devoid of enthusiasm or hope.

Mary said nothing then, but she took him to task that evening. They had dined tête-à-tête, Lord Hinterleys having already gone down to the country. For the first time Gerald showed some interest in Myrtile's absence.

" What did you say had become of Myrtile? " he enquired.

" She has gone back to France," his sister told him. " She had a little money left to her, and she wanted to go. I had a letter from her this morning. She has bought the old farm where you first saw her and is growing violets."

" Why did she want to go back? " Gerald persisted. " You were all kind to her, I hope? "

" We all tried to be," Mary answered. " Dad misses her terribly. — Why, here's Christopher! " she broke off suddenly. " Whatever are you doing, neglecting your duties in this manner? " she asked, as Christopher, still in morning clothes, was shown in by the butler.

" I've come to beg for some dinner," was the smiling reply, " and incidentally to welcome Gerald back."

Mary coloured a little with pleasure. The butler was already arranging another place.

" It's awfully nice of you, Christopher," she said.

" Very good of you to take me in like this," he replied. " There's nothing doing at the House, and I felt sure you two would be alone. I should think you must have been about fed up with that nursing home, Gerald."

" I'm fed up with everything," Gerald replied, a little wearily. " The doctors say I'm all right again, but I

don't know. I can't sleep, and there seems to be an
empty place in my head, somehow. If I begin to think,
I get the jim-jams. Give me some champagne, Richards."

" The country for you, my boy," Christopher declared. " If I were Mary, I'd take you down to-morrow."

Gerald shook his head.

" I've something to do first," he said. " By the bye,
you know about Myrtile, I suppose? She's gone back
to the little farm."

Christopher nodded. Mary, who was watching him
closely, fancied that his indifference was almost natural.

" Queer thing," he observed, " to think that she
should end up there, after all. I wonder whether she
blesses or curses us, Gerald, for taking her to the end
of the road."

Gerald sighed a little wearily.

" Curses us, I should think," he replied. "All knowledge is pain; so is memory. Last night I woke up suddenly and I remembered fighting with that great brute
on the Polish frontier. — Did Elsa tell you about the
man I killed there? " he asked, frowning.

Mary rose abruptly to her feet.

" Remember the doctor's orders," she insisted. " The
last twelve months are taboo. There are worse things
in the world than killing Bolshevists, anyhow."

" The chap had some one who was fond of him, I
suppose," Gerald said gloomily. " You ought to have
seen that woman who brought me home, Christopher.
I can't get the thought of her out of my brain. The
first time I saw her, I went to persuade her to bribe
her lover, Krossneys. I thought her the coarsest, most
brutal, most ungainly creature who ever abused the

name of Woman. Then I saw her month after month, playing a man's part. She lied, she swore, she fought, — fought with her fists if there was nothing else handy; she drank; once she almost carried me over a mile of marshland, with some outpost sentries sniping at us all the time. She was a hideous, glorious, epic figure. There was a man whom we both knew to be a spy and on my tracks. I saw her wheedle him into her room. Two minutes afterwards, his blood was streaming out from under the door."

" Gerald! " his sister entreated.

" All right," he muttered. " I'm not sure that it doesn't do me good to talk of these things. They've been a silent horror with me for so long."

Later, the doctor called to see Gerald, and Christopher led Mary across the hall into the billiard room.

" Mary," he confided, as soon as he had closed the door, " I had a reason for coming round to-night. I have seen the girl."

" Where? " Mary asked breathlessly.

" Here in London. They were opening the gates of Marlborough House as I came along Pall Mall, and I was stopped for a moment on the pavement. A small brougham came out. The windows were closed, but I was within a few feet of it. The girl was inside with a young man."

" If only you could have found out where they went to! " Mary exclaimed. " Gerald will never be better until he has seen her."

" He can do that when he likes, then," Christopher replied. " I jumped into a taxi and followed the carriage. It drew up before quite a small, detached house at the back of Roehampton Lane. I jumped out of my taxi quickly, and I was just in time to stop her as she was entering the gate."

" Go on," Mary begged. " This is exciting."

" She recognised me at once," Christopher went on, " and she made no attempt to get away. I told her that I was Gerald's friend and that he was looking for her. ' You can tell him,' she replied, ' that he can find me here.' "

" What did the young man say? "

" Nothing at all. He was very good-looking in his way, a great strong fellow, but he looked as though he had been ill. — What are you going to do about this? Are you going to tell Gerald? "

She nodded.

" I think so. I don't believe this girl means to marry him. It is much better, however, that he knows the exact position."

" I wrote down the address and here it is," Christopher said, handing her a card. " If I can be of any use ——"

" You dear man! " she exclaimed. " We must leave it to Gerald. I hope that he will let me go with him. I think he ought to find out just where he stands at once."

" I am not going back to the House," Christopher remarked. " Could we have one game of billiards? "

" I should love it," she answered. " Gerald will come and look for us as soon as he has finished with the doctor. You used to give me fifteen, wasn't it? "

Gerald came in presently and sat watching them a little listlessly. When the game, which Mary won with some ease, came to an end, she went over and seated herself by her brother's side.

" Gerald," she said, " Christopher has discovered

Pauline's address. It is quite close by here. You must go and see her to-morrow. Would you like either of us to come with you? "

Gerald began to tremble.

" She is here — in London — all right? " he demanded.

" Absolutely," Christopher declared. " She was looking quite well. Her brother was with her."

" I will go alone," Gerald decided. " I will go to-morrow. Now you have told me something worth hearing. Perhaps to-night I shall sleep."

CHAPTER XIV

GERALD, after all, derived small satisfaction from his visit on the following day. He found his destination easily, — a small, detached house in a retired back street, with a bell at the front gate and spiked railings. He was admitted without undue delay by an ordinary-looking parlour maid and conducted into a small sitting room. After waiting a minute or two, the door was opened and Madame de Ponière entered.

"You have come to see my niece, Lord Dombey?" she enquired, after a word of conventional greeting.

"Is it very surprising that I should come?" Gerald rejoined, a little bitterly.

"Perhaps not from your point of view," was the equable reply. "My niece has, in fact, been anticipating your visit."

"It would have been kinder of her," Gerald ventured, "if she had let me know her whereabouts. I have been in the hospital and afterwards in a nursing home for some time."

"My niece had other matters to consider," Madame de Ponière declared drily. "She is living in the utmost retirement, through force of circumstances."

"Can I see her now?" Gerald asked bluntly.

"She will grant you an audience," Madame de Ponière replied. "I have her permission to disclose her whereabouts, on one condition."

"She is not here, then?" Gerald exclaimed.

"She is not here."

" But she was here yesterday."

" She was forced to come to London on a certain matter," her aunt explained. " She left at nightfall. If you wish to make the journey, you can go and see her."

" Where is she? " Gerald asked.

" I shall require," Madame de Ponière said, " your word of honour that you will not divulge her whereabouts to any living person."

" I think that the dangers you conjure up are entirely imaginary," Gerald remarked, a little impatiently, " but I will give you that promise."

" My niece is to be found at Duvenny Castle in Scotland," Madame de Ponière announced. " It is a somewhat inaccessible place. Particulars of how to reach it are here."

She handed him a slip of paper.

" In Scotland? " Gerald repeated, a little wearily. " But she was here yesterday."

" She left at night," Madame de Ponière reminded him.

Gerald folded the slip of paper and put it in his pocket.

" Very well," he said, " I will go to Scotland."

Madame de Ponière looked at him through her lorgnettes for a moment thoughtfully.

" You have been ill," she remarked.

" I have been ill," he assented.

Madame de Ponière lowered her lorgnettes and closed them with a little snap.

" If I thought that you would accept it," she said, " I would give you a word of advice."

" I can at least hear it," he suggested.

" Go back to the manner of life you were living be-

fore you met Pauline — and forget her. Your visit
to Scotland will be of no service to you. It will only
end in disappointment."

Gerald shook his head.

"That," he said obstinately, "I must discover for
myself."

Gerald, following in the main the directions on the
slip of paper given him by Madame de Ponière, reached
his destination on the afternoon of the third day. He
was in the car which he had hired at the last town on
the railway route, a town which seemed to him, un-
acquainted with this corner of Scotland, almost an
outpost of civilisation. After miles of moorland, un-
broken except for huge boulders, the way had led
around a range of smaller mountains until he had suddenly encountered, when he had been least expecting it,
the tang of the sea. Many hundreds of feet below, he
saw at last his destination, a dwelling of stone as ancient
and rudely fashioned, it seemed, as the massed-up boulders on every side. The road by which it was approached was precipitous, in places almost impassable.
The last quarter of a mile was along a narrow bank,
unprotected on either side, with the spray from the
waves leaping up into his face. The road ended in a
circular sweep, surrounded by a high wall. In front
of him was a massive gate, closed and barred. The
porter who appeared in answer to the bell kept him
waiting while he communicated with the house. Finally
the gates were pushed open and the car allowed to pro-
ceed up a steep, stone-paved ascent to a courtyard
also flagged with stones and also surrounded by a high
wall. In front was another massive door, which, however, already stood open. Two men servants, both foreigners, awaited his arrival. One attended to the clos-

ing of the door and remained with the chauffeur; the other silently beckoned Gerald to follow him across the stone floor of the bare, circular hall into a room at the further end. He stood aside to let Gerald precede him.

" The gentleman will please be seated," he said.

Gerald found himself alone in an apartment not unduly large but exceedingly lofty. It was simply but magnificently furnished, but only a single rug lay upon the floor. The windows looked sheer over the sea, and the thunder of the waves against the jagged rocks seemed almost at his feet. The windows themselves were narrow — the windows of a fortress — and the depth of the window seat showed the thickness of the walls. Gerald had little time to take note of these things, however. Within a moment or two of his being left alone, the door opened and Pauline entered.

Speech of any sort, it seemed to Gerald, must be pitifully inadequate. He stood looking at her, wondering if anything in her expression would give him the clue to her mysterious behaviour. She came towards him, however, as composed and unresponsive as ever. There was nothing whatever in her manner to indicate the fact that she was greeting the man who had risked his life in a mad enterprise for her sake.

" You have had a long journey, Lord Dombey," she said.

He bowed over the hand which she had extended to him.

" A long journey, indeed," he assented, " a journey down into hell and back."

" Sit down," she invited, " and I will give you the explanation I owe you."

" Thank you," he answered, " I do not feel at home

in this house. Let me remain standing until after you
have told me what it all means. I have done your bidding. I have come to beg for my reward."

Her eyes looked at him coldly.

" I promised no reward," she reminded him.

" Not in words," he admitted, " yet you know what
I desire."

" What you desire is absurd," she declared. " That
is what I wish to explain. You have discovered, perhaps, who I am."

" I learned who your brother was."

" My brother ! " she smiled. " Well," she went on,
" listen. I am the Grand Duchess Pauline of Russia,
Princess and hereditary ruler of the Caspian Provinces,
and nearest in kin amongst living women to Nicholas,
who was murdered by the people. The man whom you
rescued is Paul, Grand Duke of Volostok, hereditary
ruler of seventeen provinces, and nearest in the male line
to the Crown of Russia. He is my cousin."

" Your cousin? " Gerald exclaimed.

" And my husband," she answered calmly.

Gerald was extraordinarily cool. The situation began slowly to shape itself in his mind.

" It has been the province of royalty," Pauline continued, " to make use of their courtiers, without explanation, in whatever way may seem good to them. I
have made use of you. I did not seek your acquaintance or your friendship. I have made you no promises.
I have kept you much farther away even from hope
than would many of my illustrious ancestresses. Yet,
in these days, you will probably think that you have
been ill-treated. I cannot help it. I and others of my
race have been ill and mercilessly treated. Yours has
been a small wrong. I made use of you and your de-

votion to free my cousin, to whom I was affianced. So far as my thanks can satisfy you, I tender them."

"You are very gracious," Gerald acknowledged, forgetting all his weariness and holding himself like a man. "May I ask, were you married to the Grand Duke when I fetched him from his prison?"

"I was not," Pauline assured him. "I was married a month after his return to England, with the consent and the approbation of my relatives here. Paul and I have but one hope and one desire — to live until the time when the people of Russia return to their allegiance, and to reëstablish the Romanoff dynasty in Russia, either through ourselves or our children. For that reason we are living here with an unseen guard provided by the English Government. When you first met us, we lived in seclusion because already four times my life had been attempted. There are still men pledged to destroy us root and branch. Here they will not succeed. We are surrounded by faithful guards, and our lives are consecrate. Not until the children live and flourish who shall carry on our name, will I or my husband take the slightest risk. The world may see something of us later. For the present we have only one thought."

Gerald stood amongst the wreck of his dreams. He seemed to be listening to the thunder of the sea, to be watching the queer-shaped shaft of sunlight which stretched across the floor. He found speech almost impossible. The silence lasted so long, however, that he was compelled to break it.

"Your Highness' explanation is complete?" he asked.

"It is complete," she replied. "You will understand that your — shall I call it admiration? — was, in a sense, an offence to me. In Monte Carlo I will admit that through sheer weariness I was perhaps a little indiscreet. The situation then seemed hopeless."

" I understand," Gerald murmured.

" The Grand Duke, my husband, will wish to offer you some hospitality," she said, touching a bell.

" It is quite unnecessary," Gerald replied.

" Be so good as to await his coming," she enjoined.

Prince Paul entered the room a moment or two later, a touch of sunburn on his cheeks, erect and handsome, a very different person from the broken prisoner of a few months ago. He advanced towards Gerald with outstretched hand.

" It gives me great pleasure," he said, " to welcome you in my very bad English to our home. You see, I reached England safely."

" I was glad to hear of it," Gerald remarked.

" Some day you must tell me your own adventures," the young man continued. " Perhaps you will give us the pleasure of your company to dinner to-night? "

Gerald shook his head.

" I have promised the owner of the car which I hired," he said, " to return it to him to-night. I must, in fact, be leaving at once."

A servant entered with a tray bearing wine and whisky. Paul served his guest himself.

" They tell me that this is the most hospitable country of the world," he observed. " Even in Russia we should not let you depart without a toast. You will wish us those things for which Her Highness and I live."

Gerald bowed and raised his glass to his lips.

" I shall drink to you and to your country," he said, " and to the good of both."

He set down his glass empty. Pauline smiled her

good-by, but they handed him over to the care of servants with the air of royalty. — Gerald drove through
the opened gates, heard the bars grind behind him, and,
looking around for a last view, was dimly conscious of
men who watched. Years afterwards, this strange visit,
with all its trifling events, assumed its proper propor-
tions in his mind. That night, however, he drove over
the moors and around the mountains absolutely without
any direct emotions. It was impossible to believe that
his visit had not been the phantasy of an afternoon's
slumber.

CHAPTER XV

AFTER they had left Toulon, the two men seemed almost to change places. Gerald, who for the last four days had been in much the same mentally comatose state as he had been since his return from Scotland, sat up and for the first time began to look about him with interest. Christopher, on the other hand, who during the whole of their journey had been continually endeavouring to amuse and entertain his companion, gradually relapsed into a rare fit of thoughtfulness. They had passed through Hyères, however, and were winding their way around the Forêt du Dom, before any direct allusion was made to the subject which in varying degrees was foremost in the minds of both of them.

"About an hour and a half beyond this, wasn't it?" Gerald asked.

Christopher nodded. It was significant that he made no comment upon the fact that Gerald had caught up with his own train of thought.

"Just about this time of the year, too," Gerald went on, ruminatingly. "I remember these orchards were just showing a little pink. And you say she's back again there, Chris. I wonder why? There wasn't any trouble at home, was there?"

"Not the slightest," Christopher assured him. "In fact, all the time you were in Russia your father seemed to rely upon her absolutely. It was a great blow to him when she made up her mind to go back."

" But what made her want to leave? " Gerald persisted.

Christopher did not hesitate for a moment. He meant to take every possible advantage of this, the first sign of any real interest in life which Gerald had shown for months.

" Because she is very finely strung," he said, " and the situation was becoming impossible for her. She was very much in love with you, and you were crazy about some one else. I was very much in love with her, as I always had been, and I was ass enough to try and persuade her to marry me. Of course," he went on, " I ought to have realised the unconquerable fidelity of a nature like hers. An ordinary woman," he went on, leaning back in his corner and discussing the matter very much as he would have done a legal point presented for his opinion, " might select and prefer one man to all others, but if, for some reason or other, he did not return her affection, she would be able, in course of time, to feel practically the same thing for another man. Myrtile could never do that. She has that saint-like fidelity which is the joy and the curse of the best women. You are a very dear fellow, Gerald, and I am very fond of you, but I sometimes get fed up with your nerves, your blindness, your Grand Duchesses and your stark idiocy."

Gerald sat up in his place and stared at his friend in amazement.

" How long have you been keeping that bottled up, Chris? " he asked.

" Ever since Myrtile turned me down," was the prompt reply. " She was as kind as she could be about it, but she did her job like a surgeon. She hurt, but I knew it was no use ever thinking about her again that way. I am a dispassionate observer now and I can see the truth."

"I suppose I have been rather an ass," Gerald acknowledged, "but you must remember, Chris, I didn't quite know what I was in for when I took on that visit to Russia, and I don't think any one could go through what I had to go through without getting bowled over. Fancy being taken care of like a baby by that amazing woman, Elsa Francks! — Having to owe her your life half-a-dozen times over! Seeing that great coarse creature, with her hank of yellow hair, and her breath smelling of drink and patchouli, standing up one moment and defying death, and lying the next without a tremor to guards who would have set us up against the wall and shot us on sight if they had known the truth!"

"She was an epic figure," Christopher declared. "I wonder what has become of her."

"Heaven knows!" Gerald answered. "We may meet her queening it at Monte Carlo, or she may have married a respectable German tradesman and buried the past. She is wealthy enough. She got that fellow Krossneys' share of the money I took out, as well as her own. — How these pine trees smell, Chris! And what sunshine! One could sleep here."

Gerald leaned back in his place with half-closed eyes, and Christopher was well content to leave him alone. This was the first time he had spoken naturally of his journey to Russia and the terrible experience through which he had passed. All through the summer months he had lain about the gardens at Hinterleys, accepting life as an inevitable burden, gaining no strength, sleeping little, all the time engaged in a morbid struggle with the tyranny of his nerves. Nothing had moved or interested him. These last few sentences of his were the first evidences of his return to a natural outlook. Physically he had shrunken almost to a shadow. There was very little left of the gay and debonair young man who had passed his arm round Myrtile's waist and drawn her into the car, mocked at Christopher's remonstrances, and, with a few careless words, built up in Myrtile's heart the fairyland at the end of the road. Yet, as they drew near the place where they had found her, he seemed to shake off some of his torpor. He sat up and looked about him with reminiscent eyes. One more bend and they would see the gate!

"Would you like to stop for a moment?" Christopher asked. "Myrtile is almost certain to be here."

This was most assuredly a changed Gerald. He was almost diffident.

"If you think she would like to see us," he assented.

He sat upright now, leaning a little forward. They were round the corner, in sight of the little grove of cypresses. And there at the gate — Myrtile! — Gerald gave a little exclamation which sounded almost like a sob. His incredulous stare had something in it alike of pain and fear.

"I wrote her days ago and said that we should be passing," Christopher hastily explained.

She stepped out into the road to greet them. Even to Christopher, her coming was almost like a vision. The small differences of clothing and circumstance seemed scarcely to exist. It was Myrtile who welcomed them, shyly but joyfully. Her eyes were fixed upon Gerald, and there was a touch of sublime pity in them as she realised the change. But from her face shone the same things.

"You will come in and see my home?" she begged.

" The car can turn in here. The road is better than it
used to be."

" I am tired of the car," Gerald said. " I would
rather walk."

They moved slowly down through the cypress avenue,
Gerald leaning a little on Myrtile's arm, Christopher
loitering behind. On one side were the formal lines of
the closely pruned vines, protruding from the rich brown
earth; on the other a flush of purple from the field of
violets. Myrtile answered some half intelligible question from Gerald.

" I am very happy here," she assured him. " There
is so much to do. I have broken up some more of the
land for growing violets, and presently I will show you
my carnations. The vineyards, too, needed a lot of
attention; they had been very much neglected. I hope
you like the colour of the house? I had it painted pink
because of the background. And you see what a lovely
verandah I have had built? By moving a few yards
one gets the sun all day."

" It is the most restful and the most beautiful place
I have ever been in," Gerald murmured. " Tell me,
Myrtile," he added, " do you know all that has hap-
pened to me? "

" Everything! Christopher has written, and I had a
long letter, too, from your father. Please do not speak
of those things which are finished. You are here to
forget."

Involuntarily he looked away towards the road and
turned back with a shiver. Whatever his thoughts
might have been, he said nothing. A little French maid,
in spotless white cap and apron, came out on to the
verandah in reply to Myrtile's call.

" A bottle of our own wine and glasses," Myrtile ordered, "some fruit, and the sandwiches I told you to have ready, Marie. Come, we have another half-hour of sunshine. Gerald, you must take the sofa chair."

Gerald sank into a sea of cushions. Myrtile, bending over him, arranged them more comfortably. Her eyes were soft with the shadow of tears. Gerald, more weary than he had confessed, seemed for a moment almost to doze.

"He is very weak," Myrtile whispered, looking anxiously across towards Christopher.

Christopher nodded.

"It is the journey," he answered. "I wish that it were over."

The wine was brought, but Gerald was now in a deep sleep. Christopher and Myrtile sat at the other end of the verandah and talked in an undertone. Presently the sun began to sink behind the forest-crowned hills, westwards. A cool breeze came stealing across the valley. Myrtile rose suddenly to her feet.

"He must not sleep any longer," she said firmly. "He ought not to be out at all as late as this."

They tried to rouse him. Three times Christopher laid his hand upon his shoulder and called him by name. There was no response. Gerald was sleeping heavily, his breathing was regular, the lines seemed to have faded from his face.

"It is the first time he has slept like this for weeks," Christopher declared. "It seems a shame to wake him."

"Don't," she begged eagerly. "You see the chair has castors. Wheel it into the sitting room, and if he doesn't wake, leave him here. Marie and I can look after him, and Pierre, my head man, is a treasure. He could carry him upstairs if it were necessary."

"We'll move him in and see if he wakes, anyhow," Christopher agreed.

They wheeled him into Myrtile's sitting room, sweet and flower-scented, without his showing the slightest sign of being disturbed. Myrtile closed the outer doors and lit the fire of pine logs and cones which was already prepared upon the hearth. Then she and Christopher stole from the room.

"This may be his salvation," Christopher declared hopefully.

There were tears in Myrtile's eyes. All the time she seemed to be listening.

"Leave him with me, Christopher," she begged. "He needs rest."

Christopher nodded.

"I'll send two of his bags down from the car," he proposed, "and some of us will come and have a look at him in a few days. His servant can stay here if you like, so that you have help if you want it."

She smiled through her tears.

"I shall need no help," she promised. "I will cure Gerald. Tell Lady Mary and Lord Hinterleys that I promise it. Only leave him alone with me. Do not come, any of you, until I send. If he wishes to leave, I can hire a car from San Raphael — he can be with you in a few hours. But I think he will be content. I think he will get better here."

CHAPTER XVI

"And now," Christopher said, as their car crawled up the last ascent, "to see if Myrtile has kept her word!"

"Personally," Lord Hinterleys declared, "I am confident. That young woman has powers beyond the ordinary human being's. Besides, our telegrams every day have assured us that all is well."

"It seems curious to me that Gerald should have been so content," Mary remarked. "Is this the place, Christopher?"

Christopher nodded. The car was slowing up. On their right was the little grove of cypress trees and the gate.

"Here they are!" Mary exclaimed. "Why, just look at Gerald!"

The two young people came down the cypress grove, arm in arm. Gerald was walking with much of his old swagger. Once more his head was thrown back; once more there was all the joy of wild spirits in the abandon of his enthusiastic greeting. Myrtile, on the other hand, seemed quieter than usual.

"Something deuced odd about the look of both of them," Lord Hinterleys remarked. "Gerald, you rascal, how are you?"

"Sane and sound, sir," Gerald answered, stretching out his hand, "thanks to Myrtile."

Lord Hinterleys looked at her curiously. Her eyes suddenly fell. She had been laughing a little hysteric-

ally a moment before. Now a fit of trembling seemed
to have seized her.

" Gerald, what have you been up to? " his father demanded.

Gerald laughed.

" Listen to that, dad," he said, " and see if you can't
guess."

The bell from the little white church was tinkling
away crazily. Gerald passed his arm around Myrtile.

" She's terrified to death," he declared. " Please
every one tell her that they're glad."

Myrtile was easily persuaded. Her father-in-law dis-
possessed Gerald as they turned towards the house.
Mary walked on the other side.

" You have now arrived in time for the celebrations,"
Gerald continued. " The feasting tenantry are in view
on the far side of the house. You will presently have
the opportunity of hearing me make a little speech in
my most perfect French, which I have just learnt by
heart."

" So you are really married! " Mary exclaimed incredulously. " Gerald — Myrtile — how wonderful it
all seems! "

" Amazing! " Gerald agreed. " Matrimony was evi-
dently my predestined Mecca. I am no longer ill. I
have never been so happy in my life. I was ploughing
for four hours yesterday, and practising approach
shots over the road to get rid of a little superfluous
energy after tea. What I really covet is the job of
Pierre, the head man, but Myrtile won't listen to it.
She says I don't understand the soil."

As they reached the house, the old curé came shuf-
fling out, beaming with smiles, delighted to find that
every one spoke his own language and that he could

talk to them about Myrtile. — Luncheon was spread out on the verandah, and Marie and a young friend from the village, with great bunches of white carnations fastened to their frocks, were waiting to serve. Gerald himself uncorked the wine.

"I propose to make a speech," Lord Hinterleys announced, holding out his foaming glass.

"It must be a short one," Gerald insisted. "The omelette won't wait."

"Then, as an omelette is my favourite dish and that one appears to be a *chef-d'oeuvre*, I drop the speech," his father assented. "I will only say, Gerald, that you have made Mary and me very happy, and that no bride in the world was ever more welcome than Myrtile to our home and lives."

Every one began to talk at once. By and by, that curious sense of unreality, the feeling that the whole thing was a scene out of an old-fashioned comedy, passed away. Gerald, who was shamelessly holding Myrtile's hand under the tablecloth, raised his glass and looked into her eyes.

"It was I, after all," he whispered, "who had no idea what lay at the end of the road. You were the wise lady and I the fool. You climbed, I pushed my way through the slough — but we found out."

All through the afternoon the villagers came and went, and the young people danced in the field at the back of the farm. Many toasts were exchanged. Every one was extraordinarily happy. Then the time came for Christopher, who was on his way back to England, to leave. Mary, who was spending the night with her father at Cannes, walked with him to the road. They paused for a moment at the gate.

"And it was really here that you found Myrtile?" Mary remarked, looking around her with interest.

"We found her on this very spot," Christopher answered, "gazing along the road to the hills. All her life she had wondered what lay on the other side. Many of us never find out. I think that Gerald has been very fortunate."

"I am glad that you are happy about it," she said, with quiet but tactful significance.

"It is because I am happy about it," Christopher rejoined, turning towards her, "that I am going to venture — that, Mary — well, I think I feel a little like the man who walked for a few minutes of his life in the moonlight and fancied that it was day. I honestly thought that I was in love with Myrtile. I know now that there is no one I ever really cared for but you, Mary."

She raised her head and looked at him, yielding unresistingly to the arm which was drawn around her.

"I am quite sure," she murmured, "that this is an enchanted land."

THE END

NOVELS *by* E. PHILLIPS OPPENHEIM

"He is past master of the art of telling a story. He has humor, a keen sense of the dramatic, and a knack of turning out a happy ending just when the complications of the plot threaten worse disasters." —*The New York Times.*

"Mr. Oppenheim has few equals among modern novelists. He is prolific, he is untiring in the invention of mysterious plots, he is a clever weaver of the plausible with the sensational, and he has the necessary gift of facile narrative."—*The Boston Transcript.*

A Prince of Sinners	The Way of These Women
A Maker of History	The Kingdom of the Blind
The Man and His Kingdom	The Pawns Count
The Yellow Crayon	The Zeppelin's Passenger
A Sleeping Memory	The Curious Quest
The Great Secret	The Wicked Marquis
Jeanne of the Marshes	The Box with Broken Seals
The Lost Ambassador	The Great Impersonation
A Daughter of the Marionis	The Devil's Paw
Havoc	Jacob's Ladder
The Lighted Way	The Profiteers
The Survivor	Nobody's Man
A People's Man	The Great Prince Shan
The Vanished Messenger	The Evil Shepherd
The Seven Conundrums	The Mystery Road

Boston LITTLE, BROWN & COMPANY Publishers